A Nice Day
for a
Cowboy Wedding

NICOLE
HELM

ZEBRA BOOKS
KENSINGTON PUBLISHING CORP.
http://www.kensingtonbooks.com

ZEBRA BOOKS are published by

Kensington Publishing Corp.
119 West 40th Street
New York, NY 10018

All Kensington titles, imprints, and distributed lines are available at special quantity discounts for bulk purchases for sales promotion, premiums, fund-raising, educational, or institutional use.

Special book excerpts or customized printings can also be created to fit specific needs. For details, write or phone the office of the Kensington Sales Manager: Attn.: Sales Department. Kensington Publishing Corp., 119 West 40th Street, New York, NY 10018. Phone: 1-800-221-2647.

Zebra and the Z logo Reg. U.S. Pat. & TM Off.

First Printing: September 2018
ISBN-13: 978-1-4201-4694-3
ISBN-10: 1-4201-4694-7

eISBN-13: 978-1-4201-4695-0
eISBN-10: 1-4201-4695-5

10 9 8 7 6 5 4 3 2 1

Printed in the United States of America

ACKNOWLEDGMENTS

I owe such a debt of gratitude to my amazing, complex, weird, supportive, wonderful family, who've given me such bountiful material to turn into fictional families. This series exists and continues thanks to the hard work and support of my agent, Helen Breitwieser, and my editor, Wendy McCurdy. Thank you to everyone at Kensington whose hard work puts my words into book form. And, as always, my everlasting gratitude to Maisey and Megan, who read and appreciate these worlds that mean so much to me.

Chapter One

Cora Preston pulled her car to a stop at the open gates of the Tyler ranch. Despite having spent her entire life in Colorado, she couldn't believe her eyes.

She had moved to the small mountain town of Gracely from Denver almost three years ago, but she'd spent most of her time *in* Gracely. Occasionally, she took the trek up to Mile High Adventures where her sister worked, and there was something soul cleansing about the views from up in the Rockies, looking down at the world below.

But *this* . . .

Green stretched out in waves beyond the sturdy wooden archway. Scattered across the expanse were little black dots she assumed were cattle, then the land covered in all that green began to roll, until far off in the distance gray, rocky, snow-capped peaks reached for the impossibly blue sky.

Cora breathed through the flutter of nerves. She wasn't here to admire the surroundings. She was here to plan a wedding.

It seemed a crazy undertaking when she'd never had

a wedding herself, a crazy undertaking when she knew her sister, Lilly, would be ten times better at it than she.

But Lilly had enough work at Mile High Adventures as PR specialist, plus mother of starting-to-be-mobile twins, and she'd given Cora this job because supposedly Cora had a "natural talent" for planning events.

Cora thought it was BS, but she wanted to make Lilly proud. She wanted to prove to everyone in her life that she'd grown up in these past few years. No more wallowing in all the ways life could be unfair, no more shrinking from being a hard-ass mother to her twelve-year-old. No more skating by.

She was reaching for the stars now, or maybe those snow-peaked mountains. Strong, immovable, and majestic.

She was ready to be *majestic*.

The gate was open, as Deb had said it would be. Cora had met the bride-to-be only once, at their initial consultation. Lilly had been there, so it had been much easier for Cora not to be nervous.

Deb was a sweet, older woman, all her children grown—some even older than Cora herself—who wanted to have the grand wedding she hadn't had as a young woman. Cora had immediately liked Deb for her clear, no-nonsense strength mixed with her desire to have a whimsical, outdoor spectacle of a wedding.

"And you are going to be the one to give that to her," Cora said aloud to herself, taking a deep breath in and out before pressing her foot on the accelerator again.

The narrow asphalt drive curved its way around, meandering along those green, fenced-in fields, cattle and horses happily grazing in different sections. When the house came into view, she could only stare wide-eyed.

It looked like a movie. The wood fairly gleamed in

the afternoon sunlight, a golden brown, with dominant glass windows reflecting the blue of the sky. The house existed in a cove of sorts, pine trees tall and proud surrounding the house except for the front yard.

The Tylers had some *serious* cash.

But before she could make it to the house that looked more like a fancy mountain resort she'd never be able to afford than a home, she had to stop.

A man on a horse was blocking the drive, and a cluster of what appeared to be baby cows ambled across.

Another man on a horse made his way toward her. When she rolled down her window, he tipped his cowboy hat. An actual cowboy hat, like this was a movie or one of the romance novels she'd read that had finally gotten her to wake up about Stephen.

"Pardon us. Just separating some calves from their mamas," the man said in a deep, swoon-worthy voice. "We'll be out of your way in just a moment." He smiled politely. At least it seemed polite. All she could really make out was his chin and his mouth because the brim of the hat shaded most of his face.

A real, honest-to-goodness cowboy hat. She knew nothing about cowboys or what they wore, but he might even be wearing chaps.

Chaps.

She wanted to giggle. Instead she forced herself to nod. She was a professional here on professional business after all.

"Can I help you with something?"

"Oh, I'm Cora Preston." Which was a stupid thing to say. Why would some ranch hand know who she was? "I-I have a meeting with Deb Tyler."

Then his expression did change, at least what she

could see of it. His mouth firmed into a grim line. "I don't suppose this is about the wedding," he said flatly.

"Well, yes." She smiled. She was the face of Mile High Weddings. It was her job to be as charming and professional as Lilly. No matter how intimidating it all seemed.

The man did not smile back. In fact, he made a noise and a movement, and then he and his horse moved away, going to converse with the man blocking the road.

Cora stared at them with a frown on her face, but when the one who hadn't spoken to her looked over his shoulder in her direction, she smiled again. *Smile, smile, smile.*

Eventually the little herd of cows was across the road, and the one who hadn't spoken rode his horse next to the group, seeming to lead them in the right direction. The one who had spoken to her moved his arm toward the house in a kind of *follow me* gesture.

Odd. She'd think whoever he was had better things to do than lead her to the house when it was clearly at the end of this long drive, but she inched along until she got to a large concrete pad in front of what she assumed was a garage that had to be bigger than her entire house back in Gracely.

Grabbing her bag, gripping the shoulder strap in an effort to center and focus herself, she got out of the car.

The man still sat on his horse, quite a few feet above her. Cora had to tip her head up and shade her eyes against the sun. She opened her mouth to speak, but the horse made an odd noise and Cora startled, which seemed to cause the horse to startle as well.

"Easy," the man murmured in a low voice as his hand swept down the horse's mane. It didn't calm *Cora* down any, but it seemed to soothe the horse.

In a fluid movement Cora could only be mesmerized by, the man swung off the horse and onto his feet in front of her. Even with him on solid ground, she still had to tip her head back to look at him. He was very tall.

And broad.

And strong.

And—

Get ahold of yourself, Cora.

"I'll take you to my mother," he said gruffly, most of his face still shadowed by the hat.

"Your mother?" Cora echoed lamely.

"Deb Tyler. My mother."

"Oh!" Oh. *Oh.* Deb had mentioned her sons were a little bent out of shape about their mother's remarrying. She'd laughed it off, but Cora knew Deb wanted her sons' approval. Micah might only be twelve, but Cora couldn't imagine not wanting him to like whomever she married.

Not that she thought that was in the cards for her, but it was a nice little fantasy to have.

With certain, ground-slapping strides, the man started walking toward the house. There was some kind of post next to the garage, and he paused briefly to tie his horse's reins to it, before walking again.

In the cute heels she was wearing, on the intricate stone walkway with lots of little dips and crannies, it was hard to keep up with him.

When she reached the porch where he was waiting for her, he slid the cowboy hat off revealing a thick, brown head of hair that looked to have been recently trimmed. He had dark brown eyes, a sharp nose and cheekbones, one of those square-cut jaws. Broad shoulders. Tall. So dang tall.

Someone could put him in a Western movie, and she'd believe he was an A-list star. She was downright ready to swoon.

Except she had a job to do. A really important one.

Lilly had stepped into Mile High Adventures over a year ago and not swooned at the very swoon-worthy sight of Brandon Evans, so Cora could be just that calm and with-it.

The man raised his eyebrows, and Cora realized that while he'd opened the door and gestured her inside, she'd been standing there staring at him.

Calm and with-it were so not her wheelhouse. But, she stepped inside and let the amazing interior take her mind off Mr. Hot Cowboy.

Wood and forest green dominated everything in this entryway. A chandelier made up of lanterns and dark metal shaped like horses hung from the high, vaulted ceiling.

Holy. Moly.

"I'll get my mother."

Cora nodded, but as he started walking toward the hallway, she thought better of it. "Wait!"

He turned slowly, looking at her as if he couldn't figure out what kind of species of bug she was.

She was the wedding coordinator, and Deb Tyler wanted the perfect wedding. Which included if not enthusiastic, at least cooperative sons. Which meant Cora had to do her best to win this man over.

"I didn't get your name."

His tight-lipped expression turned into a frown. "Shane," he said simply.

"It's nice to meet you, Shane. I'm so excited to help plan your mother's special day." She smiled brightly.

His mouth went full-on scowl, and he merely grunted before turning back toward the hallway.

Well, grunting, irritable men was something Cora Preston had learned how to deal with in the past year and a half, and it looked like she was going to be putting that experience to good use.

* * *

Shane walked down the main hall toward the back room his mother used as an office. He did his best to get his simmering irritation under wraps, because so far his disapproval of all this nonsense had only served to make Mom dig her heels in harder.

When she wasn't in her office, he headed through the back hallway toward the kitchen. "Mom?"

"Deb, the voice of doom is calling," Grandma's wavery voice said from somewhere in the vicinity of the kitchen.

He stepped into the kitchen to find Mom and Grandma at the small table they never actually ate meals at. Bridal magazines were spread everywhere. Shane tried not to scowl.

"Your wedding planner is here," he said as pleasantly as he could manage.

"Oh, shoot." Mom glanced at her watch. "I lost track of time. Poor girl. Didn't scare her off, did you?"

"Why would I do a thing like that?" he asked innocently.

Grandma gave her raspy laugh, and Mom rolled her eyes as she got to her feet. "Why indeed," she murmured loftily. "Where'd you leave her?"

"In the entryway."

Mom started toward the front of the house, and Shane trailed after her, trying to come up with some way to change her mind that wasn't antagonistic.

So far everything he'd tried had failed. He'd told her all his suspicions about Ben—that there was no record of his supposed ex-wife, that the man was the laziest ranch hand they'd ever had, that he'd lied about his references, and, most of all, that four months was not enough damn time to know someone and marry him.

Then there'd been the very foolish conversation where Shane had outright forbidden his mother to get married.

At every instance Mom went on as if he hadn't spoken at all.

His mother was too smart for this, and Shane didn't understand her insistence on forgetting that. No one in the family thought Ben Donahue was anything other than a hustling no-account. Except the two people who most needed to: Mom and Grandma.

"Where's Ben? Was he working the fence line today?" Mom asked, working her way toward the front of the house.

"I don't know where he is. *Ben* made it very clear I wasn't in charge of him."

"Oh, you two." Mom flung a hand into the air. "Acting like dicks doesn't make yours any bigger."

"Christ, Mom."

He'd lived with his mother and grandmother for thirty-two years and still wasn't used to the frank way they discussed some things a mother and son or grandmother and grandson should *never* discuss or even be in the same house while discussing.

Mom approached where he'd left the wedding planner, and Shane felt the same wave of desperation he'd been feeling since Mom had announced her engagement to scheming, lying, *thieving* Ben Donahue.

"She's skittish around horses," he blurted. "The wedding planner, that is." If he could stall this whole insane charade, maybe he could prove Ben was only using his mother.

Mom didn't even stop. "Good thing I'm not paying her to work my horses." Mom patted him on the head like he was a little kid, not her thirty-two-year-old son almost a foot taller than her. "Will you unload all that dirt in my truck and take it down to the garden before you head back to the cows?" Then, without waiting for a response, she swept into the entry with grand greetings and apologies for being late.

Shane sighed. Maybe moving the dirt would give him a few minutes of thinking to figure out how to nip this in the bud.

His siblings weren't too keen on the wedding either, but Gavin's solutions were all too violent and illegal. Lindsay and Molly had both insisted that, even if they didn't approve, they should mind their own business, and Boone wasn't around to voice an opinion at all.

Shane was the oldest, though, and, after Dad had died, the reins of this family had fallen to him. Not that he'd ever say that in front of Mom or Grandma. Still, he couldn't wait around, twiddling his thumbs, *hoping* his mother didn't make the biggest mistake of her life. He had to act—without getting thrown in jail, as Gavin's plans would surely get them.

Shane walked out the back and around the house to the garage and keyed in the code. He hung his hat on the hook, then went over to Mom's truck. He hefted two sacks of dirt out of the trunk and over his shoulder, relaxing as his body got into manual-labor mode.

Maybe he could tell the wedding planner they didn't have any money. That every last cent was tied up in the ranch and any checks written to her would inevitably bounce. Stall this nonsense.

He walked passed MacGregor with the bags of dirt on his shoulder. The horse eyed him.

"Don't judge me," Shane muttered. Sometimes the ends justified the slightly sketchy means.

He'd given up swaying Grandma to his side, and he knew telling his siblings they needed to interfere would only ensure they thought otherwise. They never cared for his telling them what to do.

A Tyler family trait, which made it a good thing they ran their own ranch. None of them could probably stay gainfully employed somewhere else without thumbing their noses at the boss.

Well, except Boone. But since his job was trying to stay a few seconds on an angry bull, Shane didn't count that much for listening to a boss.

Shane unloaded all the bags of dirt, then arranged it around Mom's garden plot in a way that it would be easy for her to put the dirt where it needed to go. On an oath, he pulled his Swiss army knife out of his pocket.

He knew exactly where Mom would want all the dirt, and it'd take him less time to do it. So, he went about cutting bags open and dumping the extra dirt in the newly turned plot she'd start planting in soon.

Once that was done, he figured he might as well go ahead and get some fertilizer from the stables while he was at it. It would give Mom the time to plant rather than fiddle with the hefting and hauling part of the garden.

He headed back for the garage. Better ride over to Gavin and tell him he was fooling with the garden at Mom's request so Gavin could get on with things with the cattle.

He grabbed his hat, but before he could walk over to MacGregor, a female voice interrupted him.

"Oh, hi. Excuse me?"

When he turned, the wedding planner was making a beeline for him. Shane scowled, but manners had been drummed into him too hard for that to last. It wasn't *her* fault his mother was falling for a lying piece of trash. He forced himself to smile. Well, not scowl anyway.

"Hello, again," she greeted, peering up at him. "May

I have a moment? Real quick. I promise." She smiled broadly. What had she said her name was? Cora?

"Sure," he muttered, slightly taken off guard by the way the sun glinted off her hair, showing off every possible shade from golden blond to reddish brown. He'd never seen a hair color like it.

"I do hope you'll be cooperative," she began as he chastised himself for thinking about someone's *hair color*. "Your mother is hoping you'll walk her down the aisle, and she thinks you'll refuse and—"

"Damn right I'll refuse," he interrupted. He was not giving his mother away to a lying son of a bitch. Not even to spare her feelings.

"But surely . . ." She opened her mouth, then closed it. There was some kind of calculation going on in that head of hers.

"Nice to meet you and all, but I've got work to do." He took a step toward his horse, but she jumped in front of him, blocking his way. He didn't worry about manners now. He glared down at her.

"You love your mother, don't you?" she asked, clearly unaffected by his glare.

"You think I don't approve because I *don't*? That woman raised three boys, two girls, and ran a ranch with only my grandma for help for the past twenty years. She deserves all the happiness in the world, and I'd be jumping up and down for joy and offering to *carry* her down the aisle in a . . . whatever those things are they carried Cleopatra around in. I'd do anything for her."

Cora blinked up at him, dark blue eyes wide. She had the lightest freckles dusted across her nose, and her pretty pink mouth twisted in confusion. She wasn't short by any means, but something about her gave off an aura of smallness. Not frail exactly, but not exactly *hardy*. He was used to hardy.

"I disapprove," he continued, because what did it matter what this woman looked like? "Because that sleaze-ball she's marrying is after this ranch and this ranch alone, and I won't let her be swindled out of this spread because she's blinded by lust."

"Lust," Cora echoed, a faint pink blotching across her cheeks.

"He's *forty-two*. My mother is *fifty-two*. You'll have to pardon my skepticism."

Cora blinked, then smiled at him, much the way his mother smiled at him when she thought he was being unreasonable. "I think maybe, just maybe, you might be letting your protective instincts as a son blind you to your mother's feelings. It's even noble, I think," she said gently. Almost sympathetically. "If you'd only—"

"This wedding can't happen. I'm going to make sure of it." Maybe that was too blunt, but he wasn't going to pretend he felt any differently to some stranger planning a wedding.

"Over my dead body," the woman muttered, then blushed when she seemed to realize she'd said it out loud.

Shane held her blue gaze that seemed to match the sky above them. *Regardless.* "We'll see about that," he returned. "Now, if you'll excuse me." He didn't wait for her response. He slipped the hat on his head and marched for MacGregor.

One way or another, this wedding would not happen. Even if he had to fight the determined, pretty wedding planner on top of his mother and grandmother and Ben Donahue.

Shane would do anything to protect his family. And that was that.

Chapter Two

Cora pulled her car into the carport next to her pretty little house on the corner of Hope and Aspen in the middle of Gracely. Lilly had picked it out a few years ago when she'd decided to move them away from Denver, and Stephen, to a place with legends about healing.

Maybe someday Cora would want to pick out a place herself, but Lilly had good taste, and it had been the perfect house for Cora and Micah to heal in, and then plant some roots in. It suited them, even after Lilly had gone and gotten married and moved up to the mountains with Brandon.

Cora sighed. Micah wasn't happy, and she couldn't figure out why. Last summer had been great, and this school year had gone well, Cora had thought. His grades had improved, he'd helped out at Mile High on the weekends, and she'd thought it had been giving him confidence.

But as the school year had ended, Micah had clammed up. Turned sullen again. He complained about going to Mile High. He complained about the basketball camp he'd all but begged her to sign him up for a few months ago.

Cora's stomach twisted painfully at the thought of forcing him to tell her what was wrong. She'd failed him when he'd first come into this world, and, even with loads of family counseling and a little bit of therapy for herself, it was hard to get over that guilt. For the first seven years of his life, she'd let him see what no child should have to see, and then she'd spent two years in that wishy-washy space of *stay or leave, be alone or hurt, accept this warped love or have no love at all.*

She squeezed her eyes shut. She was here now, and Micah was here now, and she would do right by him, even if she hadn't in the past.

So, she had to push. No matter how much the coward inside of her didn't want to.

She opened her eyes and stared at the house, then realized her neighbor and friend was standing on the porch next door staring thoughtfully at her. Thoughtfully, not like she was watching a woman who'd lost her mind and was sitting in her idling car in her driveway having a mental argument with herself.

Cora pulled the key out of the ignition and slid out of the car, forcing herself to smile brightly at Tori. "Hey."

"Hey." Tori crossed the narrow yard between their houses. "You okay?"

"Sure I am." Because Cora had spent a little too much of her life the past few years brooding and wallowing, and she'd made a New Year's resolution all those months ago. No more self-pity. No more guilt. New Cora. New *life.* She'd been doing a damn fine job.

"Wedding thing went good?"

Cora tensed at the careful way Tori was beating around the bush. Tori *never* beat around the bush. "Yes, it did. Well, mostly." She thought of Shane Tyler and his *we'll see about that.*

It was kind of sweet, all in all. After his little speech about how he'd do anything for his mother, and about the age difference between Deb and Ben, Cora understood why Deb's children were reticent to be supportive. It wasn't because they were being babies about the whole thing. It was because they wanted to protect their mother.

But it was *her* job to make sure Deb got the wedding she'd always dreamed of, and Cora would find a way to get through to the Tyler kids. She would.

But first, she had to deal with her own kid.

Tori shoved her hands in her pockets and rocked back on her heels. "Listen. . . ."

Bad news. Definitely bad news. "Whatever it is, just say it," Cora said, bracing herself. She couldn't stand Tori of all people being gentle with her.

"Will went to pick up Micah," Tori said, referring to her fiancé, Will Evans. Who also happened to be Lilly's brother-in-law. Things at Mile High Adventures were nothing if not a complicated weaving of relations and relationships.

And Will was picking up Cora's son hours before basketball camp was supposed to be over. "Why? Was he hurt? Why didn't anyone call me?"

"Micah texted Will. Said he'd ditched basketball camp and needed a ride. He claimed he'd called you and you hadn't answered, but we didn't quite buy it."

Cora frantically pawed through her purse and grabbed her phone. She scrolled through everything. No, her son hadn't called her. "Why would he do that? Why would he lie?"

"I don't know. Will was going to try to get it out of him."

Cora wanted to sink to the ground. She wanted to

stomp her foot. She wanted to go upstairs and crawl in her bed and shut out the world. Instead, she smiled thinly at Tori. "I'm sorry Will had to go to the trouble of driving out to Benson."

"You know he didn't mind."

"I know, but . . ." Cora heaved out a sigh. God, it was nice, this whole having a family and community thing. So many people to help her and her son out, so many people who loved them.

But it was also hard. She was used to only having Lilly to lean on, which meant only Lilly seeing her failures. Now she had more people to lean on, but also more people who saw when she screwed up.

Cora pushed that thought out of her head. Her therapist, Dr. Grove, was forever telling her motherhood was not a series of successes and failures. It was a complex mix of love and responsibility, and she shouldn't blame herself when Micah had setbacks.

Blame helped nobody. But Micah's setbacks shamed her anyway. "I don't know why he wouldn't have called me. I don't know why. . . ."

"Who knows why kids do anything? Will's going to try the whole man-to-man approach."

Will's Jeep pulled up in front of Tori's house, and Cora sucked in a breath. Man-to-man approach or not, she was still Micah's mother, and she had to have her own approach.

She saw Micah glance at her through the glass of the passenger-side window. She wished she could read those long, stoic looks. Micah was her son, and she had raised him, along with Lilly, but pretty much by herself. Still, so often Cora looked at him and had no idea what he was thinking or feeling.

Dr. Grove assured her that was normal for *all* parents. Cora tried to believe it.

Micah slunk out of the Jeep, and Will got out as well, following Micah toward her and Tori.

"Hey, Mom," Micah mumbled in greeting. Then he tried to walk past her into the house. She stopped him with a gentle hand to his shoulder.

He sighed heavily. "I just wasn't feeling good, okay?"

"You didn't call me," she said in the most neutral voice she could manage.

He shrugged, jerking his shoulder out from under her hand. "I knew you had your meeting or whatever. I didn't want to bug you. And you told me to call anybody at Mile High if I ever had an emergency."

"What about your aunt?"

"Couldn't get a hold of her," Micah mumbled, but his gaze slid away, and she knew he was lying.

"Go inside. We'll talk about this more in a minute."

"There isn't anything to talk about," Micah insisted, his expression going quietly mutinous.

"Inside," Cora said firmly without letting any of her simmering frustration show through.

Micah complained under his breath and stomped inside. Cora tried to smile at Will. "Thank you for bringing him home. I appreciate it."

"You know it's no problem. Look, the kid's got something going on, and it isn't not feeling well."

"Do you have any idea what it is?"

"No. I tried to get it out of him, but . . ." Will shrugged apologetically. "I deal with tight-lipped, don't-want-to-talk-about-it people on the regular." He snuck a little glance at Tori, who glared at him. "Kid's a rock."

"Yes." One Cora wanted to beat her head against. "Well, thanks, guys. I better go talk to him."

"Good luck," Tori offered with a smile.

"Thanks."

"Wine if you need it later."

On impulse, Cora pulled Tori into a hug. "Thank you."

"You know I hate it when you hug me," Tori said as she awkwardly patted Cora's back.

"I know," Cora replied, smiling as she pulled away. "That's half the fun of it." It bolstered her, this having friends who would step in and help, who'd offer wine and let her hug them even when they hated it.

She murmured her good-byes and stepped into the house. She already heard the beeps and irritating music of a video game. She stepped into the kitchen to gather her thoughts and roll her eyes. Hard.

She *hated* the video games Micah lost himself in, and yet she couldn't bring herself to take them away. There'd always been basketball to balance it out.

She marched over to where Micah was slumped into the couch, face so close to the screen of his handheld system she wanted to snap at him to pull it away. But she didn't.

"Is it the other kids?"

"Is what the other kids?"

Since she knew he wouldn't dare look away from his precious game, she allowed herself to make a face at him.

"Why you don't want to do camp?" she asked, adopting a pleasant and curious tone, instead of the accusatory one that wanted to slip out.

He shrugged. "The other kids are fine."

"The coaches then?"

"They're okay."

"So," she said, breathing through the frustration, "what's the problem?"

He shrugged again as if it were the only language he had.

"Micah, I need a reason."

"It's dumb."

"You *asked* me to go to this."

"Yeah, because you said I had to do *something* this summer." He infuriatingly kept playing the game, not once looking at her as his fingers flew over the buttons. "All my friends get to hang out at home. They get to sleep in and chill out, and I have to go to stupid camp and sweat and shit."

"Did you just say *shit* to me, young man?"

Micah rolled his eyes, all disdain and teenage sullenness, and it wasn't fair since he was *only* twelve. She was supposed to have a few more years before this.

"Whatever, Mom." He slid off the couch, his eyes never leaving the screen of his game. He started walking for the stairs.

Because she wanted to yell and demand, she let him go. She'd cool off first, then try again. Not a failure, just a regrouping. Giving him space, keeping the line of communication open, no yelling that might shut him down.

He was going to his next appointment with Dr. Grove no matter how much of a fuss he put up, that was for damn sure.

And she . . . She was definitely going to need that glass of wine.

Shane dried his hands on the towel in the bathroom and hesitated before heading out.

Mom had called a family dinner. Which she usually only did when she wanted to make some horrible announcement. Especially given that she'd summoned Lindsay home from school in Denver. The only person who would be missing was Boone, who was off rodeoing here, there, and everywhere, and was usually missing.

But worse than missing his youngest brother, or

impending doom-filled announcements, was the fact that "family" dinners now included Ben Donahue.

Shane scowled at the door. He had to get it out now, because, while he was no less adamant about making sure his mother did not go through with this wedding, he knew he couldn't keep sniping with Ben.

Shane had to find some well of calm politeness. Arguing would only make his mother dig her heels in deeper, and Ben as well. Shane had to adopt an act of friendliness, and he was pretty sure it would kill him.

But he'd give it his best shot. When he stepped out of the bathroom, Gavin was standing there, leaning against the hallway wall.

"What is taking so long? I'm not going in there by myself, that's for sure."

"We just have to stick to the plan, and everything will be fine."

Gavin rolled his eyes. "The plan sucks. The only plan I'm interested in is one where we beat Ben black-and-blue and leave him to rot in the mountains."

"What, so Mom can insist on going to find him?"

"Oh, I can leave him in a place where no one can find him," Gavin said with a little too much glee.

Shane shook his head, walking down the hall feeling like he was heading for the electric chair. "We have to be smart about this. Careful. Mom's not stupid."

"Except when it comes to this dipshit," Gavin muttered.

"Yeah, well . . ."

They stepped into the dining room. Shane's youngest sister, Lindsay, was setting the table. Molly was probably in the kitchen with Mom and Grandma helping with food.

Lindsay's blue eyes darted to the doorway to the kitchen, then back to Gavin and Shane. "Gossip time," she whispered. "Mom's moving up the date of the wedding."

"What?" Shane demanded.

"Shh," Lindsay admonished. "She's calling the wedding planner out tomorrow to see the soonest possible date they can have the wedding of her dreams. That's what she's going to announce, and the reason I'm telling you right now is so you don't tackle Ben over the dinner table."

"Tackling sounds like a plan," Gavin offered.

"No, Gavin," Shane said evenly, even though the announcement sparked his temper. "You know we can't do that. We remain calm, we agree with whatever she says, and then we get serious about proving that man is a no good, useless piece of—"

"Evening, gentlemen," Ben greeted cheerfully, stepping into the dining room from behind them. "Evening, Lindsay," he offered, all smiles and charm at Lindsay's wide-eyed look and all-too-obvious blush at the thought of Ben's possibly overhearing them.

Shane didn't particularly care. He wasn't big on hiding his judgment of lazy assholes who acted like they owned the place when they should be grateful they had a job at all. But for tonight, for his long-term goal, he'd try to force some of that judgment away.

Shane struggled with a polite smile. "Evening, Donahue. Glad you could join us."

"Well, it *is* a family dinner," he replied with a wink.

As if he belonged. Which was on purpose. He was *trying* to get under Shane's and Gavin's skin. Trying to provoke a fight, because that would get him even better on Mom's side.

Shane wouldn't fall for it, and he nudged his brother to remind Gavin not to fall for it either.

Molly and Grandma came out from the kitchen

area, Molly carrying a tray of ham. She smiled at Shane and Gavin, and Shane was quite certain Ben had no idea the smile she gave *him* was considerably dimmer in comparison.

"Hey, guys. Have a seat. Dinner is ready."

Grandma settled herself in her usual chair next to Mom's place at the head of the table. Before Shane could take his usual seat across from Grandma, Ben slid in.

It was Gavin's turn to give Shane a little nudge, and Shane forced the muscles in his jaw to relax. Mom appeared with another tray carrying bowls of potatoes, green beans, and rolls as Shane took the seat next to Grandma, usurping Molly's usual spot.

Molly frowned at him, so he nodded toward the seat next to Ben. Molly might not like Ben either, but she wasn't liable to haul off and punch him.

Shane wasn't so sure he could keep his fists to himself, and he *knew* he couldn't trust Gavin to.

"What's with the big-ass ham, Mom?" Gavin asked, taking the seat next to Shane.

"Do not swear at my table, Gavin Louis. Besides, what's wrong with ham?"

"Nothing is wrong with ham. It's just usually ham means bad news," Gavin replied.

"But turkey is worse. Turkey means someone is dead or about to croak," Lindsay offered with a grin.

Mom shook her head and began to pass food around the table. "You all are delusional. There is no hierarchy of meat and what it means."

"Meatloaf is the worst. It means Mom's about to give us more work than any one person can handle," Molly said, her smile softer than Lindsay's, but no less pleased with herself.

"You lot can always handle more work," Mom said

firmly. "Now, isn't this nice, having everyone home for dinner?"

There was an uncomfortable silence, considering everyone *wasn't* home, not with Boone absent, but marinating in that wouldn't do any good.

"Gav and I got the whole herd separated today. We'll be moving the heifers to the south pasture first thing tomorrow. Well . . ." Shane slid his most innocent look at Ben. "If we've got the fencing all mended."

Shane watched for it, and was moderately rewarded when Ben tensed. Making sure that particular fence was ready had been Ben's job today, and one thing Ben was never any good about was getting a job done in time.

In fact Shane had been considering firing Ben, at least before the bastard had started cozying up to Mom. It was just another thing in a long line of questionable timing that made Shane hate this.

"Let's not talk ranch tonight," Mom said with a big smile. She reached over and took Ben's hand in hers. Whatever tension Shane had managed to put in Ben relaxed with Mom's touch.

Shane resisted the impulse to scowl.

"I'm going to need all of you to really step in and help with this wedding, because Ben and I simply can't wait until Christmas. I'm going to talk to Cora tomorrow, but we're going to shoot for September now."

An uneasy silence fell over the dining room table. It wasn't the first time an announcement in this family had been met with that. When Boone had informed them he was joining the rodeo, when Molly had informed them she'd eloped . . . and then a few months ago moving home and getting divorced. When Lindsay had told everyone quite proudly she'd gotten a scholarship for *art*.

Those had all felt like . . . fixable things. Youthful

indiscretions. Things a person learned from, and he or she would always have the Tyler ranch to come home to if it didn't work out.

But Mom's marrying Ben was none of those things.

"At least she's not pregnant," Grandma offered into that silence.

"Mother," Mom scolded, her cheeks turning a little bit pink.

"It was why you got married the first time," Grandma returned, her gaze slowly turning to Shane.

The ham in Shane's mouth suddenly turned into tasteless rubber, and Grandma cackled happily to herself. He really didn't need to be reminded of the timing of his parents' marriage and his own birth.

"Looking a little green there, Shane boy," she said, all too pleased with herself.

But she was the only pleased one. As Shane glanced around the table he saw his brother's furious face, Molly's concerned one, Lindsay's confused one. And they were all looking at *him*.

Because in the absence of Mom's being the reasonable leader of this family, Shane had to be. He stood.

"I'm sorry, Mom. But none of us are comfortable with this."

"Now, see here—" Ben began, but Mom held up a hand.

"I didn't ask you to be comfortable," she said calmly, staring right at Shane. "You are my children, whom I brought into this world and have cared for my entire life, never once stopping to mention when I was *uncomfortable*." She glanced at Molly, who stared hard at her plate.

Shane knew Mom expected him to fold, to give in. She'd used the guilt—a fair use of it too—and it usually worked, but this was more than a disagreement over cows or money or even helping neighbors.

This was about his mother, and it was about the ranch, and he couldn't back down on that.

"If you're determined to do this," Shane said evenly, borrowing one of his mother's old tactics when her children disobeyed, "I can't stand in your way, but I also won't help."

"I see." Mom looked around the table at all her children. "And you all feel this way?"

Gavin pushed his chair back and stood next to Shane. After a moment's hesitation, so did Molly. Lindsay stared on, wide-eyed and unmoving.

"You may leave my table then," Mom said coolly.

Shane could feel Gavin coil to argue, but that wouldn't work. Not now. "Fair enough," Shane said, nudging Gavin toward the door. Molly glanced at Lindsay, and then Mom, pained. But she didn't say anything.

Shane followed them both out, and then they stood in the hall just staring at each other.

Molly was the first to speak, and she spoke directly to Shane. "Well, now what?"

He wished he had a clue, but he had to find one. And quick.

Chapter Three

Cora was running late, and she knew she shouldn't beat herself up, but Lilly would never run late. Lilly was always on time and looked perfectly put together.

But you are not Lilly. No one *is Lilly.*

Cora pulled her car up to the Tyler house and looked at her face in the rearview mirror. Her mascara was smudged, and her lipstick had long been chewed off. She'd spent the morning forcing Micah to go to Dr. Grove's office for a family therapy session since he didn't want to go to basketball camp.

It hadn't gone well. Micah had been stoic and unresponsive and a pain in her butt. She'd cried in front of him like she'd promised herself she wasn't going to do anymore. She felt like such a failure.

"But you are not a failure," she said to her own reflection. "You are a work in progress." Her mantra, and it mostly made her feel a little better.

She wouldn't have been late if she hadn't spent too much time worrying over sticking Lilly with Micah when Lilly had both twins while her husband was leading an excursion.

Lilly had assured her it was fine, and that Skeet—Mile

High's old, grizzled receptionist—was great with the babies despite his rather gruff, scary outward appearance.

Cora hadn't had a choice at that point. Leave or be super late. She'd left. Now, she was only two minutes late, which wasn't too bad all things considered. She took approximately thirty seconds to fix up her makeup as best she could.

Once satisfied with her reflection, she slipped out of her car. She glanced around the expansive yard and the ranch. She didn't see any sign of people, only cows and mountains and various machinery.

What must it be like to live somewhere so open and vast? She loved living in quaint little Gracely, and the view from the majestic mountains where Mile High was located was truly awe-inspiring. But something about the Tyler ranch touched *her*. It wasn't just beautiful. It created this odd little pang inside of her.

Which was silly. She was a city girl through and through. She'd grown up in Denver, adjusted to small town life over the past few years, but she'd never know what to do with cattle and all this *space*.

It was still a fun fantasy to have. Made a bit more fun with the image of a man on a horse, a cowboy hat pulled low, sun shining down on him like a spotlight.

Shane Tyler might be a pain in his mother's butt, like Micah was a pain in hers, but he sure was pretty to look at.

She shook her head and headed for the front door. The last thing she wanted today was another run-in with a disapproving son. Besides, she didn't want to be any later than she already was.

She knocked on the door, and Deb answered quickly. She greeted Cora with a broad grin. "Cora. Right on time, sweetheart. Come on in."

Cora opened her mouth to say she was *not* right on time. She was nearly five minutes late, but then she remembered she didn't always have to point out her flaws to everyone around her. A sad little coping mechanism she'd developed first under her mother, then under Stephen's heavy hand. If she pointed out her flaws, she got to the punch first before anyone else could.

But she wasn't that little girl anymore, and Deb was nice. So, Cora followed her into the living room. Much like the kitchen table they'd met at a few days ago, the living room was cozy and well kept. Everything looked polished and bright in the sun shining through big windows that looked out over the ranch and gorgeous mountains in the distance.

"I have a new challenge for you, Cora," Deb said, taking a seat in a comfortable-looking chair.

Cora carefully sat herself on the edge of the couch, refusing to be intimidated by the word "challenge."

"I know we were discussing Christmastime, or maybe even next spring, but I don't want to wait that long. Ben and I were talking the other night about how short life is, and we've both lost a lot already. Why wait?"

"Well, all the things you wanted for the wedding, they take time and . . ."

"And money. Which I have plenty of. Our neighbor to the north, the Fairchilds, their granddaughters grew up with my kids. Lou has an adorable little flower farm and she has a florist business to go along with it. She's recovering from a bit of an accident right now, but I talked to her about flowers, and she said she could do everything in a shorter time period."

"Oh—okay, but—"

"And I don't know if you know the owner of Piece of Cake?"

"Yes, Emily and I—"

"She's Lou's sister, used to date Gavin, in fact, and I've asked her if, for a fee, she'd be willing to move me up, and well, old family friends and all, she agreed."

Cora felt her panic rising. What did Deb need her for if she'd already figured this all out? "That's wonderful, but—"

"The dress might be the trickiest thing. My girls'll be easy of course, but . . ." The spark in Deb's eyes seemed to dim, the excitement disappearing from her face in the snap of a finger.

It was wrong to jump all over that hint at a problem, but Cora needed this job. "Deb, what's wrong?"

The older woman swallowed. "Oh, the kids." She waved a hand. "Might not have my girls as bridesmaids after all."

"Of course you will."

Deb shook her head. "Oh, Lindsay might come around, but Molly . . . Well, her and Shane always did take sides against me. I didn't think Gavin'd give a rat's ass, but he's all bristly about it too. I never dreamed I'd do something like this and disappoint my kids, but they're grown. I can't live for them anymore."

"They'll come around. You're such a good mom. I can see that just having been here twice. They're trying to protect you. It's sweet, but we'll prove they don't need to. They just have to get over this hump is all, but they will because . . ." Cora thought of her own mother. "Some mothers don't do much of anything for their kids, and you are not like that."

"Oh, I like you, Cora. You're a sweet girl, and there's some good grit under that sweetness."

Grit. Cora had never considered herself as someone who had any *grit*. She liked that Deb thought so.

She pulled her portfolio from her bag to jot down a

few notes. "Well. I'll adjust the schedule. I think we could still make it all happen by end of September?"

"I can work with that."

"And we'll have those kids of yours throwing rice and doing jigs."

Deb chuckled. "I don't think you know what you're getting yourself into there, sweetheart."

"Maybe not," Cora admitted. "I've only got one to deal with, and I'm not dealing very well."

"You have a little one?"

"Not so little. Twelve going on . . . I don't know. Surly adult." At Deb's shocked look, Cora smiled sheepishly. "I was a little on the young side when I had him."

"Ah. I was a bit young myself when I had Shane." She sighed, a wistful fondness in the sound. "That boy hasn't given me an ounce of trouble since he was twelve. Well, until now."

"Not an *ounce*? Mine is giving me nothing but these days."

"Don't feel bad, the other two boys raised enough hell for ten. And my girls have taken regularly to breaking my heart."

"So, what you're saying is it never gets better?"

Deb laughed heartily. "Better and worse all at the same time." Deb's laugh died on a sigh. "I don't know how to get through to them. After all these years, I don't know how to get my kids to be happy for me. I've got this handsome young man who all but worships the ground I walk on after twenty years of doing all this on my own. Ben Donahue might not be the best man in the world, but he's a good man to me."

"Then, we will find a way." If Cora had to face down five disapproving adult children to do it, well, she would. She was taking it as a personal mission.

* * *

"She couldn't do it without the wedding planner. She'd have to put it off again until she found a new one," Gavin suggested.

Shane stared at the wedding planner's car as he and Gavin stood outside the barn, taking a break and drinking some water. That tiny compact car had been sitting in the drive in front of the house for well over an hour. Gavin had been grousing about not letting this happen for just as long, and Shane . . .

Well, he was frustrated beyond belief by a problem that seemed to have no solution. "The wedding planner isn't the problem. Ben Donahue is the problem."

"But you said so yourself, we go after him, that only makes Mom latch on harder."

"Hence, stuck between a rock and a hard place." But Shane was a problem solver. He just needed to keep looking at this from all angles until he found one. Giving up was not an option.

"We have to do something. I swear to God she put something in the coffee this morning. Maybe not poison, but I'm telling you."

Shane slid a skeptical look at his brother.

Gavin held up his hands. "It tasted different."

"You're beyond paranoid."

"Easy for you to say, you don't drink coffee."

The front door opened, and Mom and Cora stepped out onto the porch. They shared a brief hug that had Shane frowning. That was the problem with Gavin's idea that they intercept the wedding planner. Mom befriended everyone, took everyone under her wing and made him or her feel good and welcome. They were too late to step in there since Mom had clearly already formed a friendship with Cora.

But as Shane watched, Cora didn't get into her car. She started across the yard, walking straight for them.

"What's she coming over here for?" Gavin demanded.

"How would I know?" But she'd come to talk to him after her last meeting with Mom. "She told me last time Mom wants . . ." Well, he didn't need to be specific. "Wants us involved."

Gavin snorted. "And you told her to go to hell, right?"

"Politely, yes."

"I'm done being polite."

"When did you start?" Shane asked good-naturedly, but any levity he felt at razzing his brother died as Cora crossed the drive and was now marching toward them over the grass around the barn.

She wasn't hard to look at. She wore a dress with un-furling pink flowers all over it that swished a little too enticingly along her legs as she moved at a steady clip. Her long reddish-blondish hair was swirling around her face as the gentle breeze played with it. She had dark blue eyes and a heart-shaped face, and Shane was more than a little irritated at himself for being attracted to her.

Didn't matter. They were at cross-purposes right now. Besides, delicate pretty was not his type. Mostly.

"Hello," she greeted once she approached. She was a hint out of breath, and her cheeks were slightly flushed. There was something different about her today. She wasn't really smiling. Not scowling either. Some firm, in-between expression Shane couldn't read and didn't trust.

"'Lo," Gavin returned suspiciously.

Shane nodded at her. He'd like to be curt, but it wouldn't be fair, so he smiled politely. "Good afternoon," he offered.

"I've just come from a meeting with your mother. If all goes according to plan, we'll have the wedding here at the end of September."

Shane couldn't help himself. He had to disabuse her of that notion right quick. "And if all goes according to *our* plan, we won't have a wedding at all."

She frowned, a little line appearing in the middle of her forehead and across the bridge of her nose. "What's your plan?"

Shane exchanged a look with his brother. They didn't exactly have a plan yet, but they would.

Cora chuckled. "Oh, good, I thought for a second you had some horrible idea to sabotage your mother's wedding and that my first impression of you had been all wrong." She smiled at both of them, all dazzling positivity. "Whatever differences are between you and the groom-to-be, we can work those out. Can't we?"

"No," Shane and Gavin said in unison.

Her smile died. "I was afraid you'd say that," she muttered.

"Look, I got somewhere to be," Gavin said. He turned to Shane and explained under his breath, "A few things to do for Lou's barn. Be back after lunch."

"Yeah. She doing okay?"

"Okay." Gavin tipped his hat at Cora, then cringed a little bit as if he was irritated with his own ingrained manners.

Even though Gavin left, the wedding planner didn't. Shane struggled between the urge to shoo her off and the urge to at least *try* and sway her to their point of view about this ridiculous wedding.

But she spoke first.

"Are you busy tonight?"

His jaw dropped. She wasn't actually . . .

"Oh, I'm not asking you out," she said, leaning forward

and touching his arm, something like a quick poke. She laughed a little too hard at the idea, but then her gaze traveled the length of him and back up again, before she flashed him a flirtatious smile. If he had been less of a man, he might have blushed.

"I know you love your mother. I can tell, and she's infinitely worthy of that devotion. I can tell that too. I just want to try and prove to you that you've got it all wrong about Ben."

"How would you know?"

She opened her mouth and then closed it. She seemed to ponder something for a moment and then shook her head. "Do you know where the VFW Hall in Benson is?"

He did not trust this at all, but he nodded in assent.

"Meet me there at eight tonight."

"I thought you weren't asking me out on a date," he returned.

She grinned at him, a dimple winking in her cheek. Why he wanted to grin back was beyond him. Probably just because she was pretty. Who didn't want to smile at a pretty woman?

"I'm not." Again her eyes took a little tour of his body, and he damn well had to fight the urge to fidget.

Seriously. Who *was* this woman?

"Bring your dancing shoes, though."

"My *what*?"

But she'd turned away at that, waving over her shoulder as she walked back to her car. Shane scowled after her.

He was not going to meet her or go dancing or whatever-on-earth crazy scheme she was up to. He was going to stay home like he always did, have dinner with his family, and then go over ranch paperwork while Grandma polished her sword collection.

Definitely not going to Benson. Definitely not meeting the wedding planner.

Probably not anyway.

Chapter Four

It was difficult picking out what to wear when you weren't going out on a date, but you also wouldn't mind a guy looking at you twice, but you were also employed by his mother and trying to convince him her wedding was legit.

Life was full of complications.

In the end, Cora had decided to wear the same cute floral dress she'd been wearing all day, but exchanged her flats for cowboy boots she was ninety-nine percent sure no cowboy would ever be caught dead in.

She wondered absently if Shane knew how to square dance. He didn't seem like the type, but when Deb had mentioned that she and Ben belonged to a local square dancing club, Cora had been surprised. Deb didn't seem like the type either, but Deb's face had just lit up when she'd talked about it.

So, Cora had devised her plan right then and there. She needed to prove to the Tyler children that Ben was worthy of their mother. She would start with Shane because he was the oldest and so clearly the de facto leader.

It had nothing to do with the fact that he was hot. Especially with the boots and the cowboy hat and that stoic politeness he always employed.

Okay, it had something to do with that. What could she say? She liked men. A lot. It was her great downfall that she liked going on dates, flirting, and all that dazzling anticipation. And sex. Oh, she really liked sex.

She'd sworn it off in her grand effort to get her life together, to focus on her career and on being a mom. Much as she liked them, men were far too much trouble. One preteen was all the trouble she could handle.

But surely that didn't mean she couldn't enjoy a little harmless flirting here and there.

Micah was going to hang out at Will and Tori's under the guise of walking their German shepherd, Sarge, and doing a few other jobs around their place to earn some extra money, and then they were going to ply him with pizza and ice cream till she got back.

She thought absently of how nice it would be to have a dog of their own, except she couldn't afford the time or the money or the investment in another living creature. Maybe when Micah was a little older and could really be counted on to be responsible.

She shook her head and grabbed her purse. Tonight, she had to focus on work. Tomorrow would be about regrouping and trying to get through to Micah, since Dr. Grove always suggested giving him some space between a session and then trying to talk with him about the takeaways.

She stepped outside into the slowly falling evening. The houses around them had started to fill up after its being a nearly empty street when she'd originally moved here with Lilly. Brandon's starting a chamber of commerce dedicated to drawing business owners and customers to Gracely proper was starting to have an effect.

There was a pizza parlor now, and the man who ran it lived across the street. A young couple who were teachers in Benson had bought a house a few doors down to live in the more "quaint and picturesque" Gracely. It was things like that that would bring Gracely back from the brink of a ghost town.

Cora had to believe it was possible. Her brother-in-law believed it was possible because he'd grown up here and had seen the town at its best, and because he felt responsible for its worst. But Cora had to believe because she'd once lived her life like little more than a ghost town herself, and she wanted to believe she could rebuild and be whole and vibrant.

And that was what spurred her on. Even though trying to convince the Tyler siblings to support their mother's wedding wasn't her job, it felt like something she *had* to do. It felt like being someone she wanted to be.

She drove through town, then over ranch land-adjacent highway to the much larger town of Benson. She turned into the VFW Hall parking lot and immediately saw Shane. He leaned against the bed of a gleaming red truck, cowboy hat pulled low as it always seemed to be, while the sun set behind him in a riot of colors painting the mountains like watercolors.

There were no empty parking spots next to him, so she pulled past and then into the first empty one. She wasn't surprised Shane was here. He didn't strike her as the kind of man who could resist showing up, especially in an attempt to prove a point. She was a little surprised he'd beaten her here.

And not at all surprised by the sparking anticipation

beating like butterflies low in her stomach. If hot men were her weakness, she was pretty sure hot cowboys would be her downfall.

She gave herself a hasty glance in the rearview mirror, caught herself grinning. "Business only," she said sternly into the mirror. "No flirting. Tonight is all about his mother. No. Flirting."

She jumped a foot when someone tapped on her window. She hadn't realized he'd seen her, considering he'd had that hat down so low, but Shane was standing there, a puzzled frown on his face.

She grabbed her purse, fixed her most business-like smile on her face, and nudged the driver's side door open.

"I'm sorry, were you on the phone or something?"

"No." She could've lied, but maybe the best thing for her would be to act completely herself. She wouldn't want to flirt with a guy who knew she was a little screwy, and she couldn't want to flirt with Shane, so she'd just go for the bald truth. She stood and closed the door, offering him an arch look. "I talk to myself. Doesn't everyone?"

She sailed past him, not paying attention to the way the flannel shirt he was wearing stretched across broad shoulders or to that mysterious shadow the ever-present cowboy hat gave his face.

Mysterious hot cowboy might be even more of a weakness, but she was stronger than all that. She would be.

"So, what exactly did you want to show me at the VFW Hall?" He glanced around the parking lot as people moved past them, most of them dressed in pressed plaid and poofy skirts. There was even a guy with matching pants and a vest patterned with horses.

"Follow me," Cora replied, and she was a little too

pleased when he did so instead of questioning her further.

She went through the front doors and followed the throng of people, mostly older, though there were a few more middle-aged couples, and one or two young couples more her and Shane's age.

She snuck a look at him. He'd slipped his hat off on entering the building, and his face was a maze of clear confusion. He had no idea his mother was in a square dancing club. She wondered if Deb kept it from him, or if he just didn't pay attention.

Much as Cora believed he was the dutiful son Deb described, Cora had a feeling Shane also didn't pry too deeply into his mother's personal life—aside from passing judgment on her choice of partners of course.

There was a reception area of sorts, but the crowd ambled through a door down the hall, so Cora did too, Shane at her heels. Then she found a corner for them to hide in.

"I'm not sure what watching people square-dance is supposed to prove."

She rolled her eyes at him. "Patience."

"I don't even know why I came," he grumbled.

"I assume because my charm is irresistible," Cora returned. She grinned up at him, only remembering she wasn't supposed to flirt when his gaze dropped to her mouth.

Crap.

She whipped her head back toward the crowd, searching the small sea of faces for Deb. She finally found the sturdy brunette over in the corner, a handsome man with his arms slung across her shoulders. That must be Ben. Cora could certainly see the attraction.

Cora pointed. "I want you to watch them and then tell me you really think Ben is such an awful guy."

She could all but *feel* the man standing next to her stiffen. When she glanced over at him, his jaw was tight, his dark eyes flat. He didn't appear angry, and yet she thought for a second she'd seen a flash of something close.

But he smoothed it away so tense stoicism was the only thing on his face, with the slightest hint of disapproval.

But Cora knew, she *knew*, what the Tyler siblings needed to see was their mother as a *woman*, as a *person*, not just a dutiful matriarch of a complex family.

So Shane was darn well going to watch his mother square-dance with her fiancé, and then he'd have to see.

His mother was dressed in the most ridiculous getup he'd ever seen. Her skirt had ruffles on it. *Ruffles.* His mother, who only wore dresses to funerals, was in some flouncy getup, wearing makeup.

Makeup. Bright red lipstick and sparkly shit on her face. His *mother*. Ben stood next to her, grinning like the tool that he was, and Shane thought Ben must know they both looked like utter fools.

Someone came onto the stage, talking into a microphone about something Shane didn't understand, but people filed onto the dance floor, a riot of colors and ruffles and too colorful cowboy boots.

"What am I supposed to see? My mother act like . . ." He couldn't say the words he was thinking. Partially because he was pretty sure his mother would hear him no matter how softly he uttered it and all but fly across the room to smack him upside the head.

Partially, though, because his mother *wasn't* a fool. No matter how much Shane didn't understand this version of his mother, smiling and laughing with Ben and another couple as they stepped and twirled and moved about a small square of space on the floor, he also couldn't quite bring the judgmental hammer down on it, so to speak.

"She's happy, and she's having fun," Cora said, her voice soothing some of these uncomfortable edges inside of him. "I know you want that for her."

He glanced down, the crown of Cora's head only just coming up to his nose. A riot of reddish curls that made no more sense to him than the woman who'd given birth to him *square dancing*.

Shane sighed heavily. "How do you know I want that?"

Blue eyes met his, something like consideration on her face. Her mouth curved, but he noted the dimple that had appeared in her cheek yesterday didn't with this smaller, softer smile.

"You know, yesterday your mom told me you hadn't given her an ounce of trouble since you were twelve."

Shane stiffened. Couldn't help it. Because twelve had been a grave turning point in his life, and he'd been very sure not to be trouble, just like he was almost certain his brother Boone had determined to be nothing but.

He could feel Cora's curious stare and wished he was better at hiding the way tension had crept into his body, the way everything about the age of *twelve* still stuck to him like flypaper.

"Did something happen when you were twelve?" she asked.

"Maybe I just decided my hellion days were behind me," he said, his voice sounding strained even in the midst of music and revelry.

"In my experience, twelve is when hellion is just beginning."

"You have a lot of experience with twelve-year-olds?"

he asked gruffly, hoping this conversation would go anywhere else.

"Not a lot, though mine's almost thirteen, so certainly enough."

That jolted him enough to knock some of the tension out of him. He didn't think Cora was a day over twenty-five. "You can't have a twelve-year-old." He could barely picture her as a mother, let alone one of an almost teenager.

"Afraid so."

He opened his mouth to ask how old she was, then clamped it shut. None of his business and rude besides, but he couldn't help studying her out of the corner of his eye.

"Oh, just ask," she said, rolling her eyes.

"Ask what?"

She grinned up at him then, that dimple winking to life. "I know what you want to ask. I've been down this road a few times in my life."

"What road?" he asked as innocently as he could manage.

She shrugged, still grinning, though her gaze went back out to Mom and Ben on the dance floor. "You never know the answers to the questions you won't ask."

"Guess I'll never know then," he replied.

"Suit yourself."

He clamped his mouth shut. He wouldn't be tricked into asking a sensitive question. It wouldn't be polite.

She had an *almost-thirteen-year-old.* This pretty little thing, smiling at his mother dancing some ridiculous dance with a man who would do nothing but ruin everything.

His mother was smiling, happily flushed, clearly having a hell of a time, and Shane felt conflicted for the first time. Because Cora was right, he did want his mother's happiness. He just knew this wasn't it.

"Maybe she is happy," Shane offered as concession. He'd been happy himself once upon a time, and what had happened? "Maybe she wants nothing more in this life than to marry Ben Donahue, but I can't let her do that when I am certain that man is nothing but trouble. I won't . . ." He didn't feel right bringing Molly up, how he'd failed that particular time. Not totally his fault since Molly was stubborn as a mule, but this time . . .

He couldn't let it happen to Mom. Because she might not be able to bounce back. She'd loved and lost Dad. What would being embarrassed do to her?

"I have to protect my family."

Cora looked up at him again, something sad and a little wistful in her expression. "That's really sweet," she said, looking something close to teary.

"They don't seem to think so."

Some of her sadness melted into humor. "Imagine that."

He wouldn't laugh. It wasn't funny. He took protecting his family *very* seriously, and yet something about the way she both thought it was sweet and sarcastically agreed with his family's not wanting to be protected made him want to smile back at her, to say more things to her.

This woman who'd dragged him into Benson to witness his mother square dancing of all damn things. Who smiled at him and teased him, gently. This woman he didn't know a thing about except that she was beautiful and apparently had a twelve-year-old kid. Hellion kid at that.

"You really have a twelve-year-old?"

"Really, truly. What? Does that wig you out? Or did

you have a question to ask me? Maybe to make sure you're not Ben Donahue-ing things yourself."

"For starters you're not older than me."

"But you could be ten years older than me, or does it only matter when the woman is the one who's older?"

He wasn't about to touch *that.* "Secondly, I haven't asked you to marry me."

She pretended to ponder that, and his eyes should be following that rat bastard Donahue instead of the subtle curve of Cora's mouth, yet he couldn't quite look away from her. Flirting with him when he tended to be stuffy and gruff at best.

When was the last time a woman had flirted with him without him making the first move? Applying some charm—the kind he kept hidden way down deep.

The kind he should absolutely not bring out here and now when more important than smiling at or flirting with this pretty woman was his mother's safety and future happiness.

"But you seem like such the type to believe in love at first sight and whirlwind romances that end in quick elopements." She looked innocently at him from behind her eyelashes. "I thought for sure a proposal was coming."

"Well, if you want to plan our wedding instead of my mother's, I'd consider it."

She laughed, pretty and bright, and way too intoxicating. When was the last time he'd made anyone laugh? He was usually earning groans and reproaches from his siblings, or good-natured go-to-hells when he got a little too bossy.

"I'm going to plan the best wedding I possibly can for your mother, because I think she deserves it. And, because I trust her judgment on the man she wants to marry." Cora's gaze followed the whirl and twirl of Mom and Ben, and she chewed thoughtfully on her lip.

Shane forced his gaze away from the sight of it.

Cora took a deep breath and let it out. "But if you ever show me any evidence he's hurting her, really, truly dangerous, or a threat, I'll quit." She nodded firmly. "I know she's not my mother, and I don't have a vested interest, but I won't be party to a man's hurting a woman out of viciousness."

She said it emphatically, a little too emphatically, like she'd had personal experience with men hurting women out of viciousness. He wanted to personally eviscerate whatever man might have hurt her.

But Cora wasn't his responsibility. So, he had to focus on what was. "All right. I guess I'll have to prove it to you both then."

She smiled sadly. "I don't think I've ever hoped for someone's failure more."

For the first time since his mother had announced her engagement, he hoped it a little himself.

Chapter Five

It was only noon, and Cora already felt like she'd run a marathon. She had thirty minutes to eat lunch, then she was meeting Deb at the bakery to discuss cakes, then she had to pick Micah up from basketball camp—which he'd promised not to bail on again.

Tori had agreed to give Micah a quick rock-climbing lesson after camp, and although the thought scared Cora down to her *soul*, she had a handful of vendors she needed to call today, and rock climbing would keep Micah occupied until dinnertime.

Then she promised herself she'd shut off wedding planning mind and focus on Micah. Maybe they could cook together. Micah liked that.

But thoughts of cooking turned to thoughts of vendors who would be able to offer a reception-worthy spread of food at the Tyler ranch.

It turned out planning a wedding was hard, continual work even when it wasn't your own. But she liked it, which was a surprise to her. She'd wanted to do it because it sounded doable with her limited work skills. She hadn't expected to get into it.

But she was into it. For the first time in her life she

felt vested in something outside of herself or her son, and it felt . . . amazing.

She worked on putting together a quick sandwich in the kitchenette of the Mile High Adventures offices. As an arm of this company, she was sharing space, but Lilly already had grand plans for a future office just for the wedding side of things.

"Great minds," Lilly said, stepping into the kitchen.

Cora smiled at her sister, who was carrying a squirming little boy. Cora loved having a baby niece and nephew. It was like getting to relive Micah's baby years without any of the crushing responsibility.

"You want one?" Cora asked, pointing to the sandwich she was making.

"If you're offering." Lilly leaned back against the far wall, gently untangling Aiden's pudgy fingers from her hair. "How's the wedding?"

Cora set out to make a sandwich Lilly would like, debating with herself how much she wanted to tell Lilly about how the wedding planning was going. The thing was, this whole new leaf was a bit of a balancing act. For most of their lives, Lilly had been in charge, telling Cora what to do, stepping in and doing what needed to be done.

Cora needed boundaries, so she could be the one stepping up for once. "Deb wants to move up the date to September," Cora offered, as that was relevant to all business things.

"That'll be tight," Lilly said thoughtfully.

Cora put a few slices of ham on a piece of bread. "Yes, but I thought it'd be good. The earlier we have our first wedding, the more buzz we'll get to book the next."

"True. I like the way you think," Lilly said with a grin. "But Will and Tori are eloping over my dead body, and Sam can't hold out much more on Hayley. We'll be drowning in weddings."

"Weddings we won't make any money off of because they're family and Mile High employees."

Lilly chuckled. "I *really* like the way you think. Who knew becoming a wedding planner would make you so mercenary?"

"I'm not a wedding planner yet. I have to plan a wedding first. And it has to be a success and . . ." Cora stopped herself from saying *actually happen*. But Shane's steadfast insistence that his mother was making a mistake continued to poke at her.

What if he was right? Was Cora aiding and abetting something awful that Deb would only regret? Cora could barely stomach the thought of it. She glanced over at her older sister, who had practically raised her. Mom had always been working. Dad had rarely deigned to take the time away from his real family to do anything with her or Lilly. Lilly had stepped up and been everything Cora had needed. She'd still be living with Stephen in that awful situation if it hadn't been for Lilly.

Lilly, who'd protected her as best she could, who'd stepped in and told her when she was wrong. Just like Shane was trying to do with Deb.

"I have a question for you." She handed Lilly the sandwich around the waving baby arms that tried to grab it. "Were you ever . . . When you were protecting me, did it ever turn out you were wrong about something. Or someone?"

Lilly's pale eyebrows drew together as Aiden seemed to try to leverage himself up and over her shoulder. "In what way?"

"Just that, you made mistakes right? You weren't infallible. Being an outside observer doesn't mean you automatically know what's best for someone. For me."

Lilly blew out a breath. "I often wished I could be infallible, but I suppose I wasn't. Not to mention no matter how hard I tried to protect you, you were often determined to go your own way. It frustrated me at the time, but I've also learned a little something about letting go and letting people . . . Sometimes you have to give people the space to make their own choices."

"Even if they're wrong?"

"If I could have stopped Stephen from hurting you and Micah, I would have, but aside from that? I was always a little heavy-handed, and I think letting you make some of your own choices or mistakes might have been good for you." Lilly smiled a little sadly, but seemed to shake herself out of the sad. "But I'm so proud of where you are, and what you've done. I don't think looking back is necessary."

Cora opened her mouth to explain that she wasn't looking back. She was trying to understand the now. But her cell phone trilled instead. She frowned, putting her sandwich down on a paper towel and pulling the phone out of her pocket.

Her heart sank when her display read *Benson Athletic Association*. She fumbled to swipe to accept. "Hello?"

"Ms. Preston. This is Mr. Cummings from the Benson Basketball Youth Association."

"Hello. Oh, God, is everything—"

"Your son is fine, Ms. Preston." There was a dramatic pause. "Though I'm afraid you're going to have to come pick him up, and he will no longer be welcome at any classes within the Benson Athletics Center. His behavior today has proved unacceptable. I am sorry."

Cora didn't even begin to know what to say to *that*. Except the man didn't sound very sorry. "I . . . don't . . ."

"Can someone come pick him up as soon as possible, Ms. Preston? We can discuss the particulars in person."

"Yes. Yes. I'll be right there." She hit End, trying to

breathe through a little bit of panic and a whole lot of emotion.

"What is it?"

"Micah, he . . . got kicked out."

Lilly's expression crumbled with concern and the same kind of desperation Cora felt. "I wish I knew what was going on with him."

"Me too," Cora said, her throat tight. "I have to go pick him up."

"What can I do? Do you want me to take the appointment with Deb? I've got a meeting for Mile High, but—"

"No, I've got it under control." When Lilly opened her mouth clearly to argue, Cora shook her head. "I have to do this. All of it."

Lilly closed her mouth and nodded. "Good luck. Call if you need anything."

Sandwich forgotten, Cora grabbed her purse and headed out, because no matter how much she wanted to give to this job, she needed to give more to her son. Clearly, so very much more.

She didn't allow herself to cry as she drove down the mountain. It'd take at least twenty minutes to pick up Micah. Which didn't give her enough time to figure out who could watch Micah. Lilly had a meeting, and everyone else was out on excursions. Summer was high season, and Cora didn't have time for Micah to have been kicked out of camp. Not when she had a wedding to plan in record time—her *first* wedding.

She inhaled sharply. Panic was building, but that wouldn't do. Her motto this year was *What Would Lilly Do.* Lilly would handle it. She'd find a way to juggle it all.

So, that's just what Cora would do, too.

* * *

Shane rarely pounded posts these days. It was a job left to ranch hands or summer help, or sometimes even Lindsay if she was being particularly bratty.

But a little physical labor could clear a man's mind. Shane would've preferred a long horse ride out to the far edge of the property to handle the small cattle drive, but it was Gavin's turn, and his brother probably needed the air a little more than he needed to pound things. While physical labor evened out any aggression Shane felt, it tended to only stoke Gavin's close-to-the-surface temper higher.

"Got a hand if you could use it."

Shane took a minute to school his scowl into something more stoic before he turned at Ben Donahue's voice. "Aren't you on stable duty?"

Ben had his hands shoved in his pockets and that laid-back, nothing-matters demeanor that grated against every last nerve Shane possessed. Ben smirked, tempting Shane's ruthlessly controlled temper even more.

"I know you boys think you can scare me off with the shit jobs, but let's be clear. I got nearly a decade on you, boy. I don't appreciate the bullshit orders."

Shane put down the post driver, because he was a little too tempted to use it as a weapon. He wiped his brow with the back of his forearm and took a deep breath. Ben might be older than him, but Shane knew who came out on top when it came to controlling temper. "Far as I know, you still work for me, Donahue."

"I work for the head of this ranch, who happens to be your mother."

"I'm the foreman. *I'm* in charge of the ranch hands. Which is the paycheck you collect."

"Yeah, a paycheck your mother signs. Not you."

God, how he'd love to punch that smirk off this man's face. But, he didn't have time for a pissing match.

"I have a ranch to *run,* Donahue. If you're not going to do the jobs assigned to you, why don't you go discuss that refusal with my mother." Shane didn't have much hope it'd get the stables shoveled, but he didn't want to deal with Ben directly. It could only end badly.

Ben took a deep breath and squinted out at the mountains beyond the ranch. "What exactly have I done that's got you so bent out of shape over me?"

"You want a list?" Shane retorted sharply, one of those rare impulses he couldn't control.

Ben's sharp blue gaze met Shane's. "Yeah. Maybe I do."

"You're lazy. Routinely late for work. You disappear, and no one knows where you are. You don't take orders, and it makes it impossible for me to run this ranch the way it needs to be run. If you were anyone else, my mother would have fired you by now." *Or let me do it.* "But she has stepped in and asked for lenience. Well, I've been lenient, but if you're going to come at me, I'll be straight with you."

"That's about me as a ranch hand, not about me as a man."

"In this family, in this ranch, who you are and what you do go hand in hand. Talk is cheap. If you can't show a little work ethic, I don't need to worry about getting to know you as a man. You're not the kind of man worthy to lick my mother's boots."

"I know damn well your mother's a good woman, better than me. She deserves—"

"I know what she deserves," Shane snapped.

There was something like a light of triumph in Ben's expression. That flash of temper evening out. Ben smiled, that kind of "screw you" smile that had Shane itching to throw a punch.

"She wants us to get along," Ben said in a tone of

voice Shane supposed his mother fell for, but Shane didn't. Not for a second. There was nothing conciliatory in this man. Nothing kind. The measure of a man was how he respected family—which Ben clearly didn't. The measure of a man was in his dedication to right over wrong, but, most of all, that he would work his ass off till the job was done. That was what a man did. That's what Shane's father had taught him every second of every day.

Shane had learned that lesson in a loss so severe and irrevocable, he couldn't stand anyone who hadn't had to learn that lesson.

Shane grabbed the post driver. "Ben, I didn't get along with you before you started sniffing around my mother as if that'd get you out of a hard day's work. I don't know why I'd start now."

"Because your mother wants it."

"My mother also wanted to paint the living room pink. I disagreed on that. I'll disagree on this."

"I don't have kids, let alone grown ones. I don't know how this is supposed to work, but I do love your mother."

Shane shook his head, giving the post driver a satisfying jerk against the post. "I don't believe that."

"What would it take to get you to?"

He brought the post driver down with another jerk. "There's nothing you could do that would prove it to me."

"Then maybe I'm not the problem."

That hit a little hard, but Shane shook it away. Ben was after a fight. An argument he could use against Shane in the future. Shane would be honest, but he wasn't going to get drawn into a knock-down-drag-out.

"If that's what you want to think." Another satisfying *thwack* on the post kept him from saying anything more. An argument with Ben wouldn't solve anything, because

Shane was sure he was right, and Ben wasn't going to come out and admit he was in this for all the wrong reasons.

Loved his mother? It didn't make any sense. His mother was good, hard working, and kind. Shane had never seen Ben be any of those things.

"I told your mother I'd talk to you. Try to smooth things over."

"I'd rather you told my mother you were a lazy, no-account who forged his references to get this job." Shane glanced over his shoulder, satisfied that Ben looked a little taken aback by that. "You think I haven't figured out at least half the shit you spout is lies? You think I'm just some bent-out-of-shape kid pissed because Mommy's getting married? You don't know a thing about me, or this family."

"I know your mother loves me. She's not going to give up on marrying me just because you kids don't get along with me."

Shane heaved a sigh. "Noted." He wasn't trying to change his mother's mind. He was trying to show her the truth. He had no doubt once Mom had all the facts, whatever facts Ben was keeping hidden, she'd realize she was making a mistake.

"I've told your mother everything. Whatever lies you think you've got on me, she already knows."

As if Shane hadn't already told Mom every lie he'd uncovered. "Well, then I guess you have nothing to worry about."

"Maybe I should go have this conversation with Gavin."

Shane narrowly resisted the urge to whirl around, to connect fist to jaw. But as he wasn't his impulsive younger brother, he took a deep breath instead. He laid down the post driver slowly and carefully. He turned to face Ben, straightening to his full height and looking the man directly in the eye.

"Why? So you can get what you really want? Someone to haul off and hit you so you can go cry to my mother and make us the villains?"

"You don't know me, boy."

"Ditto."

"You ain't got no right to step between us like this."

"Last I checked Mom was still moving up the wedding, still marrying you." Shane allowed himself a small, victorious smile. "That hasn't changed . . . has it?"

"No."

"But you're worried."

"Like hell I am."

Shane shrugged lazily, more than a little gratified Ben's formerly lackadaisical posture was now ramrod straight, that "screw you" curve to his mouth a flat line. "First time you've come at me directly. I've got to assume it's because you're worried about something."

"Not worried. Trying to give your mother what she wants, what she deserves. Unlike her ungrateful kids."

"She loves us too, you know. If you're not careful, you'll push her too far."

Ben seemed to consider that, and Shane refused to give him credit for having the sense to do so.

"Well, boss, guess I'll go shovel your shit then," Ben said, that flat line of his mouth turning into a cocky smile. He tipped his hat and moseyed himself back to the four-wheeler he'd driven up in.

Shane scowled after him because he had the sneaking suspicion he'd played his hand a little too clearly. If Ben actually started doing the work he was supposed to do around the ranch, without any new information about Ben's past coming to light, what argument could Shane pose then?

Chapter Six

Cora vacillated between furious and devastated, and just about a hundred emotions in between. Her sweet, obnoxious, pain in the ass, hurt, and confused little boy had thrown a basketball at a coach's head.

He had gotten himself not just kicked out of basketball camp, but *banned* from any further activities with the Benson Athletic Association. *Banned*. Her sweet little baby.

She wanted to cry and yell and pound the steering wheel, and she simply didn't have the time. She had to focus on driving to the bakery and figuring out what she was going to do with Micah once she got there.

She knew Emily, the woman who ran Piece of Cake, somewhat. Cora had gotten involved in Brandon's chamber of commerce as a representative of Mile High Weddings, and there were a few women in the group, including Emily. It had been nice to be in a meeting where her voice was considered equal to all the rest.

But having a social life or even just occasional friendly get-togethers with businesswomen in town was nearly impossible these days, and looked to be heading toward totally impossible.

"Why can't you just drop me off at home?" Micah whined, slapping his feet against the dash.

Cora reached over and pushed his feet back onto the floorboard.

"Other than the fact that you're clearly not responsible enough to be left on your own, since you threw a basketball at an instructor."

"It's basketball camp."

"Micah Zander Preston."

"It was an accident. He was being a dick."

"It can't be both, and I don't care! You don't hurt people. You don't . . ." She had to stop herself, because her voice was about to break and the tears were about to fall. This couldn't be the only interaction they had any more. Crying and anger.

She pulled into one of the spaces in front of Piece of Cake. She stared hard at the pretty brick building, the painting on the big storefront window. A giant cupcake with a smile.

Cora breathed, staring at the maniacal cupcake smile, willing herself to find some calm. Micah was acting out, and she needed to be the calm one.

"You will go inside with me. You will sit in the corner. You will not make a noise. You will endure however long this takes, and then, when we get home, we will have a calm, reasonable discussion about your behavior, and the natural consequences of that behavior."

"Are you going to make me see Dr. Grove again?" he asked, wrinkling his nose, clearly catching on to the fact that she was using some of Dr. Grove's buzzwords.

"Eventually." Cora took a second to be proud of herself. Yes, inside she was a wreck, but outside she was doing a fair job of being calm and yet firm with Micah. "How soon and how many times will depend on how that discussion goes."

He gave a disgusted, patently teenage sigh.

"One wrong move, mister, and we will camp out on her office stairs so you can speak to her first thing in the morning." And, ugh, now she sounded like her mother. The mother who'd only found fault with her, over and over again.

Though more tears threatened, Cora blinked them back. "I'm so angry with you, Micah, but I love you, baby. That's why I'm mad. I know you. . . . You're better than this. I know you are."

Some of that sullen teenage mulishness turned into something softer, more hurt. Cora didn't have the first clue if she was doing this right, but she wouldn't let her kid think she thought he was a bad kid.

"Let's go." She pushed out of the car, somewhat gratified when Micah followed without any more complaints. Though his sighs were loud enough to be heard down the block, he did as he was told when they entered the bakery. He went to a little table in the corner, parked himself in a chair, and looked down at his shoes.

"Hi, Cora," Emily greeted, coming out from behind her prettily decorated counter. The interior looked like a mix between some French bakery and some farm-y Instagram creation—all gingham and wildflowers.

"Hi, Emily. I guess Deb isn't here yet?"

Emily nodded out the window. "Here she comes. I don't suppose you have any more weddings lined up aside from this one?" Emily asked hopefully.

Cora didn't have to ask to know Emily's bakery was struggling. Every business in Gracely was struggling. Except Annie's Chainsaw Repair & Used Furniture.

The door opened, and Deb swept in, a big smile on her face. "Oh, I just can't help grinning every time I step inside, Em. Who knew those tea parties you used to have with Lou and Molly would give way to this?"

Emily grinned. "And who knew I'd be baking your wedding cake one day. I never thought . . ." Emily trailed off, squeezing her eyes shut.

"It's okay. I never thought I'd marry again either. Owen was the love of my life. But, the wonderful thing about life is it never fails to surprise you with something you thought long gone." She turned to glance at Cora. "And this little lady is working miracles to give me my dream wedding."

"Well, you deserve it, Mrs. T," Emily said emphatically. "I've picked a few designs I think you'll love. We can schedule a tasting whenever Ben's available too."

"See, not everyone is against Ben," Deb said, nodding toward Cora.

"Is Shane still giving you trouble?" Emily rolled her eyes. "Men are idiots. Especially Tyler men. No offense."

"It's imprinted in their DNA," Deb said with a laugh. "Now, let's see these designs." She moved toward a table, then seemed to notice Micah and stopped short. "Who's that?" she mouthed.

Cora stepped toward Micah. "Deb, this is my son, Micah. Micah, this is Emily and Deb. You can say hello."

He grumbled something close to hello.

"His camp . . . unexpectedly ended early today, so he's going to be my little helper." Cora smiled thinly, and Deb didn't push it. She nodded and smiled and slid into a chair at a table that looked like the surface of a log.

Emily scooted into the chair next to Deb with a giant binder, and Cora tried to find some kind of focus.

"I figured you'd want something traditional, Mrs. T," Emily was saying, flipping through plastic pages of picture after picture. "Maybe a little rustic."

"I like rustic. I want everything to fit in at the ranch."

Cora knew she had to earn her keep, which meant focusing on cakes not on her son kicking his feet against the floor in the corner. "Will the amount of people affect what designs you can do?"

Emily started talking logistics and sheet cakes, and Cora forced herself to take notes. To focus and do her *job*.

Eventually Micah scuffled over. "Can I go to the bathroom?"

Emily pointed to the back. "It's right back there, sweetheart." She smiled broadly.

Micah muttered a half-hearted thanks, which was more politeness than Cora usually got out of him. He trudged away.

"So, he got kicked out, huh?" Deb asked.

Cora startled. "Oh." But Deb looked sympathetic instead of accusatory or judgy. "Yeah, he did."

"I couldn't keep Boone in a camp, class, or court-ordered community service to save my life."

Cora couldn't believe Deb hadn't always had complete control of her family, even if they *were* trouble. Still, it was nice to hear. It was nice, for once in her life, to have someone who'd *been* there. Cora and Lilly had raised Micah without having much of a clue as to what they were doing. Mom had hightailed it out of their lives the minute she'd found a husband. Right before she told Cora she'd be better off getting rid of her baby than ever trying to raise it.

Cora straightened a little bit. Micah was a challenge, but she wasn't done trying yet. She'd brought that boy into this world, and she'd do her damnedest to make him into a good man.

"We shouldn't be talking about . . . Our meeting is about cake." She tapped Emily's binder. "Maybe Emily can copy a few of the pictures of what you like, and you can keep them to make your decision."

"Yeah, definitely."

"I want the one that looks like aspen wood, with the mountain silhouettes. If reception size becomes an issue, we'll talk sheet cake." Deb clapped her hands together. "Decision made. Now let's help you with your problem. You bring that boy out to the ranch."

Cora blinked. "What?"

"He needs some fresh air and some responsibility. You bring him out to the ranch."

"Oh, but . . . I mean, he wanted to do the basketball camp. He loved basketball! I wasn't forcing him."

"Of course not, but he's clearly changed his mind about something. If he's anything like my boy was, there's no going back."

Banned. "No, there isn't. But . . . He helps out at Mile High. I thought . . . It's so beautiful up there, and active. I thought he'd love the hiking and rock climbing and all that. It's healing. . . . It can be healing." She felt healed. Not quite the same way Lilly did, but this was still . . . She was a new person, becoming a better, stronger person. Gracely had to have something to do with that.

"Of course, Cora. The land is the truth. It's why people believe in this Gracely legend. I'd be hard-pressed to find someone who can't get a little healing from the land, but mostly it's just a little space to heal themselves. That's fine for adults, but a sullen boy with ghosts in his eyes needs to feel responsible for something. He needs to feel big instead of small. That's where the animals come in. He needs a ranch. He needs horses and hard work. Mark my words."

"I don't . . ."

"You bring him out tomorrow morning, and I'll have Shane and Gavin work up some chores for him."

"Oh, but . . ."

"Tomorrow is your day off, isn't it?"

"Yes, but—"

"You can supervise, see if you'd be comfortable leaving the boy with us a few hours here and there. If not, no hard feelings. But give it a chance." Deb reached across the table and patted Cora's arm. "I know a thing or two about raising boys. They drive me crazy, and I'd throttle all of 'em eight ways till Sunday about now, but they're fine, good men."

Emily clucked her tongue. "You might as well just agree. She won't take no for an answer."

"Oh, now," Deb said, swatting Emily fondly on the arm.

Micah shuffled out of the bathroom, still sullen, shoulders slumped, and he just wouldn't talk to her. Even that session with Dr. Grove the other day hadn't been helpful, at least not short-term.

Maybe Deb was right.

"You bring him out at six," Deb said, a little overloud, and Cora had to bite back a laugh as Micah's mouth dropped.

"Oh, I thought ranchers started work at sunrise," Cora said brightly.

Micah's jaw dropped farther, and Cora stifled a giggle as Emily covered her smiling mouth with her hand to hide it.

"We'll give him a break on that since you'll be the one driving him over." Deb looked over Cora's shoulder to Micah, who was standing halfway between their table and his seat in the corner. "Maybe next week he can start at sunrise."

"Mom?" Micah said, eyes wide and a note of panic in his voice.

It might make her a terrible mother, but all she could

think at that note of panic was *good*. Maybe her son needed some panic.

And some hard work.

Shane yawned into his jug of water while Gavin muttered irritably at the slow drip of the coffee maker. No matter how many years passed, Shane still couldn't stand the smell of coffee in the morning, but he forced himself to endure it, if only to remind himself he wasn't twelve anymore.

"Good. You're up."

Mom, dressed and alert, walked into the kitchen with that aura of determination in her eyes that never bade well for him.

Oh, Shane was not ready to fight about Donahue. He was a morning person by and large, but he needed a little time out in the fresh air before his brain truly started to engage enough to ward off whatever battle his mother was about to wage.

"I need a favor from you boys." She glanced from Gavin to Shane as if considering before her gaze focused on Shane. "Mostly you."

"Mom—"

"Before you start yapping about the wedding or Ben, this doesn't have anything to do with either."

"How could that possibly be?" Gavin asked grumpily.

Mom leveled him with a cool look, but then returned her focus to Shane. "I need you to put a young boy to work. A little grunt work, but some stuff with the horses too."

"What young boy?"

"Cora's son. Got himself into a bit of trouble, and Cora puts on a brave face, but I can tell she's worried. I told her nothing better for a troubled boy than some ranch work."

"Who the heck is Cora?" Gavin asked.

"The wedding planner," Shane muttered. "What kind of trouble are you talking here?"

Mom waved a hand. "Doesn't matter."

"It might matter."

"No. It doesn't."

Shane wanted to groan. His mother was always so bound and determined to stick her nose where it didn't belong. To help even when they had a million problems right here. It never failed that he was trying to do one thing—like, say, save his mother from making the biggest mistake of her life—and she would come out of nowhere with some new thing.

"We don't know anything about kids."

"He doesn't," Mom said, gesturing toward Gavin. "But you were just as much a part of raising the three younger ones as I was."

"That's not—"

"It's more than true. Now, stop arguing. They should be here any minute. Follow me."

Shane knew there was no point in arguing. He'd never sway his mother's opinion on both this *and* the wedding. Stopping the wedding was more important.

Besides, this means you'll get to see more of Cora.

Which was not something he wanted. Or didn't want. He was totally ambivalent about seeing more of Cora. Sure he was.

"The boy needs some hard work, a little horse time. God knows that's the only thing that kept your brother out of jail," Mom said, all but marching down the hall toward the front door.

"That we know of," Gavin offered, trailing behind.

"Ha ha. Now, Cora's a little worried about leaving

him with near strangers, so she'll be tagging along today. Just give the boy things to do, let him get attached to the horses. If you see a spark of interest in anything, nurture it. I'm sure it'll ease Cora's mind."

"What do you care about your wedding planner's mind?" Gavin asked, then shook his head as they reached the door. "Never mind. I'll never understand why you have to swoop in and save everyone."

"I guess I could ask you the same question. Unless you magically stopped checking in on Lou every day," Mom said in a sing-songy voice, opening the door to a pretty summer morning.

"That's not everyone," Gavin grumbled.

Mom grinned at Shane as they stepped out onto the porch. In the distance, Shane spotted what he assumed was the shiny top of Cora's car. Dawn was just lighting up the ranch. His favorite time of day.

That was the odd jumpy feeling in his gut. Certainly not anticipation.

Cora's car came to a stop at the end of the drive, and she popped out of the driver's seat. Instead of her usual wedding planner business-wear, she was wearing jeans. The kind of jeans you didn't see on a ranch. These were those skinny things that might as well have been made out of lace for as thin and formfitting as they were. She bent over to grab something from inside the car, and, yes, very . . . formfitting.

"Did you just check out my wedding planner?"

Shane jolted. "What? No! Gross, Mom."

Gavin snorted a laugh.

"You did. You just checked her out. Oh, that's funny."

"Why is that *funny*?" Shane demanded.

"She's a sweet girl. I like her."

"Fantastic. What does that have to do with me?"

"Oh, nothing. I guess." Mom started walking toward the car.

"What do you mean *you guess*?"

"My, you're touchy this morning." Mom waved enthusiastically as Cora walked toward them, a very grumpy-looking boy trudging behind her.

"Morning, Deb."

"Morning, Cora. Micah. So what do you think, boy? Seen anything like this before?"

The boy's blue eyes that matched his mother's darted around, and he shrugged. "Guess not."

"Shane. Gavin. This is your new coworker."

"Thought it was slave," Micah muttered, earning him a nudge from his mother, who was wearing a dark-blue T-shirt that somehow made her eyes seem even more vibrant. Or maybe that was the fact her hair was pulled back into a ponytail, leaving her pale, graceful neck visible and—

Shit, man, get a grip.

"Thanks for this," Cora said, offering them all sheepish smiles.

"Yeah, thanks," Micah said, sarcasm dripping from every syllable.

Cora looked down at her son with a pained expression that Shane could relate to a little too hard. He'd considered it his duty to help Boone stay on the straight and narrow when they'd been growing up because Boone had only been six when Dad had died. Shane had been something like his father figure.

Another failure. Because Boone had been into every kind of trouble imaginable, and Shane knew it was only his love of the rodeo that kept him from getting into serious, irreparable trouble.

So, Shane knew what it was to look at someone and

be afraid and at a loss and just desperate to figure out what to do to make everything okay.

"Well, we better get started," he said, gesturing toward the stables. "First stop. Horse shit junction."

Gavin chuckled, Micah scowled, and Cora smiled prettily up at him, the soft light of dawn giving her skin a little glow.

"And I'll make up a nice lunch for you four," Mom said. "Be back around eleven."

"Eleven? That's like five hours away," Micah grumbled to his mother.

"Excellent math skills," Cora replied crisply. "Maybe I should have put you in math camp so you couldn't throw any basketballs at any coach's head." She looked back at Shane, rolling her eyes.

"Throwing basketballs at coaches. Hmm. What do you say the kind of punishment for that would be, Gav?"

"Well, when our youngest brother started a bonfire on the baseball field before practice, I think he was on shit removal, collection, and application duty for a week."

"Arson might be a step above basketball throwing," Shane offered thoughtfully.

"Where'd the ball hit?" Gavin demanded.

Micah blinked up at them, eyes wide—somewhere between awe, fascination, and fear. "B-back of his head."

"No potential bleeding then. Yeah, we'll have to downgrade from arson," Gavin said, nodding toward Shane. "Collection then. We'll go from there."

Cora was trailing after them, and, when Shane glanced back at her, she looked vaguely perplexed.

"I hope you don't plan on giving him ideas on how to get *in* trouble all day," she said with a bit of an amused smile.

"If you plan on telling someone what to do, you have

to earn a little bit of respect first or they'll do a piss-poor job." Shane slowed his steps so he was next to Cora.

"That so?"

"Far as I can tell. Arson brother was always telling me I was a goody-two-shoes."

"You *are* a goody-two-shoes."

Shane nodded to where Micah was entering the stables behind Gavin. "He doesn't need to know that."

Shane could tell she was trying to suppress a grin, and it made him want to see it full-fledged. They stepped into the stables, and he nodded toward the tool wall.

"Grab a shovel. Part of telling someone what to do is showing them you're not afraid of doing the hard work yourself."

Cora scoffed. "I'm not shoveling. . . . You can't be serious!"

"Dead serious. Everyone in my stable works. Trouble-maker or not."

He left her there at the entrance to the stables look-ing a little shell-shocked. He was all too pleased with himself.

Chapter Seven

He wasn't serious. He couldn't be. Shane didn't actually expect her to do any of the work.

But he walked over to a wall full of tools and picked out a shovel and held it out toward her.

"But . . ." Cora couldn't think of anything to say. Except that it was Micah's punishment, not hers. But Micah was watching her with big eyes, and Shane was clearly trying to hide a smile, and she somehow wanted to prove to everyone in this awful-smelling building she could shovel a bunch of horse poop if need be.

"Every morning we muck out the stalls and put in fresh hay. Most of the horses get a good workout since they're used to get us around the ranch, but we have to keep track so we know each horse is getting enough exercise."

Shane moved to one . . . thing. Stall, Cora guessed. She didn't know the terminology, but it was like a pen, closed in on all sides, but with plenty of room for a horse.

A gigantic, hairy beast with giant eyes she thought could swallow her, even though they were only eyes, stood there. Cora couldn't bring herself any closer.

"Whoa. It's huge," Micah said, sounding awed and clearly forgetting himself for a minute because he quickly affixed a scowl to his face when Cora looked his way.

"So's the shit," Gavin said, clearly having a hell of a time.

Cora couldn't say *she* was having much fun, or that she particularly cared for either of the Tyler men in this moment, though they stood there with grins and shovels.

She didn't mind *looking* at them, truth be told, no matter how irritated. Shane and Gavin looked an awful lot alike. Same height and build—broad shoulders, toned arms, and . . . well, other things Cora couldn't allow herself to notice or think about in the presence of her son. They had the same dark hair and eyes, but the way their faces were arranged was different. Shane had a square jaw and wide-set eyes and a nice mouth. He was a sort of classic kind of handsome. Like that cowboy in an old black-and-white movie she'd fallen asleep to last night. Gavin's features were more rugged, she supposed. His nose was crooked and his mouth was all sharp angles—whether smiling or frowning or, more often, scowling. More brawler type, whereas Shane was clearly the peacemaker.

She liked that about him. Also the way his butt looked in those jeans, which she was *not* thinking about in the presence of her son.

"There are eight stalls, so we'll each clear out two. Shovel it all out here, then we'll show you how to spread in the new hay."

"Wait. . . . We're *all* going to do it?" Micah asked, looking from Shane to Cora and then back again, openmouthed enough he couldn't scale his expression back to a scowl.

"When everyone pitches in, we get more work done," Shane said simply, as if there was no question.

Cora didn't know why that touched her, or seemed like such a big, good thing for Micah to learn.

"Then I get to go home?"

Shane's mouth curved. "Your mom's in charge, kid. We're working you till she calls it quits."

"Settle in, buckaroo," Cora offered with a smile. "You've earned some hard work."

"You're going to have to do it too," Micah returned with that kind of patented disgust only kids could manage.

"I can handle it. Let's see if you can." Then she set about doing something she had never dreamed in a million years she'd end up doing: she shoveled poop. Considering she'd cleaned up leaky diarrhea diapers, projectile vomit, and the like in the years of being Micah's mom, it really wasn't *especially* awful.

Micah groaned in disgust, but Cora couldn't help but wonder if he wasn't morbidly fascinated by the whole thing. She could read the expressions on her child's face, when she wasn't second-guessing herself or he wasn't shutting her out. There was a *spark* there in his eyes as he hefted a huge pile of poop onto the metal scoop of a shovel.

Once the stalls were clean and Shane had inspected them all to make sure they'd gotten everything, Shane and Gavin led Cora and Micah through putting new hay down and then moving the horses back into the pens.

Cora looked sideways at the horse she was supposed to be leading. She didn't feel much like a leader when the horse's dark, gigantic eyes seemed to bore into her.

"She won't bite. I mean, she could, but it's doubtful."

Cora scowled at Shane. "I don't think she's going to bite me. I think she's going to eat my face off."

"I think that's gorillas." He took the reins from her,

which was a simple maneuver considering she'd been afraid to hold them in the first place and had just barely held the leather between her fingertips.

"Bears also eat faces, I'm pretty sure," she offered, following him. Well, walking next to him so that he was between her and that creature. "And, look, I don't know. Horses are still animals. It could go crazy and decide it wants to eat my face off."

"She won't," Shane assured, clearly amused with her horse reticence. He easily led the horse into the stables and gave its rump a friendly pat.

Do not let your mind go any further than that, Cora Preston.

Cora glanced at where Gavin was talking to Micah, pointing to parts on the saddle Gavin had just fastened onto one of the other horses. Cora forgot about her discomfort with horses at that avid look of interest on her son's face. She hadn't seen that in a while.

"Is your mom always right?"

"No," Shane replied flatly.

Cora waved her hand, knowing exactly what was causing that flat tone. "Aside from the Ben thing, which you've yet to prove to me isn't right, she's always right. Isn't she?"

Shane shrugged. "Maybe more often than not."

"I just love her." Because if this was the thing that got Micah to wake up and participate in life beyond his video games again . . . Cora got teary just thinking about how much she owed this woman she barely knew.

"She incites that feeling in a lot of people," Shane was saying. "For what it's worth, she likes you too. And she's got a good radar about kids who need a little hard work and a little horse therapy. Although, you can blame *her* if your kid ends up on the rodeo circuit."

Cora must have visibly paled because Shane chuckled and reached out to touch her arm. A little shoulder squeeze she was sure was supposed to be friendly and reassuring and not at all a gesture that might make her wonder what that big, rough hand might feel like against bare skin.

Shane Tyler was a *serious* problem.

"Only one out of three boys she raised ended up in the rodeo. So, you might have a one in three chance."

"How reassuring," Cora muttered.

"You guys are pro at the poop shoveling. You care if we get him up there?"

Cora looked at the horse, something akin to terror clutching her gut. The giant beast *towered* over her baby, and Shane wanted to put the little bundle she'd nursed with her own body on one. Her sweet little boy who'd spent too many years in quiet, desolate fear.

"You can say no," Shane said gently, and without an ounce of disgust or judgment. "No one would hold it against you. Horses can be intimidating if you're not used to them."

She watched as Micah reached out and swept his hand down the *giant beast's* side, just as Gavin instructed him.

"He's not intimidated," she said miserably. "Do you know what the absolute worst part of being a parent is?"

"Never knowing what the right thing to do is."

She blinked up at him, because not only was that *exactly* it, but he said it so certainly. Without even the hint of a question. "How . . ."

He shrugged, watching Gavin and Micah, and it felt like he was very purposefully not meeting her gaze. "I'm the oldest. When my father died . . . Well, I was never a parent, no, but I took on some parent-like responsibilities here and there."

Here and there. Somehow she thought it had been a little more than that. "I don't want *my* fear to hold *him* back, and yet . . ." Cora blew out a breath. "I need him to be safe and whole."

"And happy."

She wrinkled her nose at him. "You just *had* to bring that one up."

"We'll put a helmet on him. We'll guide the horse. Won't take our hands off her. It doesn't have to take twenty years off your life. Maybe just one or two."

Her heart swelled a little at that. Both at the gesture and at the fact that Shane understood no amount of precaution would ever make any of this completely without worry. She wasn't sure she knew anyone like that. Lilly was always trying to take her worry away, make it better. Her friends weren't parents. They couldn't fully get it.

Shane wasn't a parent either, and yet he got it. It was a strange mix all in one person. All in one very, very attractive person. "You're a strange man, Shane Tyler. I don't know quite what to do with you."

He pulled his cowboy hat down farther on his head, obscuring his features in shadows. "Ditto, Cora. Ditto."

They got Micah up on the horse, and the kid tried so hard to act unaffected and bored, but he wasn't fooling anyone. Not his mother. Certainly not Shane or Gavin.

The kid was *in love,* and there was something special about introducing someone to that. Mostly Shane only ever associated with people who'd grown up around horses and had always worked with them. Ranchers and ranch hands. His life was a summation of connections he'd made from the Tyler ranch.

Watching Cora's trepidation and Micah's free-falling love affair did something uncomfortable to Shane's chest. Something, much like what Cora had said about him, he wasn't sure what to do with.

Shane had instructed Gavin to take Micah around on Bodine. Although Shane thought the best course of action for his own peace of mind, and other body parts, would be to put some distance between him and Cora, he also thought he'd be the best person to stand next to her and reassure her everything was fine while Micah rode his first horse.

"I hope we're not stealing your whole morning away," she offered.

"We'll put you to work this afternoon to make up for it."

She smiled at him, one side of her mouth going up farther than the other, making him think about mouths and the meeting of and . . .

He forced himself to look ahead as Micah and Bodine passed, Gavin dutifully keeping his hands on the reins.

"We could get you up on one if you'd like."

"I would not like. I would rather shovel poop for the rest of the day. Possibly my life."

"They're not so bad."

"They are to me."

He grinned at her, already forgetting his ordering himself to look ahead. "I'm going to get you up on one. One of these days. You just wait and see." Because it was stupid to pretend he didn't want to see her. Again and again. Like this, where he didn't have to think about Mom and Ben and the wedding, just a pretty woman who smiled and flirted with him.

She pushed a stray strand of reddish hair behind her ear. "That sounds like another thing we disagree on. I'm going to start a list."

It sank some of the easy camaraderie and, yes, maybe

even flirtation, because everything that reminded him of his mother marrying that crook did.

"He lies."

Cora blinked, clearly not following Shane's train of thought, so he had to press on. "You said if you had reason to believe Ben would hurt my mother, you wouldn't be a part of it. Well, he's a liar. He forged his references to get a job here."

"Is that all?"

"All? It's a lie."

Cora studied Shane thoughtfully, blue eyes contemplating and serious. "Who hasn't lied when they were desperate for a job?"

"Me," Shane replied indignantly.

She blew out a breath, shaking her head. "You've never been desperate for a job."

He opened his mouth to argue, except, of course, there was no argument for that. The Tyler ranch had always been his. There'd never been a question or time for anything else.

"I assume you found out about his lying about the references yourself?"

"Yes."

"And did you tell your mother?"

Shane ground his teeth together and nodded. A few months ago, before the whole engagement nonsense, when he'd told Mom about the fact that they'd figured out the references were bogus, she'd already known. Ben had confessed.

But a lie was a lie.

"I'm sorry, Shane. I am. I just don't think that's the end of the world. I've told a lot of unfortunate lies because it felt like the only option I had. I can't beat myself up for it. I mean, I can and I do, but I try not to."

Unfortunate lies. Only option. It reminded him of

the other night and the odd impression he'd gotten from her that she'd been hurt by a man before.

Shane flicked a glance to where Gavin was teaching Micah how to dismount. The kid's father clearly wasn't in the picture. So, it made sense Cora had been hurt or abandoned. The kid's dad could just be dead. Shane knew full well that was possible. Still, he wondered. . . .

And had no business wondering.

Micah scurried over, and all of that preteen bluster and apathy had clearly washed away.

"Mom, this is seriously . . ." He looked from Shane to Cora, with wide-eyed enthusiasm so deep and bright, he couldn't hide it. "Can I take horse-riding lessons? Gavin says his sister gives them."

"God help me," Cora muttered, but Shane didn't have a doubt she'd agree. She was a good mom, and she wanted her kid safe *and* happy.

"Molly does a fine job with the riding lessons," Shane offered. "She's been giving them since she was a teenager. She's very safe."

"I'm sure," Cora murmured.

"And if money is an issue—"

"It isn't," she snapped, so coolly, so curtly, Shane could only stare. He hadn't expected that snap of temper from her. Certainly not over something so small. "We'll work out something, Micah, but if you're going to take lessons, you're going to have to do some work, too. Isn't that right, Shane?" She glanced at him somewhat regally, all but daring him to disagree.

"Of course. Learning how to ride means learning how to care for the horses. We could use the help, as long as it's from someone willing to listen and learn and earn a few blisters."

"But if I do all that, I can eventually ride them on my own, right?"

Micah looked hopefully at Shane, and Shane nodded toward Cora.

"Please, Mom?"

"We'll start with lessons, and we'll go from there," Cora said stiffly. It was strange to see her stiff and a little cool. Was this all because he'd been generous enough to offer an alternative if she couldn't afford the lessons? That seemed like an overreaction to him.

A bell ringing sounded in the distance. "That means lunch," Shane said, clapping Micah on the shoulder.

"I'm starving."

"Just wait until we really put you to work," Gavin said good-naturedly. "You follow me, and I'll show you what we do when we're done riding the horses." Micah trotted after Gavin.

"You want to head to the house?"

Cora's gaze was blank, and she didn't meet his. "I think I'll go see what we do when we're done riding the horses," she said, rather high-and-mighty, before she stalked after her son.

Shane could only stare in utter confusion at her retreating form.

What on earth had just happened?

Chapter Eight

It was wrong to be furious. Cora couldn't help herself. How dare that high-handed, smooth-talking cowboy so easily insinuate she couldn't take care of herself? As if he knew. When he'd had everything handed to him. All that crap about Ben lying as if it were the *worst* thing a person could do.

Well, *some* people had to lie. *Some* people made mistakes and did bad things. Clearly Shane Tyler was just perfect and well off and oh, so smart.

She was in too much of a red haze to pay any attention to what Gavin was doing with the horse or how much Micah was getting into it. The only thing she could do was stand and breathe, trying to calm that spurt of anger.

It was hardly Shane's fault he'd accidentally stumbled onto one of her sore spots, and she couldn't be mad at *him*. They were just . . . different. All the smiling and flirting in the world didn't change that fact.

She could hardly be mad at him for proving to her what she already knew. She was less. She was a ball of mistakes and failures who had lied to survive among other awful things.

She'd just thought he'd seen something different in her, and that was her own dumb fault.

Cora stopped the downward spiral of negative thoughts. She forced those old nasty voices out of her head. Some mix of Mom and Stephen and her own insecurities.

She wasn't that girl anymore. She fought her insecurities head-on, and she didn't take them out on other people like she had on Lilly for so many years.

"All right. You ready for some grub?" Gavin asked.

"Yeah." Micah bounded over to her, and it soothed some of that roiling in her stomach. She was doing something right. Maybe the whole basketball camp thing still didn't make any sense to her, but here he was grinning at her like she'd given him the world.

"You know this is supposed to be a punishment, right?" she asked him, running a hand over his hair, and he didn't flinch or bat her away.

"Well, the shit was gross."

"Mouth, Micah."

"They said it!"

She gave Gavin her best "mom" glare, and he tipped his hat. "Sorry 'bout that."

"Let's head in to lunch. And I expect you to be incredibly polite and grateful that Mrs. Tyler is providing us with food."

Micah heaved a sigh she knew meant assent somewhere deep down. Since he was letting her touch him, she slid her arm around his shoulders. Shoulders that would be up to hers in no time at all.

They walked out of the barn, Gavin leading them toward the house. Shane was nowhere to be seen. She didn't anticipate the mixed reaction she had to that. A little relief she didn't have to face him knowing she'd been unnecessarily curt with him, a little disappointment that he'd bail.

"After lunch we can do some weed spraying and some brush clearing in the pastures."

Micah shifted out from under her arm. "That sounds lame."

"The lamest," Gavin agreed cheerfully. "But after a good afternoon of that, we'll feed and water the horses. Then maybe, your mom willing, we'll get you up for another ride."

Micah looked up at her expectantly, and she knew she was sunk. Every last free moment of the next however long it would take for this to wear off, she'd be begging from the Tylers for some horse time.

Because you can't provide for your son yourself, can you?

Oof. Why couldn't she get that voice out of her head? Well, she'd have to keep working on it until it was gone. *Gone.*

They walked up to the porch, and Gavin led them inside, but before she could follow him down the hall, she heard Shane say her name.

She stopped to find him standing in the doorway to the living room. "Cora, can I talk to you for a minute?"

She winced because she knew she owed him an apology. Apparently he wasn't the kind of guy to let a little unexplained rudeness from a woman go.

"Ooh, I think your mom's in trouble," Gavin said in a sing-songy voice, which earned him a glare from Shane and Cora, and a laugh from Micah.

"Come on, kid, let's load up our plates, and maybe we can get two helpings in before we get back to work."

Cora wished she could insist on going with Micah, but she didn't avoid hard things anymore. She stepped into the pretty living room area and tried to smile at Shane.

But he was frowning at her. "Did I do something to offend you?"

She closed her eyes. "No." But that was a lie, and she might have had to lie on occasion, but she wouldn't on this. "Yes." She opened her eyes to find Shane frowning even more deeply, and who could blame him? "I mean, it's my thing. It was nothing really to do with you. So, we're fine. It's fine."

"Okay. Are you going to . . . explain said thing?"

"No." God, no. This man in front of her would not understand a sore spot or an insecurity. He would not understand someone who hadn't been a very good person in parts of her life. Who had been weak enough to be manipulated and harmed and . . . No, she might think he was easy to talk to and nice to look at, but they were just on opposite sides of the world. "We're awfully different, Shane. I'm not sure we'd ever really understand each other."

"Okay." His puzzled frown didn't disappear, but there was no other way to explain this whole thing to him. Not him.

She forced herself to smile. "Lunch then? Gavin said something about weed killing and then maybe another ride. I hope we aren't keeping you from your work?"

"No. No, it's fine," Shane said, none of the confusion in his tone dissipating.

She started walking for the hall, hoping she could find the kitchen or dining room or wherever Gavin and Micah had gone off to.

"So that wasn't flirting?"

Cora stopped mid-step. She wanted the floor to swallow her whole. Because she *had* been flirting. One hundred percent. But that was before he'd insinuated she couldn't handle her life and . . .

"Uh." Her cheeks warmed, which was so odd because she didn't blush. She usually got defensive or bold, never embarrassed. She didn't even know what to say when usually she could babble her way out of any situation.

"It felt like flirting, but if we're so different, maybe I was misreading." Except he sounded a little smug, not contrite or worried he'd read into things.

"Well, I don't know about you, but *I* was flirting," she replied, offering him an arch look.

His mouth curved, and all those butterflies she'd thought had died violent deaths just a little while ago winged back to life. Yeah, they were different. Yes, she could never really show him all those ugly sides of her, but wasn't that okay? New leaf Cora?

Except she *had* made a resolution. For herself. For her son.

"I'm sorry. I think you're hot. And nice. But I'm . . ." *A mess.* No, not that. Not anymore. "I made a New Year's resolution. No guys this year. No . . . No."

"Okay." His eyebrows drew together. "We're too different, and you have a New Year's resolution?"

"Yes."

"Are you making that up? Because I can handle a little rejection. It's July. A little late in the year to be using resolution excuses."

She wanted to laugh, and some odd part of her wanted to cry. "No, I'm not trying to spare your feelings. I'm just . . ." Sometimes honesty was the best policy. She couldn't be honest about all of herself, but she could be honest about this. "I'm trying to be a good mom and a good person, and I haven't had very much luck doing that when there's a man in my life."

"Gotcha." He made a gesture toward the hallway. "Let's get some lunch then."

Cora nodded, stepping into the hall, feeling oddly wrung out emotionally. It had just been a little conversation. An admittance to a certain amount of attraction, and a slightly more depressing admission that she couldn't act on it.

Even when life wasn't hard, it was complicated. She followed Shane down the hall, wishing she knew how to make things different.

"For the record," Shane said in a low voice, glancing back at her over his shoulder, "I'd never want to get in the way of your being a good mom or a good person, since those are things I like about you."

He dropped that serious, dark gaze and stepped into the kitchen, giving her no opportunity to respond to that, and maybe that was for the best. She didn't know what she would have said, and she was a little afraid she might have cried if she'd tried to say anything.

Shane felt broody that evening, and since he didn't care to dwell in a brood he couldn't fix, he decided to dwell on one he could.

He'd called a meeting of his siblings. They needed to nip the Ben Donahue situation in the bud once and for all.

Gavin plopped a twelve-pack of beer on the old table. Since they'd been kids they'd turned this small corner of the barn into something of a private space. When Mom got rid of a piece of furniture that still had some use, one of them would drag it out to the little room in the barn that had once been Dad's outdoor office.

Right now it boasted a table, five chairs, and a few battery-powered lamps. They'd had a mini fridge out here for a while, but it had bit the dust a few years ago, and the thrill of sneaking beer wasn't quite as big when you were grown adults.

Gavin settled himself on his chair, a worn leather beast that had once been in Dad's indoor office. Shane sat in his chair, which had been part of a kitchen set. It was uncomfortable and had a creaking, loose leg, but it still held his weight. Lindsay and Molly entered the barn, Molly with a jug of water and Lindsay with one of her ever-present boxes of candy.

There was an empty, overturned crate Boone had used once upon a time. It always stood out like an empty, sore thumb.

"Shane's got his pacing shoes on," Gavin said, opening a can of beer. "Let me guess, this isn't about the price of cattle."

"We have to *do* something." Shane couldn't control much, but he had to control this. He *had* to protect his mother. If he didn't . . .

"You told her about the reference lying, and Mom didn't budge," Molly pointed out. "Unless he's stealing from us or, I don't know, a serial killer, her mind's made up. I don't want to twist myself into knots over this anymore. Let's just support her."

"Support her into making a mistake and giving Donahue part of our ranch?" Gavin demanded.

"Is that all you care about? That he'll have a share of the ranch?" Molly returned.

"You know it's not, but it doesn't make it not a concern," Shane said determinedly. "There can't be fighting between us. We have to be a united front. Not that long ago we all agreed," Shane reminded them.

"Honestly, if he confessed to lying before we told on him, he can't be that bad," Lindsay offered, being absolutely no help at all.

"Or he's hiding even worse sins and he confessed to throw her off the lying scent," Gavin said, pointing his beer at Lindsay.

"And maybe you're a paranoid nutjob, Gav."

"Why do you like him so much?"

Lindsay huffed out a breath. "I don't really like him. I don't not like him either. But, come on, we're going to interfere with Mom's life? On what planet."

"And good for Mom for getting the hot, younger guy. She deserves a boy toy," Molly said, not doing a very good job of suppressing a grin.

"Gross," Shane and Gavin responded in unison.

"We need to hire an investigator," Shane announced. Though he shuddered at the term, Mom could have all the boy toys she wanted. As long as she didn't marry them.

His siblings' responses were immediate and all at once:

"Now you're talking," Gavin said.

"Are you high?" was Lindsay's demand.

"No," Molly said in her straightforward way.

"What is the harm in pooling our resources and hiring someone to make sure Ben Donahue isn't a no-good, thieving liar?" Even though Shane was certain Ben was without doing any investigating.

"Mom would kill us," Molly replied. "Why are you so fixated on this?"

"Why aren't you?"

"Because Mom's an adult? Because when you were sticking your nose in my life, I sure as hell didn't listen to you."

"And, as I recall, you ended up being wrong." Which he should not have said to his sister even when it was true. She'd taken a hit there. He shouldn't poke at it. "Look, we've got a tie. So—"

"I could probably break the tie."

It was as if all the air was sucked out of the barn in one instance. Because even if the sun setting through the door obscured all their views of the man in the barn door opening, they all knew that voice.

"Boone." Shane sure as hell didn't know what else to

say aside from his brother's name. His brother who hadn't been home since Christmas, and even then just for dinner. He certainly hadn't called home or returned any of Shane's calls about Mom and Ben. Boone was an occasional ghost at best.

And now he was here.

"Boone!" Lindsay screeched, launching herself toward the figure in the door, but she skidded to a halt. "You're hurt."

Boone stepped farther into the room. Actually, *limped* was a more apt term. Now that Shane could see his younger brother's face, he saw there were bandages across his temple and chin, and Boone moved stiffly.

"You look like shit," Gavin said flatly.

"Yeah, well, had the hell trampled out of me by a bull."

"You didn't think to call?" Shane managed to croak. Clearly Boone would have had to have been in the hospital with those injuries, and they hadn't known. He hadn't contacted them, hadn't wanted their help or support.

"Nah. A few broken bones and bruises. Healed up okay." Boone limped forward again. "So, what's the meeting about?"

"Mom's getting married. Which you'd know if you ever answered your phone or called." Lindsay moved like she was going to slap him across the arm, but she stopped herself.

"Married, huh?" Boone flicked a glance toward Shane. They stared at each other for a few palpable, silent moments.

It burned. The physical evidence of a failure he'd never be able to fix, most especially when this thing with Mom and Donahue felt like an uphill battle, when, stupid as it might be, he felt that same burning desire to somehow help Cora . . . except she wouldn't even tell him why they were so different.

It was almost as if the universe was trying to tell him something, except what could it be telling him? He was the head of this family, and he had to work on the things he could fix, even if it was hard. Even if it was a challenge.

He owed it to all of them.

Boone was home, and that was a step in the right direction. Surely, Boone of all people would be on their side when it came to Mom's marrying a shady man.

"You're home. Are you *home*?" Molly asked, her voice a little scratchy.

"For a bit, I guess. If Mom doesn't kick me out."

"She won't. You know she won't." Lindsay and Molly were flanking Boone, leading him toward Lindsay's chair.

Boone's gaze returned to Shane. Shane had truly never understood his youngest brother. He'd tried, he really had, but Shane believed in right and wrong, and that you always did what was right. Boone believed in raising hell and pissing everyone off.

"What about you, Shane? Going to welcome me home?"

"Of course," Shane said stiffly.

Boone's mouth quirked, and Shane noticed there was a split in the bottom lip. He was more than a little banged and bruised. "How long were you in the hospital?"

"So, tell me about this guy Mom's marrying. Some crusty old rancher type?"

"Oh, no. He's a ranch hand," Molly piped up, clearly hoping to keep Shane from interrogating Boone further.

"And handsome," Lindsay added. When all three of her brothers glared at her, she rolled her eyes. "Well, he *is*."

"He's old enough to be your father."

"Fathers can be hot," Lindsay returned.

Christ, they were all going to kill him. Spontaneous brain explosion. And yet, they were all here. Together. In their old thinking spot. If the universe gave signs, then *this* was his sign.

His family was all home. Together. If anything would get through to Mom, it would have to be that.

Chapter Nine

Cora didn't know why she was nervous. There was nothing to be nervous about. She was going to drop Micah off with the Tyler brothers, who were kind, responsible, *good* men, and they were going to give him chores while she and Deb went to visit the florist.

Micah who had grumbled and groaned and yawned and groaned some more as she'd forced him into the car this morning was now bright and alert as they passed through the Tyler ranch archway.

"I need you to tell me why you got kicked out of basketball camp," Cora blurted. Because she needed to know why there was this difference. When he'd loved basketball so much.

"You know why."

"I want to know why you *did* it. Throwing something at someone isn't like you, Micah. I know that in my soul. Something happened. Something prompted this, and I need to know."

"It's nothing. I was bored. It was lame."

That was all such bullshit. "Please, Micah. I need to . . . I'm your mother, and I love you, and I need to understand you. I *want* to understand so I can help or support or do whatever I need to do." She blew out a breath as she came to a stop in front of the Tyler house. She looked over at her son, who half the time seemed like this alien she'd never understand.

He didn't look at her, but he also didn't beg her off again. He sat there, staring out the window, obviously thinking things through.

"Dad knew," he finally said on little more than a whisper.

It was a sledgehammer to the chest. So hard and painful she could hardly speak. "What?" she managed to gasp.

"He sent me a basketball. At camp. I didn't want to be there anymore." He stared hard out the window. "I didn't want you to freak," he muttered, pressing his forehead to the glass.

"You have to tell me if he contacts you. It's important you tell me. You know that." She wasn't sure any of those words actually came out of her mouth. Everything felt too tight and painful, so much so she could barely breathe.

Micah flicked a glance her way. "You're crying," he said, and his tone was so flat and detached she knew she was making this worse, but how could she not cry when her baby was in danger and he didn't want to tell her?

"Yeah, but I'm not broken, Micah. I'm upset." She was terrified, but she didn't want to tell him *that*. "It does upset me that he tried to contact you when he isn't supposed to, but I have to know so we can deal with it."

"I got kicked out. It solved the problem. Besides, this is all cool. I want to do this." He pointed toward the Tyler stables.

"Baby, I need you to promise me. Really promise me, with no caveats, that if something like that ever happens again you will tell me. Right away. I might cry. I might freak, but then I'll calm down, and I'll handle it." She thought about how old he was getting. How he was trying to protect her and how he shouldn't have to. He was still a *boy* and shouldn't have to do this, and yet he was so *mature*.

She took his hand in hers, and though he didn't hold on, he didn't pull away. So, she squeezed. "We're in this together. You have to tell me not just so *I* can handle it, but so that we can handle it together. We're a team, baby."

"So, if Dad sent you something, you'd tell me?"

Hell. "Would you want me to?" she asked, *praying* the answer would be no.

"Yeah." Micah looked at her then, and she saw some spark of the boy who'd started to emerge since they'd moved here. All this time she'd been worried about giving him space, and his father had contacted him. "I don't want him to hurt you again."

Oh, God. If hearts could break, hers was a thousand pieces on the floor. She held Micah's hand in hers and looked directly into his eyes. "He doesn't get to hurt us anymore. Neither of us." She didn't want to say the next part, but maybe she did need to start treating Micah like a partner.

It felt wrong, but it was what she'd wanted all those years of feeling insignificant and pointless. She'd wanted someone to consider her a partner, not a thing to be hurt *or* protected.

"After my appointment, I'm going to call our lawyer and ask what we should do about this. Okay?"

Micah nodded.

"And you've told me everything?"

He nodded again.

Cora pulled him into a hug and held on tight. "I love you, baby. I promise, I'll do everything in my power

so he can never reach you again. I promise you that."
Whatever it took. No matter the cost, emotional or financial.

Weirdly, she thought of Shane and his reaction to Ben's lying. She would lie, steal, cheat, fight to keep her baby safe and unharmed. She would do *anything*. Shane would never fully understand that. He was too good, and had maybe had things a little too easy in his life.

But this wasn't about Shane, even as he stepped out of the house, shading his eyes against the rising sun as he stared at their car with a frown.

Cora cleared her throat and pulled away from Micah. "All right, my little cowboy, time for you to get to work."

"Gross, Mom."

She grinned at him, gratified when he gave her a little smile. "I love you."

He rolled his eyes and moved out of the reach of her arms, pushing the door open. "Love you too," he muttered so quietly she almost didn't hear it.

But hearing it was a balm to her soul. He loved her. Wanted to protect her. She was raising a good kid, and she'd made mistakes, but she was overcoming them. And that bastard Stephen wouldn't touch Micah's life again. Even if she had to ask Lilly and Brandon for help.

She got out of the car, ignoring the little hitch in her chest at the sight of Shane and Micah talking on the porch. Micah looked up at him, clear hero worship all over his expression, and Shane just had the kindest smile with everyone.

Shane Tyler. Still a major problem.

She walked across the yard and up the steps. Micah had disappeared inside.

"I sent him to get a jug of water from Mom. Real cowboys stay hydrated."

"How very responsible," Cora returned with a chuckle. "You okay?"

It was then she realized she hadn't fixed her makeup, and it was probably clear as day she'd had a teary moment there in the car. Oh well. She looked out over the mountains, taking some solace in their sturdy strength. Was she okay? "I'm still working on it," she murmured.

She glanced at him then, noticing the shadows under his eyes and the hint of stubble on his chin. "Are *you* okay?"

He raked a hand through his hair before pulling the cowboy hat onto his head. "You ever wanted to be a spy?"

She laughed, surprised by the odd question and maybe even a little charmed by it. By him. *He won't understand you. You swore off men.*

But he grinned down at her, and she forgot all that. It was nice to forget, and nice to know good men existed somewhere in this world. In *her* world.

"I had some Nancy Drew fantasies. I guess that's more sleuthing than spying."

"It'll do, Nancy. Call me Joe Hardy and come solve a mystery with me."

Cora's expression turned skeptical, but Shane noted she also didn't stop smiling. There was probably something a little wrong with him given that he was still asking for her help after she'd been very clear she wasn't looking for a romantic complication to her life.

And neither are you.

Except he couldn't quite remember that in her general proximity. All he could think about when she was within viewing distance was the fact he liked being around her. He liked making her smile, and the way she studied him. She didn't outright argue with him like his siblings always did. She listened, even when she didn't agree.

When it came to this stuff with Ben and spying and investigators, siblings couldn't be counted on to deal with it rationally. Gavin went too far, and the girls went not far enough. Boone's being home only made it more complicated. There was too much going on *inside* of his family, a family who didn't understand what it was like to be used by someone for what you had.

He needed a little outside help. And if that was some kind of rationalization to be in Cora's orbit more often than not, so be it.

"What exactly did you have in mind?" she asked, still skeptical, but *listening*.

"So, I suggested hiring a private investigator to the kids last night."

Cora wrinkled her nose. "The kids?"

Shane winced a little. "I'm the oldest. Old habits. Et cetera. Sometimes I call them kids."

She pressed her lips together, but she couldn't hide the smile. "Okay, Dad." When he glared, she laughed. "But isn't a private investigator kind of heavy-handed?"

"Maybe. Maybe it is, but I've been trying to get my mom to see the truth about Ben for a while now, and I can't seem to." He couldn't let time run out. Couldn't let this happen to Mom. "The suggestion of a private investigator was something of a last resort."

"But your siblings don't agree?"

"They can't decide how they feel about it. The thing is, it would be an answer. If an investigation came back clean and there was truly nothing in Ben's past that might make me think he's a threat to my mother, I would drop this. I would find a way to get along with the guy. It would be an *answer*. I need an answer, and neither Mom nor Ben will give it."

"And, you, being you, you've asked in a hundred different ways."

"I have. All I ever get is they love each other, and maybe they do, but that doesn't mean he's not dangerous." God knew. "Cora, I don't know how to let her make this mistake. And you said if there was any evidence that he might hurt her, you would help."

"Yes. Yes, I would." Her smile had died, and she looked so grave. Off in some other world. There was a heaviness about her that he'd thought he'd seen when she'd walked up, but she'd pushed it away. It was back now.

"Because someone hurt you once?" he asked gently, hoping to get to the bottom of her as much as he hoped to get to the bottom of Ben.

She didn't meet his gaze. Instead she stared at the mountains like he so often did when he didn't know what to say or do. When he was looking for answers that didn't seem to appear anywhere in this world. He always hoped the mountains had the answers. They never did, but that never kept him from looking.

"I know what it's like to have someone make you think he cares about you when he doesn't." She smiled sadly. "Shane, I can't imagine your mother being that person."

"I wish I couldn't. But even the most invincible people aren't immune to losing sight of the truth when feelings are involved." He'd witnessed that firsthand. Experienced it. "Everyone has a weakness, and there's always someone to pay for that weakness. Even the invincible."

She cocked her head. He had the urge to explain it all to her. To sit her down and tell her everything that had happened to this family and how he couldn't let it happen again. But he was selfish enough to want to keep his weaknesses from her. His failures.

"I suppose that's true," she said after a while. "But I don't know how I can help you spy."

"Ben doesn't trust me. He doesn't like me."

He was gratified to see a spark of humor back on her face. "Gee, I wonder why."

"Regardless of why," he replied with feigned sternness, "I can't go snooping around him or his stuff. Neither can my siblings. He knows that we're out to get him."

"Ah. But he doesn't know I am."

"Exactly. With Micah doing chores for us and stuff, plus the wedding planning, I figure you'll be around a lot. You could do some eavesdropping and potentially some snooping."

"That sounds . . . not wholly on the up-and-up."

"It isn't."

"I didn't know you had it in you," she said, with something like admiration in her voice. As if doing something wrong was something to admire.

He wasn't proud of any of this, but it had to be done. "I don't want to do anything sordid, but I'll do anything if it means I might protect my mother from hurt. I don't just mean emotional hurts. If they get married, this ranch is part his. That might sound cold, but this ranch is my blood as much as my mother is. It's my life. My father is buried on this land, my grandparents. My life, my family, and my history are all here in this ground, and I can't trust someone with part of that until I know for sure he or she is worthy of that trust."

"It must be very special to have all that," she said quietly.

"It is. And it's important to me." He didn't add that

he felt bad for her that she clearly didn't have anything like this to belong to. "I know you care about my mother."

"I do. She's been very good to me for absolutely no reason at all."

"So, you don't have to consider this a favor for me. You can consider this a favor for her. I don't want you doing anything you're uncomfortable with. If you say no, you want nothing to do with this, I'll never ask again. But I had to ask."

"And this is definitely not flirting?" she asked, and clearly she tried to ask it seriously, but she ended up smiling mischievously at him instead.

"Not yet anyway."

She laughed a little. "Well, I'm going over to the flower farm with your mother this morning. Then I have a meeting in the afternoon with a future bride. I don't know when we could make this happen."

"Leave Micah with us for the whole day. Come back to pick him up around five. Mom will insist you both stay for dinner without my even having to put the idea in her head. I'll figure out something to get us all together—a fire pit and s'mores or something. While that's going on, you and I can sneak off and do a little digging."

"That sounds like flirting."

He grinned. "First you have to find something on Ben."

She shook her head, but the lightness and easy humor were back. "This is kind of ridiculous, you know?"

"Yeah, but I'm willing to do a lot of ridiculous things to keep my family safe. To keep this place whole."

She met his gaze then, her blue eyes serious and searching. "I guess that's one of those things I like about you, Shane."

He realized then how close they stood on the front

porch. The beautiful pearly light of dawn teasing the red of her hair into prominence, the delicate blue of a morning sky reflected in her eyes. He couldn't remember a time in his entire life when he'd wanted to press his mouth to someone else's so badly. It was something akin to a stabbing pain, wanting to know what she felt like under his palms. Wanting to inhale her scent until he couldn't smell anything else.

The front door slammed open, knocking him back to the here and now and some sense. Micah bounded out, Gavin following at a much slower pace. And then, to Shane's surprise, Boone limped out behind Gavin.

"Don't look so surprised, big brother."

Shane wasn't sure he'd ever stop being surprised to see Boone here. To see all the physical evidence of his brother's injuries.

Boone's gaze flicked to Cora, and there was a little flare of something in his eyes that Shane did not care for at all.

"Boone, this is Mom's wedding planner and Micah's mother. Cora, this is my youngest brother, Boone."

"Oh, the troublemaker," Cora said with a bright smile. "I've heard a little bit about you."

"I just bet," Boone said with a grin.

Shane attempted not to tense, but it was hard when he noticed that Micah was looking back and forth between Boone and his mother with something akin to interest.

"Let's get those chores done," Shane said gruffly and abruptly. He tipped his hat to Cora. "Enjoy the flower farm."

"I will." She reached out and ruffled her hand over Micah's hair. "Take care of my baby."

"Ugh, Mom. Come on," Micah groaned, slapping her

hand away and hurrying down the stairs and away from his mother.

But Shane held her gaze, because he could see all her concern and worry and he knew that concern and worry all too well. "I will. I promise."

Her smile warmed, and she nodded before disappearing inside to find Mom. When Shane turned to go down the stairs, he found both of his brothers staring at him. Micah was a few yards ahead, happily playing with Ben's dog, King.

His brothers didn't budge. Just blocked his way and stared.

"What?"

"Oh, nothing," Gavin said in a tone that was clearly not *nothing*.

"So, have you actually made a move or are you still the pine in silence type?"

"Fuck off, Boone." Shane didn't push past his brother like he would have liked to have done, mostly because he was a little afraid even a friendly nudge would send his brother toppling over.

"Pine in silence type it is."

"Who said I'm pining, silent or otherwise?"

"The grin she flashed at me. You'd made a move on her, she wouldn't be looking at me."

It burned, but Shane knew Boone was after a reaction, and he wouldn't give it. "If you want to believe that, you go right ahead." Shane, for one, wouldn't.

He would try really hard not to believe that.

Chapter Ten

Cora could hardly believe what stretched before her. Rows and rows of colorful, delicate blooms. It was like a Pinterest picture, complete with little red barn in the distance that apparently acted as Lou Anderson's florist shop.

"I can't believe this exists," Cora offered to Deb.

Deb smiled, though Cora noticed the woman wasn't her usual cheerful self this morning. Not that she was sullen, or even quiet, just a little muted.

"The Fairchild girls had it a bit rough growing up. Their grandparents did everything they could to give them the opportunity to do what they really wanted with their lives." Deb sighed. "Poor Lou," she murmured as a young woman stepped out of the barn.

Cora didn't have time to ask what was poor about her, because Deb was propelling them forward, calling a greeting to the woman.

"Morning, Lou. This is my wedding planner, Cora," Deb said, pushing Cora forward.

Cora smiled and held out a hand. "It's nice to meet you."

Lou smiled politely, but there was something off

about the right side of her mouth. The right side of her face was mostly obscured by the flap of a bandana that seemed to hold back a short cap of blonde hair. When she shook Cora's outstretched right hand, Lou used her left hand, which made it awkward.

"Welcome," Lou offered.

"Your place is amazing," Cora said enthusiastically. "I've never been to a flower farm before."

Lou's one visible green eye radiated pride and excitement. "We're very proud of it. Obviously what we've got blooming now won't be available in September, but I've got some pictures and mock-ups in the office."

"It looks good as new. You must have really been working on it."

"Gavin's been helping."

"Oh, I know. He's always sneaking off to come over here."

Lou laughed, though it didn't sound very happy. "Care to stop him?"

"You know Gav just wants to help," Deb said gently.

"Well, he shouldn't."

"As if I could tell a man with the last name Tyler not to help. Owen might have died years ago, but it seems to be imprinted in the DNA."

Lou glanced back at Cora, and she was so completely lost. She tried not to feel out of place. After all, Deb and Lou were old friends and neighbors. Cora was *just* the wedding planner.

"We had a fire," Lou explained. "In the barn." She gestured to her bandana-covered face with her gloved right hand. "I'm about the only thing that survived. But we're rebuilding, and Lou's Blooms will be up and running and ready for this wedding by September."

"I'm glad. We've got at least two more weddings

scheduled for the year with Mile High Weddings, and we'd like to use as many Gracely-local vendors as possible."

"I'm your girl," Lou said, walking them toward the barn. As they got closer, Cora could see that, though the front looked completely finished, the building itself was still in the stages of being rebuilt.

They walked through the door, and everything inside was mostly wood. Unfinished walls and rafters, the smell of sawdust and flowers, and just the strangest underlying hint of smoke.

There were buckets and tables and big shelving units labeled with things like *purple lace* and *floral tape*. Even though it clearly wasn't a finished florist-type space, there was a lot of evidence Lou Fairchild knew exactly what she was doing.

She led them over to a long table along the far wall. There were cutouts in the walls for windows, clearly, but plastic covered them.

"Windows go in next week," Lou said with a careless wave toward the plastic. Then she tapped her non-gloved hand to the table. She had pictures all set out and a few bunches of flowers arranged together. "Pictures are of the flowers I'll have in September. I brought in some possible color schemes with different flowers. Em told me what cake you chose, so I thought focusing on greens and whites would be good, but I've got some more colorful options to consider too."

Cora studied the flowers, the color schemes. It was all beautiful, but Lou was right. For the things Deb had been looking at, the white and green with maybe some brown accents would be the prettiest.

Deb made an odd squeaking noise, and when Cora looked over she realized the woman was crying. Alarmed, Cora reached out. "Deb?"

"Oh, it's so stupid." She waved a hand in front of her face. "Don't know why I'm getting emotional."

"Well, weddings are emotional," Lou offered, eyebrows drawn together. "But you seem sad, Mrs. T. Not emotional."

Deb sniffed and then made another sound, something like a swallowed sob. "Boone's home," she managed to croak.

"Ooh," Lou said, because she knew all the history and all Cora knew was he'd been in the rodeo and was a troublemaker.

"Ben thinks I should kick him out, and we had a big fight over it, and then I started wondering last night if Shane and Gavin aren't right about this whole thing. I'm not at the end of my life yet, but what's a woman my age doing getting married?"

Lou and Cora looked at each other, both wide-eyed and a little lost. In Cora's experience, Deb always knew what to do and never wavered. Cora wondered if, in all the years Lou had known Deb, she'd ever seen any uncertainty. Cora kind of doubted it.

"I just don't know what to do. I'm willing to do something I want for myself and the man I love, even if it irritates my kids, but I'm not willing to turn my back on my kids for some man."

"Well . . ." Lou looked helplessly at Cora with a shrug.

"If he loves you, he'll understand how important your children are to you," Cora said firmly.

"He can be so hard sometimes." Deb sniffled, using the tissue Lou had handed her to dab at her eyes and nose. "But then so can I."

"Deb Tyler, you are the least hard woman I know," Lou said firmly. "Except maybe my sister."

Which earned a watery chuckle from Deb.

"If he's making you feel like there's something wrong

with you, hardness or loving your children, well, he isn't the man you think he is," Cora said. Much as she hated to butt in, she knew that all for a fact.

Deb looked at Cora then. "He's not a bad man."

Cora really hoped Shane talking to her about his Ben doubts weren't transparent, because this wasn't only about that. It was about Cora's own experiences. She knew a thing or two about bad men. "Then he will prove that by apologizing and coming to his senses. Sometimes . . . Sometimes another person can make you feel like you're wrong when you're not. They can . . ." Cora looked from Deb's to Lou's interested face and felt her cheeks warm, but she pressed on. "They can seem loving when they're not."

Deb reached out and took Cora's hand and squeezed. "Thank you for that. That's an excellent reminder."

"We all need it sometimes." But inwardly, Cora felt something like dread twisting in her chest. Shane was so certain Ben was bad, a liar or maybe worse. If Ben was making Deb—this strong, determined, resilient woman—doubt her actions, maybe Shane really was right.

Which meant Cora was going to have to help Shane spy. She'd agreed this morning thinking they wouldn't find anything, *hoping* they wouldn't. Now . . .

"Oh, silly cold feet. Ben's a good man. If I hadn't married Owen because we had one little argument, well, I'd have five less kids. That's for sure. Well, four anyway." Deb smiled and pointed to the pile of white and green flowers. "You're right, Lou. This one will look the best. Now, which flowers will you have in September?"

Cora paid attention, making notes of flowers and prices and dates, but her stomach churned. She couldn't help but wonder if she was planning a wedding she was going to be involved in stopping.

* * *

"You got good instincts, kid," Shane said as Micah managed to get off Stan in a smooth move.

"Yeah?"

"That's only your third dismount, and you were smooth," Molly said with a kind smile. "Still need some work on the getting up, and the rein holds, but you're making great progress in a short period of time. We get a few lessons in, you'll be a pro in no time."

Micah grinned, the apples of his cheeks hinting a little red. "Cool," he said, clearly failing at nonchalance. The kid was hooked, and a hard worker all in all. As long as there was the promise of more horse riding in the future, he did what they asked of him, and once he'd figured out that hurrying through a job didn't get him to the ride any sooner, he'd started to do a more thorough job.

"Why don't you take Stan here into the stables and rub him down?"

Micah's eyes widened. "By myself?"

"If you think you can handle it."

Micah nodded, as if doing a bobblehead impersonation. "Yeah, yeah I can handle it. I'll do a good job." He looked up at the big horse adoringly, then flicked a suspicious glance back at Molly and Shane. He ducked his head, and Shane suspected he was trying to hide his excitement from them.

Micah made a clicking noise, clearly mimicking what he had heard Shane and Molly do, and then gently pulled on the reins. Stan, the horse Molly used for most of her lessons and therefore used to inexperienced riders, easily obeyed and walked with Micah's guidance into the stables.

"He's so sweet," Molly said.

"Good kid," Shane agreed. "Mom knew what she was doing when she suggested this."

"She usually does. Speaking of . . ."

Shane braced himself for a lecture from his younger sister.

"I was thinking that maybe instead of pushing Mom about Ben, we take an alternative tact. Let her marry Ben, if that's what she wants, but that doesn't mean we couldn't suggest some . . . legal protection."

"Are *you* going to suggest that to Mom?" he asked incredulously.

"Hell no, that's your job." Molly's grin flashed but faded quickly. "She's not going to listen to us about the whole thing, but maybe we can appeal to her practicality."

Shane didn't know why the idea didn't appeal to him. It was smart. It would save Mom from the kind of embarrassment he'd suffered, but . . . She'd still be hurt. He couldn't abide the thought.

"We'll think about it," Shane said.

"We? You speak for all of us now?" She shook her head. "Of course you do." Her tone wasn't so much bitter as it was sad. "This isn't working. The way we are."

"What does that mean?"

Molly shook her head. "I don't know," she muttered. "It's like we're all separate, fighting separate battles, not letting anyone else in."

"We're not doing that."

She laughed, and this was bitter. "So says you."

"Mol—"

She held up a hand. "No, I'm just . . ." She swallowed, squinting off into the sun. "The divorce stuff came through today, and I'm pissy and taking it out on you. Not fair."

"Hey." When she didn't look at him, he reached out and took her by the shoulders, giving them a squeeze until she raised her gaze. "You know if you ever need a shoulder to cry on, I'm here."

She looked patently miserable. "Tylers don't cry, remember?"

"We could. I mean, I'd rather cut my balls off, but *you* could."

That earned him a watery chuckle, and she leaned into him with a sigh. "You really do hold us all together. I'm just starting to think the rest of us need to do some holding back."

"I . . . don't know what that means."

She pulled back, any trace of tears gone, and she smiled. He knew she wasn't okay, but he also knew if she wanted to let herself go, she would.

"You don't have to know what it means, I don't think. Think about talking to Mom about a prenup or something similar. Talk to Gavin about it, and I'll talk to Boone."

"I could talk to Boone."

Molly grinned. "I don't want to clean up any blood. You take the moron. I'll take the idiot."

Shane nodded. "Fine, fine. And Lindsay?"

Molly hesitated. "She likes Ben."

"Yeah, I know."

"I don't know why Mom's doing this. It sucks, and I'm wrapped up in my own crap, and it *sucks.*"

"I'll take Lindsay then."

"I wish I could crawl into a cave and come out in a year."

"You'd miss an awful lot."

"Yeah, well." She shrugged. "I'm going to go take a very long shower and have a very long, private cry. I'll see you at dinner."

Shane nodded and offered her a wave as she turned and strode to the house. Once he was sure she was gone, he rubbed his hands over his face. Tylers might not cry, but they sure got swindled when it came to love.

He'd made the mistake himself, he'd let Molly make the mistake when he hadn't thought to lock her in her room till she saw some sense, and now Mom was about to make it too.

Not on his watch.

Shane stepped into the stables to check on Micah. Shane tensed momentarily when he saw Boone was with him, helping get Stan all cleaned up.

"Knocked him out," Boone was saying. "One strong punch, right to the jaw, bam," Boone said, grinning and replicating the movement with the hint of a wince.

"Can you teach me?" Micah asked in awe.

Shane stepped forward. "No, he can't." What was his brother thinking, telling these kinds of stories to a young, impressionable kid? "Violence is hardly an answer."

"Don't listen to Shane. He's an old stick-in-the-mud," Boone stage-whispered.

Shane wished he could find it funny, but Micah was his responsibility. He'd promised Cora he'd take good care of the kid, and Boone's bullshit stories were certainly not taking care.

"You can wash up for dinner."

"Can I?" Boone replied, with that cocky grin and the faint hint of tension laced underneath all that lazy cowboy.

Shane didn't know what he'd ever done to piss his brother off, what made them so much like oil and vinegar. It got him thinking about Molly's saying they were all separate, fighting different, solitary battles.

A truth he didn't care for because he'd been fighting it his whole life.

"Well, I'll see you up at the house, kid. Whisper a few

sordid stories to you at the dinner table." Boone winked and then limped away.

Shane bit back all the retorts, all the lectures. They'd never worked. Why would they work now when Boone was a man? Limping and injured and perfectly happy not to let the family in.

Christ, his family was a mess, and Shane didn't know what to do. Except put one foot in front of the other.

"Stan looks good. You hungry?"

"My mom should be getting here soon," Micah grumbled.

"She should. But I have a feeling my mom is going to invite you both to dinner. My mom's a pretty good cook."

"Really?"

Shane nodded. Appealing to a kid's stomach was rarely the wrong choice. "Never had better in fact."

"My mom sucks at cooking."

Shane tried not to laugh. He doubted Cora would be happy to hear that estimation. "I bet she tries really hard though."

Micah shrugged, stepping out of the stall. He dutifully pulled the gate closed and latched it. Shane couldn't help but be impressed that the kid would be that conscientious.

Micah shuffled after Shane, kicking at the dirt, hands deep in his pockets, shoulders hunched. Something clearly heavy on those shoulders.

"Good day?" Shane asked, hoping to open up the line of conversation. Maybe *someone* would depend on him a little bit, and he could be a little less of a failure.

"Yeah. The horses are cool."

"Good."

Silence reigned except for the sounds of their feet hitting the grass as they walked across the yard toward the house.

"That thing you . . ." Micah trailed off, glaring at the ground and stomping on it like it had done something to him. "Violence . . ." He shook his head vigorously.

Shane watched him and wondered if Micah had taken such an interest in Boone's story because someone had been picking on him. It could have been why Micah had gotten himself kicked out of basketball camp. Kids could be cruel for the dumbest of reasons.

"Violence is hardly an answer," Shane repeated. It was something his father had told him once. When Shane had gotten into a fight at school because Pat Butler had called a girl in their class fat and Shane had told him to shut his ugly mouth. Shane had earned a split lip and a black eye, but he'd broken Pat's nose and felt pretty good about it.

Until the lecture from his father.

"So, what . . . what do you do when someone's bothering you if not knock them out?" Micah mumbled so quietly Shane had to really strain to listen.

Shane thought back to his father's speech. In the end, it hadn't been the lecture he'd expected. It had been neither outright censure nor fatherly delight. Something measured and tempered that had stuck with Shane for all the years after.

"Actions have consequences. Negative actions typically have negative consequences. I try to avoid the negative consequences if I can, which means finding positive ways to deal with a situation. It doesn't mean you never throw a punch, but it means violence is always your last resort. Because no matter how little you mean it, violence leaves a mark."

Micah's head whipped up then, and he looked at Shane with something in his expression Shane couldn't read. It might have made Shane uncomfortable if they hadn't reached the porch stairs.

He heard the faint rumble of an engine and looked south to the entrance of the ranch. "That'll be your mom," he offered.

Micah looked out into the distance, where the sun was flirting with the peaks of the mountains. He watched, his face tense as Cora's car approached. Then he flicked another glance at Shane before his gaze drifted toward the stables.

"Well, thanks."

"For what?" Shane asked, his own gaze on the now stopped car and Cora stepping out, the early evening light making her hair look more gold than its usual reddish hue. His chest kicked something strange as her mouth curved when her blue gaze met his.

"The horses and stuff. I like it a lot. I like it here," Micah said it all in a rush, likely embarrassed to admit he liked something.

"You're always welcome here, Micah. Promise."

Micah nodded jerkily as Cora reached the stairs.

"Hey, guys. All horsed out?"

"I think if he had his way he'd still be on one, but our stomachs got the better of us, didn't they?"

Micah nodded. He didn't exactly lean into his mother when she slid her arm around him, but there was something Shane could see in the slight movement of his shoulders. A relaxation. A comfort.

Shane opened the door and stepped inside, gesturing for them to follow. "I think I smell meatloaf. Anyone not a fan?"

"Anything is better than my own cooking," Cora said with a chuckle. "Isn't that right, baby?"

Micah groaned, probably at the endearment, but he gave Shane a meaningful glance as they stepped inside. As if to say *see, she is a terrible cook*.

Shane closed the door and then walked behind them

as Cora led Micah toward the dining room. If his gaze dropped to the way her pants skimmed her—

He jerked his eyes back up to the back of her head, except she'd glanced back at him and caught him in the act of checking out her ass.

She, however, didn't frown or narrow her eyes or so much as look flustered. Instead, she winked at him.

He was toast.

Chapter Eleven

Dinner was amazing. Not just the food, though partially that. Also, the company. Cora had never seen anything like it. Though she'd had some dinners with the Mile High crew, and those could get a little loud, it was just three men and three women plus her and Micah. Sometimes with the addition of Skeet. It was very adult and friendly.

This was like watching a fireworks display. Bursts of color and noise, some bigger and brighter and louder than the rest. The occasional whistle of a fizzle, a tense silent moment as everyone waited for that next thunderous boom, and then all light and dazzle again. An engaging, otherworldly display she couldn't look away from.

On the occasions when she could tear her gaze away from Shane and the way he all but led the table in their circuitous teasing and boisterous conversation, she looked at Micah, who watched as if he was as in awe as she was.

It was strange to be able to watch her son be engaged and happy and not feel that stab of guilt. Usually Micah's being happy only reminded her how terribly she'd failed him up to this point. But there was something about the warmth of the Tyler dining room, even with the occasional tense moment when Ben added something and everything in the room seemed to pause, hold its breath, and wait.

No explosions ever came. It was a careful dance, mostly made up of laughter and love, and no one ever acted as though she and Micah shouldn't be there or didn't belong, which was its own wonder.

Especially as Shane easily maneuvered the conversation into the suggestion of starting up the fire pit and roasting marshmallows, while everyone jumped onto the idea, easily including Cora and Micah in the plans.

"You men go get the fire started. I want to show this boy my sword collection," Grandma Maisey said, pushing back from the table.

Cora looked frantically around as everyone acted like that was a completely normal sentence and kept clearing dishes.

"Cool," Micah said, practically leaping from his chair.

"Grandma," Shane said, nodding toward Cora, who was still sitting there like a landed fish. Gaping. Speechless.

Maisey waved a hand. "Oh, don't worry, sweetheart. There's no touching. Most stuff's behind glass or hung up. Only time anyone ever got hurt was when a bird flew into the room and I stabbed it. And birds hardly count as anyones."

"Sure," Cora said. "That's totally normal. Swords. My child. Dead birds." Micah trailed happily after Maisey while Molly and Deb cleared the table. Gavin and Boone had disappeared, arguing over how to best roast a marshmallow, and Cora was left sitting at the dining room table feeling a bit like she'd been hit like a gong.

"He'll be fine. I promise," Shane said, pushing back from the table himself. He gathered the last of the plates and handed them to Molly when she came back into the room.

"Your grandmother collects swords?" Cora said, because maybe if she repeated it, she could wrap her head around it.

"Yes. She has one that dates back all the way to the French and Indian War. She's quite proud of it," Shane said seriously.

Cora shook her head, and Shane grinned. She couldn't help but smile back. He had a handsome smile, with a warmth to it that made her heart give one slow, delicious flip. She thought back to when they'd walked in and she'd caught him checking out her ass.

She'd never been with a good, decent man before. There were a lot of reasons for that, mostly her own insecurities and issues, but there was also this odd assumption that good and decent had to be boring.

The things Shane sparked in her chest were hardly boring, and just because someone was good and decent didn't mean he couldn't be a little bad. . . .

Cora jumped a little when someone cleared his throat. Her cheeks heated when she realized Ben was still sitting at the table.

"Guess I'll go get the fixings and take them outside," Ben announced, making it somehow sound like a challenge.

All that smiling warmth from Shane had faded, but there wasn't *some* of the tension and anger she usually saw in him at just the mention of Ben. There was almost a thoughtfulness in his expression. "That'll be fine, Ben," he said.

Which was clearly not the reaction Ben expected, since he blinked at Shane and frowned. Still, instead of explaining himself or anything else, Ben simply stood from the table and walked stiffly into the kitchen.

Leaving Shane and her alone in the dining room. Not alone *alone,* because she could hear the sounds of Deb and Molly and Ben in the kitchen.

"Let's take a little walk."

She nodded, knowing what he really meant. *Let's go spy.* If it hadn't been for this morning and seeing Deb cry, and Cora's overlong conversation with the lawyer about what they could do to further protect themselves from Stephen, she might have felt a little bad about the idea of spying on Ben.

But she was churned up, and the idea of stepping in and protecting people felt like something she *could* do. If she could stop Deb from facing even a modicum of the unhappiness Cora'd had with Stephen, she would gladly do some spying.

Shane led Cora out the front door and into the early twilight. The warm summer air smelled like sunlight and something flowery, likely Deb's garden. Then there was always that faint hint of manure on the breeze. It was oddly appealing as a mixture.

He led them across the yard, but instead of a right toward the stables, he took a left. A part of the ranch she hadn't seen much of. But his steps were slow and easy, and the silence was comfortable.

Still, Cora wasn't one to revel in a lot of silence. "Micah was good?"

"Micah was great," Shane said without hesitation. "He's got a good understanding that if he does the chores well, he earns more time with the horses, and he takes that seriously. A few more weeks, we'll be able to give him some unsupervised chores. If he wants. If *you* want."

Cora took a deep breath. She'd been accepting help Micah's whole life, because she hadn't been in the kind of place to help her child. Now she could, and there was a selfish part of her that wanted to do it alone for once.

No help from Lilly, no help from a handsome man she one hundred percent had the biggest crush on.

But that *was* selfish, and she wanted Micah to have everything. She'd never be able to give him a horse, but she could give him this access. She could take Shane up on his generous offer, especially since it *was* generous. And Micah would be working to earn something.

"As long as it's what Micah wants, it's what I want."

Shane nodded. He pointed ahead to a large building Cora hadn't seen before since it was tucked away behind the barns and stables and a cluster of trees that must have been planted a while ago. "This is the bunkhouse. We have a variety of men who work for us. Some seasonal. Ben's got his own cabin over there. Typically it'd be the foreman's, but . . ." Shane shook his head. "It's things like this. I don't want to hate Ben, but he conned Mom into letting him live there when he should be in the bunk like the other men."

"Do you have a key? I don't know if breaking and entering is our best bet for snooping."

Shane took a deep breath, staring hard at the cabin they were slowly walking toward. "Maybe we shouldn't do this," he muttered.

"It was your idea."

"I know but . . . between some things Molly said to me, and some things I said to Micah, I'm starting to think I've gone about this all wrong."

She was going to give him a bit of a good-natured hard time about being a goody-two-shoes, afraid of doing something wrong in order to do something right, but he'd *said some things* to her son.

What did that mean?

Cora stopped in her tracks, and Shane stopped with her, looking at her questioningly. Cora took a deep breath so she didn't overreact.

"What did you say to Micah?" she asked, trying to sound curious instead of demanding. Interested instead of panicked.

"Boone was telling him stupid bullshit stories about the rodeo, about fighting, and I told him to ignore it. That trouble wasn't worth it."

"Oh." Stupid of her to be worried. To be panicked. Of course Shane had a good head on his shoulders. He didn't even want to spy on a man he hated and thought was going to hurt his mother.

"Do you think he was being bullied at that camp? Or maybe at school?"

Cora's entire body went cold. A dead, awful cold she'd experienced so many times in her life. Usually at the hands of Stephen, when he used that subtly furious tone of voice, and she'd known . . . she'd always known . . .

"What do you mean?" she whispered.

"I told him violence wasn't a good answer most of the time, and he asked why not. What else could you do. So, I just wondered if maybe someone was bothering him."

Cora blinked back the unexpected tears. Yes, her son was being bothered, bullied, and all by his own father.

"I'm sorry. I'm upsetting you." Shane stepped closer, reached out, and touched her shoulder. "I shouldn't have mentioned it."

She looked up at him, at his warm, concerned brown eyes. Regret and just goodness shining in them. "How did you answer?" she managed to ask.

"I told him what my father told me when I was a kid. Actions have consequences, positive and negative, and it's always best to work toward a positive consequence, because violence leaves a mark no matter what."

She could only stare for a few minutes. At this beautiful man with the perfect words. *Violence leaves a mark no matter what.* Yes. It did. Stephen had only physically hurt Micah once, but she knew the violence Stephen had used on *her* had left a mark on Micah. One she couldn't fix or erase.

She swallowed at the lump in her throat.

"I didn't mean to upset you. I'm sorry."

"I know." Shane would never hurt people just to exert control. Shane would never manipulate or undermine. He wouldn't tell her she was weak or stupid or that it was all her fault.

Violence leaves a mark no matter what.

She was tired of the mark it had left on her. She'd never get rid of it, but for a moment, just a few moments, she wanted to forget. So, she moved up onto her toes and pressed her mouth to the corner of his.

Perhaps another man would have been strong enough to allow that kiss to be a friendly brush of lips. But there was so much more than friendly pulsing through him when Cora's lips touched the corner of his.

Because his mind blanked, there was nothing to do but slide the hand on her shoulder over and onto her back, pulling her closer to him, adjusting their mouths so they really touched, so his head bent to meet hers, so he could kiss her like he'd been trying not to dream of doing for days.

She melted into him, easy and pliant, but the oddest thing was he felt a little like he'd melted too. Into her, into the kiss. He wanted his hands in her hair, his skin on her bare skin, and yet some part of him was content with this kiss in fresh air as the sun fell around them.

Her arms slid around his neck, drawing him closer, as if his arms banded around her weren't bringing them close enough. He forgot about pretty much everything.

All the concerns and confusions and worries of the day melted into pleasure, into Cora.

He was content to learn the taste of her—sweet and bright—with a light brush of tongues. He wanted to exist here where the softness of her skin, of her body pressed to his uncompromising one felt like a new kind of heaven he'd never experienced.

There was a well of want inside of him that no amount of pressure or closeness could seem to fill. It only seemed to go deeper and deeper, like the kiss itself.

Where does wanting ever lead?

It was a thought he wished he could ignore, but there was too much going on right now to remind him of all he'd lost over a simple thing like *want.* So, he eased away, though his body protested, though Cora's body moved with him, leaning into him, and he was a man who would always hold a leaning woman up.

Especially her.

Her eyes fluttered open. Her lips curved into a smile he wanted to kiss until smiling was the only thing either of them ever did.

But that was a fantasy, and this was real life.

She sighed dreamily though, eventually putting her weight on her own feet instead of against his body. "Well, I knew it would be good. I'm not sure I knew it would be that good." Her hands slid off his shoulders, and he had to all but force himself to release her.

He realized his hat had fallen off somewhere in the interaction. Using that as an excuse to collect himself, he bent down and picked it up, hitting it over his knee to knock off the dirt. *That good.* Yeah, that was for sure.

But he had to control *that* good. Keep it at a manageable level. Not let want overtake reason. That being said, it didn't mean it couldn't happen again. . . .

And again . . .

He cleared his throat. "Not that I'm complaining, because, believe me, I am very much not. Why did this conversation prompt a kiss?"

She stared up at him, that hint of tears and vulnerability he'd seen there before the kiss hidden under something else, something he couldn't put into words. All of it was still there, but she'd rearranged it so something like strength was the predominant mask she showed.

He had a sinking suspicion it *was* a mask.

"Well, I guess it's wrapped up in the fact that I haven't had a lot of good, nice men in my life." She let out a huff of breath. "I didn't think they existed until about a year ago. My sister started working for Mile High Adventures last spring, and the guys there are all really good, solid guys. They've always been so kind and encouraging with Micah. I know he looks up to them, and that's been so important. But they're not like you. You're really good at making people feel like . . . I don't know how to explain it. I just know those were the words Micah needed to hear. And he would've never listened to them from me."

"Cora . . ."

"The point of all that is I'm really glad you could give him that, and so that's why I kissed you. You helped when you didn't have to. I know you did it because you thought it was the right thing to do, because you, your whole family, they just step in and help. And care. Plus, you're really hot, especially in a cowboy hat."

Shane managed to laugh. "I'm glad I could say something he needed to hear."

"And I *know* you mean that." Cora looked behind him, at the pastel sunset streaking across the sky, clearly thinking something through. "But I shouldn't have kissed you. I'm sorry."

"Cora, like I said, I wasn't complaining. There's nothing about the kiss you need to apologize for."

"Except that's the kind of kiss that leads to other kisses, and I'm not sure . . ." She chewed on her bottom lip as she moved her gaze back to him. "I'm not sure I'm in a place to do this. Because you are nice and good, and I'm still kind of figuring out how to be all that."

"So it's that resolution thing again?"

"Kind of. And it's about me, not you. You're great."

"Someone hurt you," he said gently.

Her expression shuttered and blanked. Shane wondered if part of this wasn't just the fact that she didn't want to go into that. The hurt. The scars whatever happened must have left. He knew he had his own that he wouldn't want to touch with a ten-foot pole, especially with someone he liked.

"What are we going to do about Ben?" she said resolutely.

He could've refused the change of subject, but he wasn't about to push her any more than he would've pushed her little boy this morning when they'd talked about violence. "Molly suggested I ask Mom to do a prenup. That way, even if Ben is trouble, the ranch will be safe. If things went sour, Mom would still have the ranch. Her pride."

"How could her pride be intact if she got treated that way by someone she loves?" Cora asked, all that *emotion* swirling in her eyes.

"That's where I'm stuck. I'm starting to wonder if it would even make a difference. If I found evidence he was a murderer, would it change a damn thing? For whatever reason, she loves him. I don't know how to fight that. It's all been running around in my head. Talking with Micah about violence and the marks it leaves. Talking with Molly about the way our family is. Nothing is working, so we have to change our approach."

"How?"

"Honesty." He'd been on the fence before, but kissing Cora, talking to Cora about how *good* he was, and just the honest way she'd talked about not being ready . . . It was the answer. It had to be. "I knew Ben was a liar almost from the start, and I never gave him a chance to be anything but that. Maybe instead of fighting him and Mom, I need to talk to them. Openly. About my concerns and what we all can do to move forward together. As a team."

Something moved over her expression. One of those unreadable feelings he wished he could label and fix for her.

"I wasn't going to tell you this, because I thought it would just make you angry, but maybe . . . maybe you're absolutely right. This morning your mom was upset. Crying. She'd had a fight with Ben and—"

"What did the thieving, lying, scheming piece of shit do to her?" Shane demanded, white-hot fury sparking through him.

Cora smiled indulgently. She reached out and placed her hand against his chest. They both looked at it for a second. He felt her move as if she were going to take it away, but when he gently placed his own hand over it, she stilled and smiled up at him.

"I like that you're a good, protective son. It speaks to so much about you and your mother. They fought over Boone. She didn't give details, and I didn't press. Maybe I should have. Maybe I should've asked her what was wrong and said things related to her. Maybe instead of holding back because I was afraid of opening up to my crap, I should have connected to it and . . ."

He rubbed his hand over hers, and she stepped a little closer, the smell of her perfume infiltrating the smell of summer and ranch.

"I don't know what happened between them. It could've been a simple argument. God knows I've seen my sister and her husband argue a million times over. But they love each other wholeheartedly, and they'd do anything for each other. It could be just a fight that people have because people have fights, but if I hadn't been too afraid of giving something of myself, maybe I would've found out."

"Tylers aren't known for their heart-to-hearts. As wonderful as my mom is, as connected as we all are, there's a separateness. Molly said something I'd forgotten. When I was a kid, Dad always used to tell us Tylers don't cry. Scraped a knee, mad about some prank Boone played, Tylers don't cry."

"That's silly. Kids have to cry," Cora said, frowning.

"I don't think he could stand to see us hurt. I also think that saying might've dug into each of us a little warped. So, I think you're absolutely right. I think we need to forget fear, and embrace a little connection."

Her mouth slowly curved. "You look like you're going to be sick."

"To be honest, I look that way because I *feel* that way."

She moved her fingers under his hand, against his chest, watching their fingers touching with consideration. A consideration that hit him a bit like a punch to the gut. That *need* and *want* he couldn't allow to take over.

"How about this. Instead of spying on Ben tonight, we think about getting to the bottom of this in a new way. You can talk to Ben one-on-one. Man-to-man. Lay out your concerns and your feelings, and we can go from there. I think that's a good idea."

"Even if it sounds horrendous in every way."

She chuckled. "How about this. To ease the horrendous, and sort of pre-reward you for your emotional bravery—"

He snorted, but she continued.

"*I'll* be honest with *you*. I have a lot of insecurities, and the fact that you're a good guy is intimidating to me." She swallowed, but her eyes never left his. "I really like you a lot, and I'm attracted to you. But I don't know how to build a relationship. Especially when I've got a kid and this job I'm trying to succeed at. I'm so afraid of failing that I don't want to try."

He took a step forward, but she held him off by withdrawing her hand from his. He stopped too, because he knew she was doing the thing they were all scared to do. Opening up, explaining, allowing herself to be scrutinized and judged. "But even though I'm nervous and unsure, I want you to take me out to dinner some time. On a date."

"You name the date. I'll figure out a place."

"But it's a bargain. If we go out, you have to do the Ben heart-to-heart."

Shane shuddered. "Please stop calling it that."

She laughed, so he allowed himself to as well.

"On one other condition," he said, pressing his lips together so he wouldn't grin down at her.

"What's that?" she asked with a little smirk.

He didn't answer her. Instead he leaned down and kissed her again. He soaked up the way she melted into him in the hopes it would blot out all the fear inside of him.

Chapter Twelve

When Cora dropped Micah off at the Tylers the next morning, there was a new kind of nervousness fluttering around in her stomach. Though she trusted the Tylers with Micah, most especially Shane, it wasn't easy to leave her baby somewhere while she went off and worked. She wasn't sure that wormy little feeling of guilt would ever go away.

Watching Micah bound over to the Tyler front porch where Shane, Gavin, and Boone had already congregated was a balm to all that worry though. Micah was excited, and every day he tried to hide that excitement a little less. He'd loved basketball camp, and being on teams and whatnot, but this was something else. It lit him up in a way she'd never seen, and she wanted that light to grow and grow and grow.

Before she could back out and head over to Mile High to take care of some paperwork, Shane held up a hand and started walking over. She didn't mind waiting, not when she got to watch him walk. Cowboy hat down, shoulders back, a self-possessed swagger that never fell toward arrogant. Just a man who knew what he was doing and was going to work damn hard to do it.

She allowed herself a dreamy sigh before she rolled down the window at his approach.

"Morning," he offered, tipping his hat in what must be some kind of ingrained gesture. She liked it, liked pretending he was some romantic, Wild West cowboy about to sweep her off her feet.

Get a grip, girl.

"Morning," she returned.

"So." He leaned his forearm against the top of her car.

"So," she replied, grinning stupidly at him.

"I don't suppose you've figured out a night you've got free."

"I don't suppose you've had a heart-to-heart with your potential future stepfather."

He winced, then shuddered dramatically. "All of those words need to stop being uttered."

She laughed. Oh, she liked him an awful lot too much, and it was hard to care on pretty mountain mornings when he was this nice to look at.

"I'm working on it." Though, she had to admit, part of taking her time making arrangements for Micah was seeing if Shane would push it. If he'd ask again, or simply let it all fall apart. Maybe a little warped, but she needed a few days to be sure of this. "Finding someone to watch Micah without him getting angry about being too old for babysitters is a bit of a balancing act."

"He could come," Shane offered easily. So easily, as if there wasn't a question or an ulterior motive.

Cora glanced at where Micah stood looking enraptured at Boone. None of the guys she'd been with, including Micah's own father, had much cared for Micah's presence. But Shane seemed so sincere. Her son could just *come* on their date.

But it opened a whole well of . . . things. Feelings and

complications that already existed because Micah was wrapped up in the Tylers now.

"I'll make sure Boone's not a bad influence, if that's what's worrying you."

Cora wasn't sure what to make of the way Shane talked about his youngest brother, but she didn't have the same impression of Boone that Shane seemed to. "I'm not worried about your brother's being a bad influence. I wouldn't leave Micah here if I thought anyone would be one."

"Boone's a good kid, but he's been out with the rodeo for too many years. He cusses and tells inappropriate stories and takes too many risks."

Cora had to stifle a laugh. "First, you might want to accept that your brother is no longer a 'kid.' I don't think he's that much younger than I am."

Shane grunted with a frown. "I've told him to watch his language, but he doesn't listen to me much. I'll work on it though. And if he can't knock it off, I won't let him be around Micah."

Cora felt something like awe wash through her. She'd raised her child with an abusive man in their lives for too long. She worried about everything when it came to Micah—but not language or inappropriate stories. It was ludicrous and yet somehow adorable Shane would consider all that something to keep her son away from. "Micah will survive all that."

Could Micah survive her ruining all this if she dated Shane and it didn't work out? She chewed on her bottom lip and looked from Micah to Shane. "I already know the answer, but I have to ask, for my own peace of mind. If we do this date thing, try to start something, and it went ugly . . . I need to know Micah could still have this."

"Not a question. He's always welcome here, and there

are plenty of people he could work with if he ever didn't want to work with me. Molly's doing most of the horse teaching. Gavin could handle all the chore instruction. Micah's got a place here no matter how he or you feel about me."

"What about how you'd feel about me?"

Shane moved so that his elbows rested on the rolled down window of her car door, his body leaning down and in so that his face was close to hers. She could smell what she assumed was his soap or deodorant, clean and piney. His eyes were a dark brown, serious and completely focused on her.

"Nothing that could happen would change the fact that Micah is welcome here. That's a promise, and I don't go back on a promise."

She wanted to sigh dreamily again, and all those anticipation nerves she was supposed to be avoiding, to be a better mother, a better person, they were back tenfold, and she wanted to roll around in them.

Shane was a *good* man. Not her usual mistake. Surely it wouldn't be so bad to anticipate a little. *Indulge a lot.* A man who didn't go back on his promises . . . Well, that wasn't something she'd predicted. She should be flexible. She couldn't eradicate *all* fun from her life just because she was a mother and a career woman.

"Our first date should probably be just us," she said, trying to keep how much she *wanted* out of her voice.

His mouth curved. "I can deal with that." Then that curved mouth leaned closer. "They're in the stables," he murmured.

She darted a gaze to the stables, then to the front porch where they'd been, finding both empty. Anticipation was like a drug she couldn't get enough of—until it all crashed to a halt. "Your mother isn't though."

Shane whipped his head back toward the house so

quick it was a miracle he didn't hit it on some part of the car door.

Deb *and* Molly were on the front porch, clearly watching Cora and Shane with avid interest. Cora didn't know exactly how all this worked. Families and ties and good people.

Shane cleared his throat. "Well, it's not as though I'm going to pretend I'm not going out with you." Then he leaned in through the window and brushed his lips across her cheek. It was quick and more friendly than romantic, and yet it was a clear . . . *thing*.

Deb and Molly would know, and when Cora screwed this all up—which she inevitably would, because when did she not?—everyone would know she was to blame, because it could never possibly be Shane the Great.

She pushed away that thought ruthlessly. Those kinds of insecurities had no place here. She wanted to *build* something, not be beholden to something. Grow something like Lilly and Brandon and Will and Tori had. Not codependent, insecure mind games. Something real. Cora had to believe she was capable of that, and, if she *was*, Shane was by far the best chance she'd ever take.

"I'll let you know when I pick up Micah what evening I'm free. Maybe we can go square dancing."

He laughed. "I'll suffer through a lot of things for a woman I like, but it won't be dancing. I can promise you that."

"Hmm," was all Cora said in return before tapping her steering wheel. "Well, I gotta go. See you soon."

"He's in good hands," Shane assured, patting the door as he stepped away from it.

"I know," she responded, and she did know that. It was a gift in and of itself, and some piece of the many pieces that made up what she liked about him. She gave a little wave, then turned around in the lane and headed off the Tyler ranch and toward Mile High Adventures.

When she arrived at the pretty wood cabin that made up the main offices, she was about ten minutes later than she'd planned. Punctuality was one of those things Lilly was always getting on her over, and it was one of the things she had a hard time managing.

On a little sigh, Cora got out of the car and headed for the office. Before she even opened the door she heard the wailing of two babies. She could barely remember Micah's being a baby, those sounds, and all the work that went with quelling them. She'd just been a tired heap of nerves, hoping she could find some way to make Stephen love her and take care of them.

She much preferred the present. She opened the office door to find the kind of chaos that had her pressing her lips together. Hayley and Sam were helplessly handing a screaming Aiden back and forth, while Tori awkwardly held Grace, and Skeet desperately jangled a rattle at her.

"Well. This is quite the picture."

They all glanced at Cora, and, as if they were all of one mind, their expressions went from embarrassed to relieved in a New York minute.

"You know what to do with these things," Tori said, moving toward her quickly. "Take it."

"Tori," Cora admonished, dropping her bag and taking the screaming bundle into her arms. Cora snuggled Grace close. "What's a matter, baby? And who on earth left you with these people?"

"Lilly had some appointment, and Brandon and Will were supposed to be back before she had to go, but there was more damage to the trail than they thought, and they're still out there clearing debris," Sam explained, grimacing at the wailing baby in his arms.

"Then that madwoman left them with us," Tori added.

"Grace is just hungry. Did Lilly leave bottles?"

"Yeah, but she said not till ten."

Cora waved that away with one arm. "I'd wager Aiden needs a diaper change. Which one of you is going to take that?"

"I'll get the bottles," Hayley blurted, already rushing for the kitchenette.

Cora rolled her eyes. "Can't believe you all are scared of a diaper change." She marched over to Skeet and handed Grace off to him. He held the baby with an ease that surprised Cora, but he still looked extremely uncomfortable with her continued screaming.

Cora focused on the other crying baby and marched over to where Lilly had a little box of baby supplies. She set out everything she'd need before gesturing for Sam to give her Aiden.

With more care than necessary for thin glass let alone a child, Sam transferred the baby. It was sweet, all in all, and Cora couldn't help but wonder if Lilly had orchestrated this whole thing so everyone would stop being so darn afraid of their new additions.

Cora expertly changed the diaper and talked Hayley through preparing the bottle. She made Sam take Aiden back, and, while he was still fussy, Cora instructed Sam to walk around the room while holding Aiden, and that calmed the baby down considerably.

Then, she ordered Skeet to hand Grace over to Tori, who sat on the couch. Cora talked her through feeding Grace her bottle.

"Thank God," Hayley breathed, once both babies were happy. "I don't know what we would have done without you."

"Survived," Cora said. "Just as Lilly intended." But it felt good to be needed, to be useful. To be reminded there *were* things she was good at. Things were on the right track. Things were good.

And *she* could make them even better.

"How come you can't teach them to shit in a box like a cat?" Micah asked, wiping his sweaty forehead with the back of his arm. Kid needed a haircut before the summer heat kicked in and—

And that was none of Shane's business. It was getting a little hard to draw that line, because it felt like falling back into old habits. Having a younger kid around to worry about. No different than his siblings, because the kid had a mother who could take care of him fine and well just like his siblings had, but Shane felt a certain amount of responsibility, of stake in his good care.

Micah wiped his forehead again. They currently weren't shoveling shit, so Shane didn't know where the question had come from. Instead, they were fixing a warped part of the fence, a good primer in ranch maintenance.

The ranch didn't particularly need another ranch hand, but having a kid around to do the grunt work was still a help for all of them. If Micah got good at it, learned some responsibility and horsemanship, he could work his way up to ranch hand in his teens.

That was probably thinking too far in advance, all in all, but Shane liked plans. He liked having a say in the future of this ranch.

What he did not like was the fact that he was going to have to take today as an opportunity to talk to Ben. Mom had driven down to Denver to go shopping with Lindsay and she wouldn't be back until tomorrow. It assured Shane the kind of privacy he preferred.

Shane heaved a sigh, glanced at his watch. "Well, it's

three. Why don't you run over to the stables and see if Molly's ready for your lesson while I finish up here."

Micah hesitated, looking at the stables, then at Shane. "But this is the last post, right?"

Shane didn't smile, though he wanted to. He nodded earnestly.

"Then I should finish, right?" Micah's eyebrows drew together. "Or should I be on time for my lesson?"

Micah was a different kind of kid than Shane was used to. His younger siblings had been wild, argumentative, and bullheaded. The varying sullenness he remembered from Boone and Lindsay's childhood days, but there was a need to earn approval and a need to do the *right* thing in the boy that didn't remind Shane of any of his siblings.

It reminded him of, well, himself, and it created a new wave of affinity for the boy. Because it was hard to be this age without a dad, and it was hard to want to protect the people you loved and do the right thing and not know how to do either.

"When the boss gives you the go-ahead to leave a project unfinished because you've got something else to do, you say thanks and accept it. If you didn't have anything else to do, you would stay and finish the job. But I'm going to need you to learn how to be a good horseman if you're going to want to earn yourself a spot on my crew."

Micah blinked. "Your crew," he said, almost to himself. "Like a ranch hand?"

"We can hire you officially when you're fourteen. How old are you now?"

"T-twelve. I'll be thirteen soon though. November."

Again Shane fought the impulse to smile indulgently at the kid. Micah didn't need indulgence. He needed to be treated like a young adult. Someone Shane would trust to earn some adult responsibilities. "So, you focus on getting good with the horses, do your chores well—which will earn you a few bucks under the table—and the more we trust you, the harder you work, the better shot you've got at a real job here when it's legal."

Micah stared at him, wide-eyed and wondering.

"Well, go on now. Don't keep Molly waiting. If she's not in the stables, come on back, and we'll go find her together."

"O-okay." Micah took a few halting steps toward the stables, then looked back at Shane for one long, considering moment. Then he was off, racing across the field between him and the stables.

Shane watched him go, remembering that feeling of freedom and excitement. That all this was his. Oh, he hadn't felt that kind of exhilaration in about twenty years, but it was still there. Deep under all the responsibility and worry and hard work, that little seed of utter freedom.

This is mine.

But he had to protect what was his. He sighed heavily, glancing over at Ben's cabin. Ben was assigned to the branding crew this morning, but they should be done with their work by now, which meant Ben was likely there.

Alone, with no possibility of interruption from his mother.

Shane was not a man who shirked a responsibility, so it was weird to find himself dragging his feet, finding excuses, taking too damn long to finish up the fence maintenance. Hard work, protecting his family, these were not things he shied away from.

Being open and honest were. Allowing some of that

strength to slip, in order to put plain what it was that worried him. Because he didn't worry. He fixed.

Which wasn't working for this particular situation. So, Shane cleaned up his tools and placed them in the back of the work vehicle. He reminded himself this was all a part of protecting his family, and for that, he would do anything.

He drove over to Ben's cabin and didn't let himself stop to think or even plan what he was going to say, though that might have been prudent. But he needed to man up and do this.

Shane walked across the yard and rapped on Ben's door. When Ben opened it, Shane noticed with an odd bolt of concern that the man looked a little haggard. But he scowled at Shane, and it was easy for the concern to melt away.

"What do you want?" Ben grumbled, standing in the opening, clearly blocking it.

"May I come in?"

Ben narrowed his eyes, not bothering to hide how suspicious he was. "Let me guess, you're going to threaten me."

"No, Ben."

"Pay me to disappear?"

Shane blinked. That hadn't even occurred to him. He noted, with a sinking heart, that the man seemed a little eager.

"Would that work?"

Ben's expression hardened. "No, it damn well wouldn't, asshole."

Shane felt some mix of despair and relief. Hell, if it were that easy, this would all be over. But it would mean Mom was just as big of a fool as he'd been years ago, and he didn't want that for her.

"We should talk," Shane said forcefully. "Talk, not bicker like high school girls."

Ben snorted, and Shane thought maybe that was something akin to a laugh. After a few seconds of study, Ben moved toward the side and let Shane step in.

The cabin was ruthlessly neat, which wasn't what Shane had expected. There didn't seem to be any personal belongings, which struck Shane as off. Wouldn't a man have his own things around? His boots by the door or his hat on the rack?

Or maybe Shane was just looking for things to be off and wrong. Maybe he needed to stop looking for everything bad, and start with a blank slate.

"You got a piece to say, you go ahead."

Shane nodded. He noted Ben did not offer him a seat, so they stood like squared off brawlers on opposite sides of the room.

"I don't like that you lied about your references, and I've let that color a lot of our interactions. Because to me trust is paramount, and by marrying my mother you are asking to be part of our family. I need to be able to trust you."

"Funny, I see it as just marrying your mother, and it's got nothing to do with you."

"She's my mother."

"And a grown woman," Ben replied with a negligent shrug.

"Maybe if you could tell me why you lied," Shane offered, trying to maintain his calm, his control.

"Nope."

Shane clenched his jaw so he wouldn't retort irritably. He breathed in through his nose, out through his mouth. "I'm trying to bridge a gap here."

Ben folded his arms over his chest. "You think I'm stupid, boy?"

"I'm still your boss. Don't 'boy' me." Which was not the right tact to take, but he'd told Cora he'd be open and honest. That didn't mean he'd ignore disrespect. Or general assholishness.

"You want to pretend to hold hands and be friends now because your mom ain't budging. Maybe if you show her you've cozied up all nice, you think you can whisper a few key things into her ear and change her mind. No. I'm not falling for it. I won't lose her because of you, or any of you."

"Maybe if you gave us an inch, you wouldn't have to be worried about losing her because of us."

"If I tell you why I lied, would it change anything? Or would you still see me as a younger man looking for a cushy ride? Like I said, I ain't stupid, and I'm not falling for this. I might've once, but I've lived and learned."

"Yeah, me too," Shane muttered. Lived and learned not to trust someone to ever have his best interest at heart. Learned to be implacable because giving something to someone else he hadn't been sure about had always led him to loss and hurt. So he always did the right thing, the good thing, even when it was an uphill battle or a sure failure.

Ben gestured at the door. "You can go now."

Shane could. He could go and write Ben off, and yet that wasn't what he'd come here to do. Much as he hated it with every fiber of his being, he'd come to the conclusion that talking it out was the right thing to do.

"I don't trust you, Ben. I don't much like you. But I love my mother, and I want her to be happy. No, I can't sway her opinion. Not sure I ever could. But I also can't stand the idea of her getting hurt. The possibility of it physically pains me."

Ben's expression didn't change, but he also didn't move to kick Shane out, so Shane kept talking. Honest as he could.

"I also worry about this ranch, and what my mother's marrying anyone would do to it. My great-great-great-grandfather built this place and turned the very earth we're standing on, and it's a part of my soul. The fact of the matter is you haven't given me any damn reason to feel comfortable with your sniffing around either. So, all I'm asking for is a little honesty. A piece of yourself so I can try to accept that I've got nothing to worry about."

For a second or two, Shane held his breath. Something had changed in Ben's expression, almost a softening. A sadness instead of an anger, and Shane was both hopeful and terrified the man would offer something worthwhile. That a little truth and honesty were really the answer.

"Ain't nobody ever done anything good with a piece of me," Ben said, though his voice had a hint of gravel to it that hadn't been there earlier. He gestured toward the door again, and Shane sighed.

There was no getting through to this man, so he turned and walked away. He'd been honest, asked for honesty in return, and gotten jack. There was no reasoning with someone who didn't have a shred of decency in him.

Shane jerked the door open, but before he could step outside, Ben's quiet, strained voice stopped him.

"I don't want your damn ranch. All I want is Deb."

When Shane looked over his shoulder at Ben, the man was scowling.

Ben pointed outside again. "So, why don't you fuck off and leave me alone, huh?"

But something awful had happened in that moment. Shane had seen a flash of insecurity, maybe even fear in Ben's eyes, as if the admission had cost him something. As if he was a man like any other, not good or some evil boogey man, but a complicated middle ground.

Which was the absolute last thing Shane wanted him to be.

Chapter Thirteen

Cora wanted nothing more than a massage and to sleep, both at the same time. She didn't think phone calls and babysitting should make her quite so exhausted, but she had put a lot of steps in keeping Aiden happy by walking him around the office. Then Lilly had insisted they take a hike out to a place they could possibly get a permit to hold weddings at.

Cora wanted a giant steak and a glass of wine before that sleep and massage, but pizza would have to do. She couldn't possibly face cooking or the near hour it would take to drive to a restaurant that served steak, *or* listen to Micah bitch about either.

Luckily, since they'd eaten with the Tylers last night, it meant they hadn't had pizza last night, which meant they could have it tonight. Parenting at its finest.

As she drove through the archway to the Tyler ranch, some of her exhaustion eased. It didn't go away or anything, but it softened. The set of her shoulders relaxed of its own volition.

She didn't have any right to feel all those things when this wasn't hers, but the ranch was something like magic. The people in it magical as well.

That little insidious voice always telling her things wouldn't work out whispered that this wasn't hers and never could be. She was kidding herself setting up dates and talking about honesty and heart-to-hearts when she knew without a shadow of a doubt she'd never be able to tell Shane about her past.

Shane was a protector. A solver. Not only would he look down at her for what she'd allowed, but he would treat her differently. Probably like she was something fragile or breakable, or worse, the stupid, weak girl she'd been when she'd been desperate for Stephen's love.

It was unfathomable to think of admitting anything about that time to Shane.

When she drove her car around the bend, and the big, pretty house came into view, Shane and Gavin were standing in the yard with her son. Playing catch. Such a stereotypical father-son activity, it about ripped her in two.

The Tyler ranch couldn't be for her, but couldn't it be for *him*? Her past would be a secret worth keeping if Micah was getting the kind of male companionship she'd always wanted for him.

Shane turned and waved at the sound of her car. The giant grin splitting Micah's face didn't even dim at the sight of her. Things were improving like they had been before Stephen had interfered and ruined everything.

Cold fear washed over her. Could Stephen find this place? Could he ruin this for Micah too? For her? She was taking precautions with her lawyer, but the basketball camp debacle proved laws and all the precautions she took on her own couldn't keep them safe from Stephen.

The only thing that kept her from running was the fact that Stephen wasn't all that interested in them. *He* never showed up, which would have broken the restraining order. He only ever *sent* things. A reminder he had more than they ever would.

She wouldn't live in fear, though it was a constant, gnawing worry that someday he might *act*, not just *scare*.

Cora brought the car to a stop with so many emotions pummeling her she was a little afraid if someone even smiled at her, she would cry.

She had to be stronger than that for her baby. She'd promised herself she would be. She couldn't go back on that promise.

Cora forced herself out of the car with a bright smile on her face. "I thought you hated baseball," she offered to Micah as cheerfully as she could manage.

Micah shrugged. "Shane said I was wrong and he'd prove it to me."

There was so much joy in that simple statement. Cora was reminded she had to believe in good things. That they were possible for Micah and her. If she believed, it could be true. It could work.

"Baseball is awfully slow and boring if you ask me." Cora smiled sweetly at Shane and Gavin, who both put their hands to their hearts simultaneously as if they'd been mortally wounded by the same bullet.

"Only someone who doesn't understand could possibly call it slow and boring."

Cora shrugged her shoulders. "If you say so."

"That does it. We're going to have to take you both to a Rockies game and prove it to you."

"No way. Seriously?" Micah asked, wide-eyed.

"We can get back and forth from Denver in a day if we catch a day game. And if your mom agrees."

Cora didn't relish the prospect of heading back to Denver. She hadn't been back since they'd escaped

Stephen, and there were no happy memories to make her want to return.

But, the smile on Micah's face was everything she needed to know. He was excited. He wanted to do it, and it was the kind of normal activity she wanted to be able to offer her child. "I think it'd be great if we can coordinate it."

"Great. We'll work something out. We Tylers are headed up to The Slice is Right for dinner. Do you guys want to come?"

Micah looked expectantly at her, and Cora hesitated. This was getting to be almost too much. Too involved. If something happened . . . She pushed any doomsday thinking out of her head. Bad things could always happen, but living life trying to avoid them wasn't living.

"That'd be great. I was planning on picking up a pizza for dinner anyway." It dawned on her then that Deb wasn't here. "Are you just going out to eat because your mother isn't here to cook for you?"

"Naturally," Shane replied.

"Don't you think it's a little bit ridiculous two grown men can't cook dinner for themselves?"

"As if my mother ever let us near a kitchen. It's not our fault she raised us a little useless," Gavin offered.

"It's not like *you* can cook, Mom," Micah piped in.

She glared down at him. "Which is why I know how important it is that you learn how to."

Micah rolled his eyes, but he quickly turned to Shane. "Is Boone going?"

Shane and Gavin both tensed, but Shane did the best job of smoothing it out and replying to Micah blandly.

"Haven't seen him around today. If it's okay with your mom, you can go find him and invite him."

Micah looked up at her so hopefully she couldn't

have said no if she wanted to. "Just in the stables and the house. Otherwise you need to stay within eyesight."

Micah bounded off toward the stables without a second look, and Cora tried not to worry. It was good for him to be exploring things on his own, learning things on his own, and, if her heart was being ripped out of her chest while she let him wander around without supervision, well, she'd have to learn how to deal with that.

"He'll be fine," Shane reassured.

Cora smiled thinly. It didn't *help* her worry any, but she appreciated that he'd try.

"I'll go see if Molly wants to come," Gavin said. "Might call Lou and Em."

"Yeah, whoever wants to," Shane agreed, but his eyes never left Cora, and she couldn't pretend she didn't like *that*.

Gavin walked toward the house, and Shane gestured toward the driveway. "Want to take a walk? Like, say, this path that will give us a direct line of sight into the stables, and also keep the house in view."

"You're a smart man, Shane Tyler."

"I know a thing or two about worry." They walked in a comfortable silence for a few moments before Shane broke it.

"So, I talked to Ben."

Her eyebrows went up, though maybe she shouldn't have been surprised. In her experience, most men didn't do much of what they didn't want to—and she knew Shane didn't want to. But Shane wasn't like most men she'd known. "How'd it go?"

"I don't think it went well, but I don't think it went awful. Which, quite frankly, doesn't help me any."

"What did he say?"

Shane shook his head. "A bunch of bluster about not owing me an explanation. He wasn't going to explain himself to anybody for anything, and I was getting pretty damn irritated. Sure it was pointless and all. But as I was leaving, he said he didn't want anything to do with the ranch. All he wanted was my mom."

"Aww."

Shane scowled. "Not aww. No awws."

"Of course it's an aww. He loves your mother, and he was willing to offer some piece of truth after not wanting to, to prove it. I think that's progress."

"I know you're right. A very weird kind of progress." Shane stopped walking and turned to face her. He had such a handsome face, so strong and honest. Even when he smiled with mischief in his eyes. "So. Your end of the bargain?"

God, he was cute. "I don't have a definitive answer, but I have a couple potential things. Will and Tori are going to see if Micah wants to go on this rock climbing thing, which I'm hoping he declines with all of my heart. If he doesn't want that, Sam and Hayley are going to see if he wants to do a camping thing with them, and Brandon and Lilly will come up with something if all else fails."

Shane reached out and brushed his fingers across her temple. Cora's stomach wobbled as he slowly tucked a strand of hair behind her ear, his fingertips touching every inch of skin they could. She couldn't remember if anyone had ever touched her quite like that. Gently and reverently, with his eyes on her like she was the center of the universe.

"I'll work with whatever day."

"Good. And it will be soon," she assured, because,

oh, she wanted more of this, of him. More than a few minutes, even in this beautiful place.

"You know, in the meantime . . ." His mouth inched toward hers, and, because she was feeling a little giddy over all this *want* and anticipation, she blinked fake innocently up at him.

"In the meantime what?"

He grinned. Still touching her face, his mouth inching closer.

"Mom!"

Cora jumped back with a start, though that was probably silly. Micah was jogging out of the stables and probably hadn't seen a thing.

She would have to tell him what was going on, though. Probably before she went on a date with Shane. Because this wasn't just some date for the heck of it. It wasn't a night out to get all the edginess out of her system. It was Shane. And it was somehow scarily important.

Figuring out how to explain it to her twelve-year-old was beyond daunting.

"I guess 'in the meantime' will have to wait," Cora offered with an apologetic smile.

"I can wait. Long as it takes."

And she had no doubt that that's exactly what he meant.

Stuffed with pizza, his cheeks hurting a bit from smiling so damn much at Cora over the table, Shane walked out of The Slice is Right feeling good. Light. He was still worried about Mom, Ben, the wedding, Boone, et cetera, and et cetera. But it wasn't the same as it had been.

Part of it was hanging out with his family. When

nothing felt at peace, just being around them for a meal often reminded him they were surviving. Tylers endured. Always had. Always would.

The conversation with Ben had helped some as well. It wasn't the kind of closure Shane would have preferred, but Cora had been right when she said it sounded like progress.

But part of being able to believe that was Cora herself. He would never have come up with the idea of talking *openly* with someone on his own, and he certainly never would have *done* it without a nudge. Cora had swept into his life and rearranged something he didn't quite understand yet. She'd eased some tenseness that had been inside of him.

He walked with Cora and Micah to their car, listening as Micah chattered on about the level he'd beaten on the old-school arcade game inside. Gavin and Boone were waiting for Shane back at his truck across the lot. Molly had taken a ride back to the ranch with Lou and Em a little earlier.

"Well, guys, thanks for coming along. We enjoyed the extra company."

"It was cool," Micah said, and Shane was noticing more and more he didn't even try to tamper his enthusiasm. "Mom usually makes us get carryout and eat at home."

"Well, I don't carry quarters around, so you wouldn't be able to play all those games anyway. We're lucky Boone came prepared."

Shane caught Micah's glance toward where Boone and Gavin were waiting by the truck. It was strange to know the kid had some hero worship for Boone and mostly tolerated Shane and Gavin. Weird to be in some kind of competition for affection with his baby brother.

Probably unbeknownst to Boone, who wouldn't have cared either way.

Shane tried not to care because he knew the important thing wasn't who the boy looked up to. It was that the boy had someone *to* look up to. And Shane had some work to do on remembering his brother was a grown man who had done a lot of cool and interesting things.

"We'll see you tomorrow?"

"It's actually my day off, and I think Micah should probably take one, too," Cora offered somewhat apologetically.

"I don't want a day off," Micah interrupted.

Cora looked at Shane and Micah, some kind of argument going on within her. Shane had been the one to put her in the middle of it.

"Why don't you call me in the morning. You can decide which one whenever. We'll be around."

"Thanks, Shane." She took a step toward him, sort of half reaching out her hand before she pulled it back and stepped away from him and toward her car. "Thanks for tonight. We had a really great time. I'll call tomorrow."

Shane tipped his hat and waited for Micah and her to get in the car and get buckled. They pulled away before Shane turned and walked back toward his brothers.

When they started making kissing noises and falsetto *woo-oo*s, he flipped them both off.

"Man, I haven't seen you this hung up on somebody since Mattie York," Boone offered.

Luckily Shane was halfway through moving into the driver's seat, so the immediate tension that went through his body was offset by forward motion.

Boone was mostly clueless about everything that had happened with Mattie as far as Shane knew, but Gavin was aware of bits and pieces. Shane had tried to hide it, but some things couldn't be hidden when you were family and in business together.

Shane considered briefly Cora's words about being honest with people. Giving them pieces of yourself to better understand the situation, or maybe better understand theirs. Shane rejected the advice for this particular moment. His brothers didn't need to know about the mistakes he'd made. Not on this. But he could focus on one truth that he wasn't embarrassed of. "Yeah, I'm hung up on Cora. Why wouldn't I be? She's great."

"She's hot," Boone offered from the back, clearly wanting to get a rise out of Shane. "Don't know why you'd mess around with a woman with a kid, though. Haven't you had enough responsibility in your life?"

"I don't mind responsibility. Besides, I like the kid."

"Hard worker," Gavin added. "Good touch with the horses."

"Yeah, he's a funny kid. But you really want to play daddy to a kid who's already half grown?"

"He tried to play daddy to me, and we're only two years apart. I don't see why this would be any different," Gavin offered. He grinned at Shane. "Especially if you're getting sex out of the deal."

"You *are* getting sex out of the deal, aren't you?" Boone asked as Shane pulled out of the pizza place's parking lot.

"What's it to you?"

"Well, we know Gavin isn't since he spends every free moment fluttering over Lou."

"I don't flutter, asshole."

"And I can barely walk these days without wanting to saw my damn leg off. Molly's worked up about the divorce, and if Lindsay is sleeping with anyone I'll personally saw his balls off. So . . ." Boone trailed off, and

Shane had the unfortunate, horrible, scarring realization that their mother was the only member of the Tyler family currently getting regular sex.

Due to the uncomfortable silence that descended, Shane had the feeling they'd all come to that horrifying conclusion.

"Let's go drinking," Boone offered.

Shane snorted, but Gavin elbowed him and gave him a meaningful look. "We could go to Branded Man's. Just for an hour or so. I'll text Moll she's in charge at the ranch tonight. She won't care."

Shane caught on. They hadn't really welcomed Boone home as they might have normally done if Mom hadn't been so pissed at him. The injuries, and the fact he hadn't told them about the injuries had only stoked her anger with him higher.

It'd be a good thing to take him out, just the three of them. In an environment Boone could relax in.

"Yeah, sounds good." Shane made a U-turn and headed back toward the other side of town. Branded Man's was no Main Street tourist stop. It was mostly a glorified shack on the north side of Gracely. It wasn't much frequented by anyone who didn't work land somewhere around Gracely.

The parking lot was little more than a postage stamp of dirt people arranged their trucks in whichever way they could. Blocking someone in would ensure a fist-fight before you were allowed to leave. Shane carefully parked his car.

"I haven't been here in something like ten years."

"I'm surprised you've ever been here," Boone offered, clapping him on the shoulder from behind before he slid out of the truck.

Shane sighed, but he followed his brother toward

the sound of Merle Haggard singing about drinking. Inside, the room was filled with smoke. Since the owner didn't employ anyone and acted as bartender himself, he didn't have to follow any of the state's smoking regulations.

Shane coughed a little as they made their way toward the long, worn bar. Boone laughed at him and ordered three beers from Peach, a name all locals knew better than to make fun of him for, who slapped three bottles onto the bar in rapid succession. He shook his head when Boone pulled out his wallet.

"On the house. Saw that tramplin' you got while back."

Boone held up his beer toward Peach. "Thanks, Peach." He then made a beeline for a table in the corner.

"How come *we* didn't see the trampling?" Gavin asked as they settled themselves around the table.

Boone shrugged. "Pretty sure it was on TV. Nothing stopping you."

"Except knowing where the hell you were, what outfit you were with, and so on."

Again Boone shrugged negligently. Shane kept his mouth shut because he couldn't trust himself to say anything that wasn't a lecture. Because he'd made sure to know all of those things, but it hadn't occurred to him to check on how Boone had done in his event. He hadn't wanted to know, because Boone's success in the rodeo only ever felt like a failure to his mother.

He hadn't protected Boone. Hadn't kept him on the straight and narrow. Shane took a long, deep drink of the beer. A nice double of whiskey might dull the guilt, but he'd be driving them home, which meant this beer was it.

Gavin pushed back from the table. "Be right back. Think I see someone I know."

Shane watched Gavin walk away, but he didn't see whomever Gavin thought he knew, so he turned back to Boone. His little brother who was home and injured. His little brother who probably needed to be reminded he had a place here. No matter what.

"We're glad you're home."

Boone quirked a sardonic eyebrow. "Are you?"

"I am. We've missed you around here, and I know Mom's being a little cool, but it's only because she's been worried sick."

Boone took a long, deep sip of his beer. "Probably not going back to the rodeo," he mumbled, studying the wall hard.

Shane nodded. "Because of the injuries?"

Boone shrugged, which was as good as a yes in Shane's estimation.

"You've got a place with us."

"Maybe I don't want one," Boone said, his ice-blue eyes landing square on Shane and holding.

Shane fought his first impulse, which was to tell Boone exactly what to do. Come home. Stay home. Work the ranch. If they had all five of them running things, they could maybe convince Mom to expand, and it could support all of them. If they were smart, if they were careful.

But he knew that's what Boone expected of him. Boone wanted demands, something to fight against.

Shane was done giving that to him. "I'll support you in whatever you do, Boone. Just let me know how I can."

Boone's frown went from belligerent to confused. "Right now you can support me by getting me another beer." He drained the one he had. "Or ten."

Shane sighed. Boone wanted to get drunk, Shane

would let him. He could keep an eye on him now. He wouldn't always be able to.

"Oh, shit."

Shane swiveled at Boone's muttered oath, then repeated it. Somehow Gavin was in the middle of an argument that was heading straight for a fistfight. With Lou's ex.

Oh, this was so not going to be good.

Chapter Fourteen

When Micah asked for the thirty-seventh time—yes, thirty-seventh, she'd counted—to go to the Tyler ranch, *before* she'd even finished her coffee, Cora decided the whole thing was stupid.

Micah had gotten up voluntarily at five in the morning and was currently *begging* her to go do *grunt* work. Her child wanted to do *chores*, and she was refusing him because it might mean they were spending too much time with the Tylers?

It was idiotic, and this whole thing was Shane's fault for bringing it up last night anyway. *He* could listen to her kid yammer on and on and on all morning. She was going to . . . do something somewhere quiet. So damn quiet.

She texted Shane that they were coming over, then got dressed while Micah stood outside her bathroom door, going on and on about the different horses he'd been allowed to ride, Boone's fantastical rodeo stories, a barn cat that had curled up in his lap one afternoon.

She loved her son more than anything. Beyond sun, moon, earth, universe, and so forth. And it was *beautiful* he was so excited about something to the point of chattering.

God, she wished she could tape his mouth shut. Just for a few minutes so she could apply her makeup in peace.

But Micah did not stop. Even when she handed him a bagel to eat on the way in the hopes she could enjoy the pretty drive out to the Tyler ranch in some semblance of morning stillness. But Micah just kept talking through mouthfuls of bagel, all but bouncing in his seat when they crossed under the archway for Tyler ranch.

Even though Micah's constant chatter had set her on edge, the edginess eased here. Oh, she was so screwed. Too wrapped up in Shane and too wrapped up in this place far too quickly and easily.

But hadn't that been what Lilly had felt when she'd started working at Mile High Adventures? And look how that had turned out.

You are not your sister.

Cora pushed the nasty voice away. No, she wasn't Lilly, and she'd never be quite like Lilly, but that didn't mean she couldn't make some good happen in her life. For Micah. For herself.

She pulled to a stop in front of the house, glanced at her excited, exuberant son. It swelled in her chest, that they could make it to this point, and she wanted to embrace this. Nurture it. Prove to Micah he could be enthusiastic about something without the fear it'd be ruined or taken away. "Before we get out, you have to do one thing."

"What?" Micah asked, craning his neck toward the stables.

"Look me in the eye, and tell me how much you love this."

Micah flopped back in his seat, glaring at her. "I'm not doing that."

"Then I'm driving us back home."

"Mo-o-om," he whined.

"Just look me in the eye, and say, 'Mom, I love ranch stuff. It's the best, and I want to do it every day. And if I ever change my mind about that, I'll tell you, and explain why.'"

Micah rolled his eyes so hard it had to hurt. "Yeah, all that, whatever."

"Look me in the eye, Micah, and say it."

He huffed out a breath and scowled at her. "I love this and if I stop I'll tell you why," he grumbled, dramatically folding his arms across his chest. "Happy?"

"If you are, baby." She reached over and cupped his face with her hand. Again, he rolled his eyes, but he didn't pull away. "I hope you know that's all I want. For you to be happy."

He pulled away from her hand and reached for the door. "You should be happy too, Mom," he mumbled before scurrying out of the car.

Cora inhaled deeply and looked at the house, where the three Tyler men stepped out onto the porch, along with Molly. Maybe she didn't belong here, and maybe she never would, but she'd take the slice of happy it offered while she could.

She stepped out of the car, Micah already to the porch. Yeah, this was good. This was happy.

Molly walked up to her. "Hey, I've got some horse stuff to do, but then I'm heading over to Lou's to help with some flower stuff. Shane said it's your day off. You want to come? Em will be there for a bit. A fun little girl's day . . . with weeding. But also ice cream."

Cora smiled. It was hard to find friends, and ever since Tori had gotten engaged Will was always trying to interrupt their girl-only time. Tori usually told him to shove off, but it was nice to be the one getting invited to do something. And something different. "That sounds great."

"'Kay." Molly glanced at her watch. "Give me about an hour. If you don't want to hang out with the boys, Grandma's inside polishing her swords."

"Right."

Molly laughed. "Don't we seem so normal from the outside? Then you get to know us and . . ." She made an explosion noise before clapping Cora on the back. "See you in a bit."

Cora walked the rest of the way to the porch where Micah was looking up at Boone, rapt with whatever he was saying. When her gaze moved to Shane, she hurried the rest of the way toward him.

"What happened to you?" she demanded, reaching out to gently rub the spot next to his busted lip.

"Uh . . ." His gaze slid to Gavin, as if Gavin would answer, but Cora spoke first.

"Oh my God. What happened to *you*?" Gavin's eye was puffy and bruised, and there was a bruise on his jaw as well.

"You should see the other guy?" Gavin offered hopefully.

Shane's fingers curled gently around her arm. "Why don't you come inside, and I'll explain everything."

She looked over at Boone, but his face didn't boast any new injuries added to the fading ones he'd always had.

"I'll take the kid up to start the shit shovel," Boone offered, nudging Micah toward the stairs.

Shane opened his mouth, but Boone waved him off. "Save your orders, Cap. I'll keep on schedule."

"I'll make sure," Gavin said quietly to Shane after

Boone left the porch. Gavin turned to Cora, his cowboy hat in his hands. "Look, everything was one hundred percent my fault. Shane was just trying to keep me out of trouble."

She nodded at Gavin before he took the stairs down into the yard. Slowly she turned to Shane, something in her chest feeling weird and jittery—and not in a good way. Bruises and cuts and . . . It was a little sickening to be reminded of how well she knew that morning-after feeling.

"What happened?" she managed.

"It's a long story," Shane said sheepishly. He gestured to the porch swing. "Want to sit?"

"Do you have work to do? I don't mean to—"

"Gavin and Boone can handle it for now. You look . . . shaken."

Yes, she felt that. She blew out a breath, feeling silly. It wasn't the same, but Shane had said all those things about violence the other day and . . . She went ahead and sat on the porch swing, her gut twisting in knots.

"Did you two get in a fistfight?"

"I wish," Shane replied. He stretched back and then placed his arm behind her shoulders. Slowly, carefully, as if he expected her to bolt.

She felt uncomfortable, but she didn't want to bolt.

"So, after the pizza place, we went to a bar. Sort of a welcome home to Boone."

"A bar? You don't seem like the bar type."

"I'm not. In fact, I don't think I've been in one in something like a decade. At least, not that kind of bar. But, Gavin saw this guy he has a weird history with and . . ."

"Was he drunk?"

"No." Shane shook his head. "We'd barely sat down

when the other guy threw a punch and . . . Well, I tried to break it up and got a split lip for my trouble."

"You didn't hit back?"

"I tackled back. Busted the guy's jaw. He deserved it though, after what he did."

Cora had to breathe deeply against the hard wave of nausea. *You deserved it. If you did what I asked, I wouldn't have to hit you. If you cared more. If . . .*

"Cora?"

She shook her head, leaning away from Shane's body. "I'm sorry I just . . . I don't like that word. *Deserved.* No one deserves to be hurt like that." She couldn't bear to look at him. He'd see too much. She knew for a fact he'd see far too much.

"I agree with you to an extent, sweetheart. But this guy was partially responsible for Lou's fire, Lou's injuries. He can stand a busted jaw."

Cora whipped her head up. "He set Lou's fire?"

"He had a role in the setting of it." Shane searched Cora's face for something, and she hoped to God he didn't find it. Sometimes she was afraid she had *abuse survivor* written across her forehead. She couldn't stand to be that to him.

He rubbed his thumb back and forth across her jaw. "You okay?"

She studied the cut on his lip, the slight puffiness to it. Found a truth she could give him. "I don't like seeing you hurt."

The unhurt side of his mouth curved. "I don't mind that." His thumb kept brushing her jaw, his other fingers lightly resting on her neck, occasionally pulling a strand of hair between two fingers.

She wanted those fingers everywhere, because it would blot out all this other stuff. She knew it would. She didn't want other stuff, old hurts and fears, ugly reminders. She just wanted him, and that feeling he offered when he touched her. The flutter in her chest, the rapid beating of her heart, the low, tugging ache in the pit of her stomach.

"If you want to change your mind about going out with me—"

"No." The word was out of her before she even had time to think about it, but it was true. "No," she repeated. "It's just complicated."

"How? Explain it to me."

She couldn't. She just . . . couldn't. So, she changed the subject to something she could. "Micah's going on an overnight camping trip on Thursday."

Shane didn't move. Instead, he kept himself still, his thumb resting on her jaw, his fingers barely touching her neck. He wanted to smooth his fingertips everywhere. Slowly, to learn every last soft spot and curve. Every dip and swell.

Still he kept himself motionless. Until he was sure he could speak without sounding strangled. "No curfew, then?" he said carefully.

"None."

He nodded, once, then slowly drew the tip of his thumb down the line of her chin. "Thursday, huh?"

Her mouth curved, some of that haunted uncertainty going out of her dark blue eyes. Her dimple appeared, and he touched it with his index finger.

"So, I'm all yours," she said, her smile deepening.

His whole body tightened at that, head to toe, groin most especially. He was a careful man, always had been. It was somehow in his makeup and reinforced by everything that had happened in his life. He didn't take sex lightly, no matter how often his brothers told him he should.

He took it even less lightly with Cora, who felt like some kind of miracle. The kind he didn't want to break.

"Are you going to kiss me, or do I have to be the initiator again?" She grinned up at him.

"Hey, I'm trying to be gentlemanly, like my mama always taught me to be," he faux-drawled.

She laughed, leaning close. "Be a little less gentlemanly," she returned, her lips close to his.

"I'll work on it," he managed, before taking her mouth with his. He didn't let himself go completely, though he was tempted, both in general and by her words. But there was a time and place, and his mother's porch with any number of passersby wasn't it.

Her mouth was soft and sweet, with a sharp hint of cleverness, as if she knew everything she did to him no matter how hard he tried to keep it reined in. She leaned into him, her hands cupping his face, her fingers brushing against the short bristles of his hair. He wrapped his arms around her, pulling her tight and close, so he could feel her breasts pressed up to his chest, so she could likely feel what she was doing to him.

She sighed against his mouth, and distantly he knew it throbbed where he'd been elbowed, but the pain was drowned out by the feel of *her*.

"I like you an awful lot, Cora," he murmured against her mouth.

Blue eyes stared up at him, wide and serious, even as that slight curve to her now wet lips stayed. "I like you too, Shane," she said, and it wasn't any big admission. Of course they liked each other.

But it felt big, mixed with that kiss, with his heart beating hard against his chest, against hers.

It was only when that beat slowed that he heard someone approach. He glanced at the yard to see Micah standing there a few feet away from the stairs.

"Boone said he can't find the four-wheeler keys," Micah said flatly.

Cora jerked, seeming to only just realize Micah was there. She leaned away, plastered a fake smile on her face, and looked at her son.

"You're not getting on it, are you?" Cora asked, her voice sounding a little rough even to Shane.

He shouldn't be pleased by that.

"No," Micah returned, still that odd flatness to his voice and expression.

Shane pulled the keys out of his pocket and tossed them to Micah, watching the kid's expression carefully. But Micah had certainly learned how to put his displays of emotion on lockdown if he wanted to.

The boy caught the keys, then, with one last inscrutable look, turned and walked back to the stables. Shane noted he didn't jog, bound, or run. He *trudged*.

"He's not happy," Shane offered to Cora.

Cora frowned. "How do you know that?"

"My mom didn't really date when I was a kid, but this whole Ben thing? Beyond the very real concerns I have, there's also that weird . . . You don't want your mom with someone. You just don't. And any time that person is nice to you, you think it has to do with what that person is trying to do with your mom."

Cora took a deep breath. "I guess . . . that makes sense. I mean I've dated, but casually. I've kept him out of it."

"You've apparently kept him out of this, too."

Cora looked up at Shane, her eyebrows drawing

together. "You try talking to your twelve-year-old about dating and see how you like it."

Shane chuckled, rubbing his hand down her now straightened spine. "I'm sorry that came out disapproving. I don't disapprove of your not telling him. That's certainly your decision to make."

"I just haven't found the right words," Cora returned, looking at where Micah had gone, chewing on her lip.

"He wants you to hook up with Boone."

Cora jerked her gaze back to Shane. "He does not."

"Boone is fun and exciting, and I am a boring stick-in-the-mud who makes him follow the rules."

"That isn't true."

It was nice of her to say so, but Shane understood too much of this. He'd been the fatherless kid. He'd helped raise four other fatherless kids. "It is true, both that he thinks that and that I'm a boring stick-in-the-mud. I'm okay with that, but you should be, too."

"Okay with your stick-in-the-mud-ness?"

Maybe. "Okay with the fact that he likes someone better than me. That he might wish you were with someone else." Shane hoped that all came out like he didn't care, or like he was above it all. Above the need to make that kid worship *him.* But that would only backfire, so he did have to find a way to be okay with it.

"I care what Micah thinks . . . to an extent. His liking Boone better doesn't suddenly make me want Boone more than I want you. I'm not attracted to Boone."

Shane raised an eyebrow. Girls had thrown themselves at Boone since way before Shane had thought Boone should be catching them.

"I'm not saying your brothers aren't cute," Cora conceded.

"Oh, now it's both my brothers."

She laughed, nudging him with her elbow. "Now you're just giving me a hard time."

"Yeah," he admitted, pulling her close again. "And I'm about to be very ungentlemanly."

"Oh, good," she said, grinning up at him.

Steps thumped on the stairs, and Molly spoke, overloud. "Well, hello."

"Go away," Shane returned, pulling his hat down to cover his and Cora's faces so he could kiss her again, but Cora pushed him away.

"Stop," Cora chided with a grin. She got off the porch swing, much to his disappointment. "I'm going over to Lou's with your sister."

"And it looks like we have a ton to talk about," Molly said with an evil sister gleam in her eye.

"Be nice," Shane warned.

"Oh, I'll be nice to Cora. We'll see if I be nice to you once I get all the dirt." Molly linked arms with Cora. "*All* the dirt," she repeated, pulling Cora inside.

Cora waved with a grin and disappeared with his sister.

Shane gave himself a minute . . . or ten, to think about anything other than the current erection he was sporting. Because the task that lay ahead was going to be just about as unpleasant.

He had to face the kid, and he had the sinking suspicion it wouldn't be easy at all.

Chapter Fifteen

Despite the ups and downs of the morning, Cora was excited to be heading over to the flower farm. She wanted to explore it a little more, both from a personal interest standpoint and from a Mile High Weddings standpoint.

She smiled to herself, because she was starting to sound like her sister, and a couple years ago she never would have believed that was possible.

Molly drove her truck across fields and back toward the north edge of Tyler property, where Cora had never been before. The summer green was getting a little brown, but the sky was a beautiful blue, and the mountains acted like honorable sentries in the distance. The cows dotted pasture ground, the occasional ranch hand in a four-wheeler or on horseback waving as Molly drove.

"Mom doesn't like it when I cut through the back, but it cuts off about twenty minutes. And she won't be home till this afternoon, so I figure I'll have till dinner before she scolds me about it."

"Did you grow up with Lou and Emily?"

"Oh, sure. Lindsay's so much younger than me. Lou

and Em were my only hope for female companionship my own age for a while there. Plus, small towns. You didn't grow up here."

"No, Denver."

Molly wrinkled her nose. "I tried to live there for a few years with my ex. Worst years of my life, and not just because he was a dickbag."

Cora laughed. "Yeah, I relate."

"Micah's dad?"

Cora tensed and tried to find a way to play it off. Play it down. "Yeah, he's not . . . the greatest." *Ha ha, understatement of the year.*

"But he's still around?" Molly asked conversationally, concentrating on the path.

"Alive, but not around." Cora squinted out the window, trying to get a handle on her whirling emotions. Stephen seemed to keep coming up, a bad penny as always. She didn't want to talk about him. Couldn't, even if Molly had a shitty ex, too. "I don't like to talk about him."

"Got it. Well, just a head's up, we're not just helping Lou with work. This is a little cheer up mission over similarly shitty exes. I guess you saw the shiner my idiot brother got."

"Shane said he got in a fight."

Molly rolled her eyes, waving at a ranch hand who opened a gate for her and closed it behind them. "Gavin and his hair-trigger temper, I swear. Most easygoing guy alive unless he thinks you wronged him, then *boom.*"

"But this wasn't about him."

"No," Molly agreed as the truck rumbled along. Cora saw rows of colorful blooms, so she knew they must be on Lou's property now. "But I'm not gossiping until I hear what's going on with you and my brother."

"Oh. Well. We're, uh, going to go out on a date."

"Hmm. And there's already been kissing. PDA is gross and mean by the way. It's like rubbing it in to the PDA-less."

"Sorry," Cora offered, though she knew Molly was just teasing her. Cora glanced at the brunette. Her profile reminded Cora a lot of Deb. "I like him."

"Aw," Molly offered without a hint of cynicism or sarcasm. "Our Shane . . . He's such a good guy. I think you're perfect for him."

Cora scoffed. "Hardly perfect."

"You're outgoing and determined and funny. You tease him, and he lights up. He needs a little light now and again. And, I can't pretend to know what having a kid is like, but Shane's good with them, so it's not like that's a problem." Molly glanced over at Cora briefly, her expression one of mock horror. "Oh my God, I sound like my mother meddling."

Cora laughed. "I hate to point it out, but coming over to cheer up your friend under the guise of helping her work *also* sounds like your mother."

"Shit."

"I guess it's a good thing your mom's awesome."

Molly smiled. "It is a very good thing." Then she grimaced. "Hopefully our taste in men isn't the same."

"I don't think it's catching. My sister married a great guy after my mother and I displayed nothing but horrible, horrible, awful taste."

"So Lindsay has a prayer?"

"I think so. If Shane lets anyone near her ever."

Molly laughed hard at that as they pulled up to Lou's barn. "Lindsay's sneakier than all that."

Before they'd even gotten out of the truck, Lou appeared from the barn. A ways away there was a house. Nothing as big or as extravagant as the Tylers. In fact, it looked rather worn down, but loved and well-lived in. That must be where Lou lived, and maybe the grandmother Lou had referenced the last time Cora had been here.

"What are you guys doing here?" Lou asked suspiciously, the bandana haphazardly tied over the side of her face as it had been last time. "Didn't forget a wedding thing, did I?"

"You know you didn't," Molly called cheerfully, tramping over to where Lou stood. "You remember everything. I was just feeling antsy over there with all that testosterone, and Cora has the day off her wedding stuff, so we wanted to come play with the flowers and feel like girls for a bit."

"Cutting snapdragons today for market." Lou frowned at them. "I don't need help."

"But you could use it," Molly said cheerfully. "Besides, you should talk to Cora about supplying for more weddings than just Mom's. That'd be another stream of revenue. And you know people doing these outdoorsy weddings want local shit."

"You're a real eloquent businesswoman, Mol," Lou said grumpily, but there was a slight curve to her mouth. "And I know why you bitches are here." She flicked a glance at Cora. "You can be exempt from being a bitch. I don't know you well enough yet."

"It's okay. I can be a bitch."

Lou's mouth curved a hint again. "So, you know all about my sad sack of a situation. I can tell by that slightly sympathetic, slightly terrified look on your face. The question is, who told you? Shane or Molly. Which version you heard depends on which mouth blabbed. Molly exaggerates everything, and Shane makes everything about his idiotic brother."

"Oh. Well."

"Mostly me," Molly offered. "And not everything. Just what you already heard from the busybody police of Gracely. So, what are we working on?"

Lou let out a hefty sigh and motioned them to follow her. They tramped around the barn and to a big, white tunnel thing. Lou opened a door, and inside there were rows and rows of tall, gigantic snapdragons, the like of which Cora had never seen before.

"Wow," Cora breathed. "This is amazing."

"Isn't it? Lou's got the greenest thumb in Colorado, I'm just about sure," Molly said proudly.

Lou grunted. "I'm doing some cuttings for the farmer's market. I'll show you two how to do it once. If you fuck it up after that, you're gone."

"She's just the friendliest," Molly said, slinging her arm around Lou's shoulders.

Lou flinched and hissed out a breath.

Molly withdrew her arm. "Sorry."

"Don't be," Lou said jerkily, though clearly the casual touch had hurt her. Cora's heart twisted. Even though she didn't know quite what Lou had been through, she knew what it was like to be physically hurt and not know how to truly deal with it, not know how to accept help or love.

"I don't know why Gavin has to get in my business," Lou said, stomping back toward a table filled with tools. "And Rex isn't even my business anymore. Fighting with him was stupid."

"Oh, please, you two have been all up in each other's business since you met in grade school," Molly said, following her. "And of course it was stupid. It was men. But, he *was* just trying to protect you. That's how they all are."

"Well, I don't need protecting. I'm no one's victim,"

Lou said resolutely, pointing a pair of clippers at Molly. "Especially a Tyler. No offense."

Cora ducked her head in the blooms and tried to ignore the flutter of uncertainty. There was nothing to be uncertain about. The Tylers were protectors, and if Shane ever knew what she'd been through, he'd treat her like a victim.

She just couldn't let that happen.

Shane watched Micah all morning and afternoon, even when he was supposed to be overseeing branding but had sent Gavin to handle it instead. The kid acted normal, if decidedly less chatty, and yet Shane felt as though something was off.

Wrong.

He couldn't put his finger on it, though he could only assume it had to do with Micah's seeing Shane kiss Cora this morning. What else could it be? Yesterday the kid had talked a mile a minute, and, yes, Boone wasn't here to regale Micah with tales of the rodeo, having mentioned something vague about some kind of appointment in Benson, but Micah wasn't usually *silent* with Shane.

Shane didn't think.

He *knew* kids were hard, and yet this was some whole new weird level. His siblings he could yell at. Control and maneuver—always in the name of protection, but he could do it confident in the fact that he was their brother and he had the right.

He couldn't do those things with someone else's kid, no matter how much he liked said someone else or her kid.

"Molly's here. You can clean up and get ready for your lesson."

Micah didn't bound into action. Didn't smile or respond. He just slowly began to clean up the buckets he'd been using to wash down a few horses the hands had brought by, done for the day.

Even though Cora was on her way, Shane couldn't take this any more. "You okay, Micah?"

Micah shrugged, dumping out the buckets where he was supposed to and lining them up exactly where they went. It was a precise kind of focus Shane hadn't seen from him before. The kid did his chores right, but there was a careless, kid-ness to the way he breezed through them.

Until today.

"You know, you can talk to me about . . . things."

Micah stopped what he was doing and looked at him then, his expression the same blankness from this morning. "What things?"

"Any things. Questions about the ranch. If you want to unload about something that's bothering you." Shane hesitated. Hell, in for a penny. "If you want to talk about this morning."

Micah stood there looking like an adult, like a *man*. A careful man, doing a lot to hide everything behind a wall of strength and *got this handled*. It was eerie. And not just because Micah had seemed to grow three feet before his eyes, but because Shane felt such a . . . *kinship* with all that. He understood it in his bones. He *was* it.

"What about this morning?" Micah said, and it gave Shane a little chill, the way Micah could employ this cold, emotionless mask.

But Shane had started this, and he wasn't a man to start things without finishing them. "You know, I don't like the guy my mom's . . ." Okay, it seemed a little off to bring *marrying* into this conversation. Shane recalculated. ". . . with. Haven't since the beginning. I'm trying to get over it, but, you know, I know what it's like to watch your mom. . . . I just, I know this might be strange for you." And boy was Shane bungling it. "I get it."

"No, you don't," Micah said, so sure and certain, before he strode out the exit of the stables, toward where Molly and Cora were approaching.

Shane watched him go. Surprised, baffled, and something else. Something that surprised him just as much as Micah's walking away.

That little brush-off had hurt. Personally. Not just a *Cora will be disappointed* kind of hurt either, and different from brush-off hurts from his siblings. He knew his siblings loved him, even when they were pissed and directed it at him. They had to love him. They were bound to him by blood and this ranch and life.

Micah was bound to him by nothing. Micah could think Boone was the coolest till the day Shane died. Micah could spend his whole life wishing his mom had wanted someone else.

"But she doesn't," Shane muttered to himself, readjusting his hat on his head. Plenty of women appreciated a hardworking, cautious man.

Not Mattie.

Not Mom.

Not Molly.

It was a stupid line of thought. He had nothing to do with who Molly or Mom had or would marry, and Mattie . . . Well, they'd been in high school. It wasn't at all comparable. There was no pattern.

Cora entered the stables, wrinkling her nose, presumably at the smell. She was still a city girl at heart, but he thought it was kind of cute on her. Molly and Micah stood outside, talking something over.

"So, I just saw your mom and Ben making out."

"Oh, God, why would you say that to me?" Shane asked, disgusted down to his soul.

Cora laughed, and most of the weirdness with Micah faded away at the sound. They'd figure Micah out. Together. With time.

"Poor Molly had to witness it. There were tongues."

"Stop it. I mean it."

"I think he touched her ass," Cora continued, eyes sparkling with humor. Each horrible thing she said brought her closer to him though.

"Why are you being mean? What have I ever done to you?"

She laughed, low and husky, and he sort of didn't care what other words might come out of her mouth, because she was close, and he could smell her perfume and soil. Every worry or concern was obliterated by it.

"Because after listening to Lou telling me stories of how much of a goody-two-shoes you've always been, I'm all too tempted to debauch you, but, you know, people, so I can't. So I have to be mean and boner-killing instead."

"Boner . . . killing. Wow." He shook his head, more than a little enraptured by the happily mischievous tilt to her mouth. He lowered his voice, and his mouth so it was close to hers. "Lou doesn't know everything about me."

"Oh really?"

"Really. But you'll have to wait until Thursday to find out." Instead of kissing her on the mouth like he wanted to, he simply pressed a quick peck to her forehead and stepped around her. "Have to go check on the branding. See you later," he offered, not daring to look back.

"Now who's mean?" she called after him.

He chuckled as he stepped out into the late afternoon sun. For a brief second, he thought Micah scowled at him, but it was gone in a blink, his face back to blank as could be.

Shane must have imagined it. His insecure imagination playing tricks on him.

Things were fine. Things would be fine.

Chapter Sixteen

Cora practically bounced as she watched Micah shove a random conglomeration of crap into his backpack. She'd already warned him he was going to have to carry it, since Sam and Hayley would be carrying all the supplies they'd need to camp, but Micah didn't listen.

She was having a hard time focusing on making him listen because Shane would be here to pick her up in two hours. A date. A *real* date. It felt like she hadn't had something just for her in ages upon ages.

She was going to have sex. *Good* sex if those few and far between kisses were anything to go by. That had been ages and ages too.

She didn't have to feel guilty about it, because Micah would be off doing something fun for him.

Micah rocked back onto his heels from a crouched position that looked nothing but uncomfortable to Cora, studying her in that quiet, thoughtful way of his. He'd been doing it since he was two, and, a decade later, Cora still couldn't figure out what it meant. What he might be thinking. Good, bad, or in between.

She'd talked to Dr. Grove about it and been assured

it was normal. Kids needed their interior space to work through hard things too.

"You could come with," he offered carefully.

Cora tried not to grimace at the thought of sleeping in a tent. With bugs. And animals creepy crawling around at night. She shuddered.

Micah's expression softened a hint. "You're such a baby."

"A happy, warm, comfy bed-sleeping baby," Cora agreed.

His mouth quirked at that as he zipped up his back-pack.

"Did you pack your toothbrush?"

"Mom, there's no running water. Sam and Hayley have those toothbrush wipe things."

"Right." Camping really was beyond her, but she was glad Micah liked it, and not just because it meant she got a date with a hot guy out of the deal. With sex. Actual alone-in-her-house sex.

Micah got some time with his *interior thoughts*. Which was supposed to be good. She wished it felt good not knowing what he was thinking, what he was feeling.

"There isn't anything you want to talk to me about before Sam and Hayley get here?"

"No."

Cora didn't know whether to let that be or press, and it was the constant fight in this motherhood thing. Always trying to figure out the right lines to draw. But whether Micah wanted to talk to her or not, it wasn't as if Shane was *just* a date or *just* some sex. This wasn't a date to have some fun or scratch an itch. It was the kind of date you went on to try to build something.

And half of her foundation was Micah, which meant making sure his foundation was solid. "I am . . . I'm . . ."

Interior thoughts and space. She blew out a breath. "Shane and I are going to go out on a date."

Micah didn't look at her. "Okay."

"I thought you should know."

"Why?"

"Well, you'll be telling me when you're going on dates whether you like it or not, and you like Shane, so I thought you'd be happy. Or at least okay. Because, you know, he might come over sometimes and it might be . . . Well, it'd be fun, the three of us. Wouldn't it?"

Micah adjusted his backpack, still not looking at her. "I think I hear Sam's Jeep," was all he said before heading toward the door.

"Micah." Cora followed him, not sure what was twisting inside of her. Worry. Fear. Irritation. "You do like Shane."

"Yeah. He's fine. It's fine. Whatever. Can I go now?"

Cora placed her hands on her son's ever-growing shoulders. He'd be taller than her in no time. A *man* in no time. "Baby, be straight with me. We promised each other that."

"I hate it," Micah spat, so acidly that Cora took a step back, shocked to her core.

"But—"

"It's a dumb idea, and I don't want you kissing him or going out with him or any of it!" He said it so vehemently, so sure.

"But you like him," Cora replied weakly. Where on earth had *that* come from? "You like all of them." Which reminded her she was the adult in this situation. She had to be strong, not weak. "Shane's a good man, and I like him a lot. And he likes me, *and* you. He's the kind of guy . . ." Ah, hell, she couldn't start talking about relationships and foundations and futures with a twelve-year-old, but she needed to explain it all somehow. She reached for him. "Baby—"

"You'll tell him," Micah exploded, backing away from her, tears shining in his eyes. "About everything that happened with Dad. You'll tell him and everyone will know and they'll treat us different. It'll be all pity and weird looks and . . . I hate it. Everyone at Mile High does that. You're going to ruin everything at the ranch, and it's the only place I have."

Cora could only stare. She hadn't expected an outburst of emotion, but more . . . She hadn't expected *this*. Micah to feel exactly the way she felt—that on the Tyler ranch she could just be her. Not Lilly's messed up sister or an abuse survivor, but *Cora Preston*.

"I'm not going to tell him," she whispered.

Micah straightened at that. "What do you mean?" he asked, blinking furiously so that none of those tears fell. She had to keep her own eyes as wide as possible to keep *her* tears from falling.

"I'm not going to tell him or anyone all of that," Cora said, more firmly this time. "I don't . . . I don't want any of that pity either. So, we just won't talk about it with them. That's okay. We don't have to tell everyone we meet about our past."

"Really?" Micah's eyebrows drew together, and he bit his thumbnail, an old anxiety habit he didn't do often anymore. "But isn't that lying?"

"No. It's . . . It's keeping some things private. That's okay."

Micah studied her. "You're really not going to tell him?"

"Really." She'd already decided she couldn't, and now she had even more reason not to. Micah didn't want her to. So, it wasn't even selfish anymore. She was doing it for her kid. It was the right thing to do. For both of them.

The knock on the door caught them off guard, eliciting a flinch from both.

"You still want to go?" Cora asked, placing her hand on the knob. "You don't have to."

"I want to go."

"Because if you want to talk—"

Micah tugged on the door. "I want to go."

Cora let go of the door so Micah could open it. She forced herself to smile at Sam and Hayley. "Hey, guys."

"Hey," Hayley greeted cheerfully. "Our little camper ready?"

Micah rolled his eyes, likely at the word *little*. "Did you bring hot dogs?"

"And marshmallows," Sam assured. "We'll be out of cell range, but I'll have the Mile High walkie on me."

Cora smiled at Sam, grateful for his assurances. "Thanks."

"You could come with?" Hayley offered with a grin.

"Yeah, hard pass," Cora returned. She gave Micah a squeeze before he could escape. "You guys have fun."

"We'll be back by four tomorrow. Keep him at Mile High till you pick him up."

Cora nodded at the plan. "Thanks, guys."

Sam and Hayley turned toward the Jeep, and Micah followed, but he looked back at her over his shoulder, gripping his backpack strap. He retraced his steps, standing at the bottom of the stoop looking up at Cora.

"You really won't tell him everything?" Micah insisted.

Cora stepped down so she could pull him into a hug. "I really won't," she assured, kissing his temple. "Be good and careful."

He nodded and pulled away, then bounded off toward

Sam and Hayley, *finally* a little hint of happiness and enjoyment in him.

Cora waved and smiled as Sam drove his Jeep away. She tried to get over the weird, sick feeling in her gut as she took a step inside. Micah was safe and having fun. She was going to have her own kind of fun. Nothing had changed except she had even more reason to stay the course she'd already decided on.

It was okay. She was doing the right thing. For her. For Micah. Hell, even for Shane. Because they could build a foundation on the present instead of on some horrible past. It made sense.

All the sense in the world.

Shane pulled his car up to the address Cora had texted him. She had a pretty green house in the old mining housing section of town, a narrow structure way too close to her neighbor, at least in Shane's estimation.

Still, he supposed the house suited her, though she'd clearly forgotten to water the pot of colorful blooms on her porch that were wilting and browning at the edges. He stepped out of his truck and ignored the worming thing in his gut.

Nerves were silly. Cora was Cora. He wasn't a teenager or even a man unsure of his feelings or hers. Truth of the matter was, they'd had plenty of buildup and assurances before they'd gotten to this point.

And kisses. The kind that kept a man up at night, and distracted in the middle of the day, and a little bit bow-legged in the morning and—

"Okay, enough of that," he muttered to himself, stepping onto the first stair.

"Stay," a voice called out from across the yard.

He glanced over at where a woman was standing on

her porch, clearly having yelled the "stay" command to her German shepherd sitting in the middle of the yard between the houses.

Yes, the neighbors were definitely too close.

"Ma'am," Shane offered when the woman stared suspiciously at him, tipping his hat politely. Some of that suspicion on her face relaxed into something closer to shock.

A man stepped out onto the porch with her, and they exchanged muttered words, gesturing toward him as he took the rest of the steps up to Cora's door. When he snuck a glance their way as he lifted his hand to knock, they were both just standing there. Staring.

"Damn neighbors," Shane muttered.

The door swung open, and Shane forgot about neighbors, close or otherwise.

She made his heart kick on a good day, but this was something else altogether. Skin, for starters. Miles of it, creamy pale, a delicacy he wanted to spend the rest of the day tasting. Her hair was down, some riot of golden waves around her shoulders, and subtle touches of makeup that suddenly made a man have impure thoughts. As if he needed any help in that department.

"Hi," she offered, bright pink lips curving into a smile made for hot nights and rainy days. "Am I over-dressed?" she asked, swinging her hips slightly so the flowy dark green fabric fluttered around her thighs.

He tried to bring his gaze back up to her face and failed. "No, you'll do just fine."

"You seem a little distracted, Shane."

When he finally managed to tear his gaze from her legs, he found her grinning.

"You better not invite me inside, or I might just show you why."

She pulled her bottom lip between her teeth, making a considering sound, and, if not for the yip of that damn neighbor's dog, Shane might have bent down and taken some of what he wanted in a kiss.

"Your neighbors are watching," he offered instead.

"Oh." She glanced across the way, then waved at the couple still on the porch before pulling Shane firmly inside. She closed the door, leaning against it. He told himself to look around, to compliment her on her house or something, but all he could do was look at her.

"If I kiss you, it's only going to mess up your makeup."

"I could probably fix it," Cora returned. "If necessary."

How could there be any other option but to step toward her, cage her against that front door, lean his mouth to hers and—

A loud knock startled them both.

On a heavy sigh, Cora rolled her eyes. "Just give me one second, okay?"

"Uh, sure," Shane complied, taking a few steps back, hoping the raging erection he was currently sporting wasn't as noticeable as it felt.

Cora opened the door. The woman from the porch stood on the other side, holding a bowl. She pushed it toward Cora.

"Hi, Cora. Could I borrow a cup of sugar?" the woman asked, smiling and batting her eyelashes and clearly checking Shane out, not paying attention to whatever Cora's answer would be.

"You don't bake, Tori," Cora replied, forcing the bowl back at the woman. "And that's a bowl, not a measuring cup." She gestured back toward Shane. "Tori, this is Shane. Shane, this is Tori. She's leaving now," Cora said firmly, giving the woman a little push.

"Is he a real cowboy?" Shane heard the woman ask in a low voice, as Cora nudged her firmly out the door.

"I'll tell you all about it later," Cora said, then closed the door on Tori.

"Nosy neighbors," Shane offered, shoving his hands in his pockets. Because if he didn't lock them in, he'd reach out and touch her. Kiss her like he'd been planning to, and then it would take the kind of restraint he'd really rather not employ to usher her out the door and into his truck so they could go into Benson for dinner.

It was the first time in years he wished he had his own place, and not just because of his wounded pride that he'd lost that opportunity.

"Nosy friends, more like," Cora replied. "Tori's actually marrying my . . . Well, my sister's brother-in-law, I guess he'd be. They both work at Mile High with Lilly and—" She waved a hand. "Anyway. Where were we?"

Shane cleared his throat. *Far too clothed*, he wanted to say, but he was supposed to be a gentleman. "Ah, maybe we should go. I said I was taking you out, and I'm not sure where we were would lead us out the door any time soon."

She looked around the little entryway as if pondering some great problem, so Shane did as well, noting the clutter of young boy and professional woman, mixed up and shoved into a little corner. Sneakers and high heels, some flowery printed scarf tangled up with a fleece jacket. It felt . . . right. Cora. Made him glad to be here even aside from the potential for sex.

She met his gaze again. "I don't want to go out."

His stomach dropped, something like panic catching in his chest. "But, I thought—"

She stepped toward him again, this time reaching out, her hands landing on his chest, fingers splaying there.

She looked up at him, blue eyes dark and damn near mesmerizing enough to drown in. "I want to stay in."

He maybe wasn't the quickest man in the world, but he wasn't a slow one either. Everything inside of him tightened, and damn near yearned. But there was a protocol. A plan. A certain way you did things with a woman you were interested in. "You're all dressed up," he managed, a feeble excuse at best. If all his blood hadn't rushed south he might have come up with something better. "You'd want to go out after all that work, wouldn't you? I mean, I don't know much about women, but I heard my sisters complain about getting fancied up plenty growing up."

"All that work doesn't need to go outside to be enjoyed," Cora replied, hands sliding up his chest to his shoulders as she moved onto her tiptoes, against his chest, her mouth just out of reach.

God, he wanted that mouth. Those curves. He wanted all of her so much he practically throbbed with it, but there was still some semblance of brainpower left. Obligation. He should take her out first. He should. "But—"

"We have approximately eighteen hours in this house together, alone, and then God only knows when the next time will be, at least until school starts again. How do *you* want to spend it?"

"Sold." He reached out, lifting her off her feet in a smooth maneuver if he did say so himself. She laughed, breathlessly, then latched her mouth onto his, a potent mix of lips and teeth and tongue.

She might kill him, and he'd enjoy every second. "Where?" he murmured against her busy mouth.

"Upstairs. I have condoms upstairs," she managed to say between fervent kisses to his mouth, his jaw, his temple. Her hands tangled in his hair, and he wanted to do the same. Lose himself in every inch of her. Lose these horrible clothes keeping them apart.

"Upstairs it is," he said, heading for the narrow staircase behind them, groaning as her body moved against his until he thought he might black out.

But he wasn't about to do that. He was going to carry her up the stairs, and, then, he was going to have her. All of her.

"Oh, but you can't carry me upstairs," she said, again through a shower of her mouth against his skin.

"Like hell I can't," he returned, setting out to do just that.

Chapter Seventeen

A man had never carried her before. Not when she'd been a child, not up the stairs, and certainly not to bed. But Shane was doing all that as though it were easy as pie. As though she weighed about half of what she did. As though he wanted her as much as she wanted him.

She'd been worried there, for a second or two, when he'd been so adamant about taking her out, but she'd realized quickly that was so very Shane. To want to do things in the right order. To make sure he was taking care.

Right now, this was the only way she wanted to be taken care of.

"My room is the first one."

He reached the top of the stairs, not even out of breath as his mouth streaked over her neck. He nudged the already ajar door open with his boot and stepped in, fastening his mouth to hers, lips rough, tongue demanding.

Oh, yes, there was something deliciously dirty underneath all that goody-two-shoes. He didn't even put her down. She'd hooked her legs around his waist, and his hands cupped her ass as he moved her slowly against the *very* impressive erection in his jeans.

If it went on much longer she might shatter right there. Especially when his mouth lowered again, down her neck and then her chest over the fabric of her dress. He found the hard peak of her nipple through the fabric and closed his mouth over it, with heat and a little bit of teeth.

She arched, electrified, desperate, needy. "Let me get the condoms."

"Are you sure you don't feel like I'm moving you too fast?" he murmured into her neck, his tongue tracing some tendon there, eliciting a gasp from her.

God. *God* he was good at this. Too fast? "Shane, I'm not even half naked. This is *glacial*. Maybe childless women can dawdle, but a single mom has to take the chances she's offered."

He chuckled, something kind of dark and edgy in the sound, in him, and she wanted to revel in the fact that she brought it out. He lowered her to the ground, slowly, making sure her body slid against his erection as he put her on her feet.

She managed to unwrap her arms from his neck, her breath coming in short spurts from the sheer excitement of it all. "Just give me a second," she said, quickly walking over to her bed and getting down on her hands and knees. She reached under the bed, pushed the two plastic bins out of the way, then dragged out the heavy gun safe where she kept all the things she wanted hidden from Micah.

She punched in the code, then lifted the lid. Inside was a wad of cash she kept stashed away just in case Stephen ever messed with her finances. A few art projects Micah had made in school she was afraid he'd throw away if he had access to, all the legal papers regarding Micah and Stephen in an unmarked folder, the little pistol she'd finally stopped carrying around out of fear, and a box of condoms she'd bought the other day, thinking of Shane specifically.

She grabbed it and snapped the safe back shut, turning to face Shane while she was still crouched by the bed.

"I . . . have never seen condoms kept in a safe before."

"Well, you know what they say, gotta have *safe* sex." She smiled when he laughed at the horrible joke. "Seriously, though, I can't let my kid see I have condoms."

"Yeah, I get that. You're saving him from being scarred for life."

"Oh, did you find your mom's condoms once?"

Shane grimaced. "Well, everything inside of me just shriveled up and died."

She pushed the safe back under the bed and got to her feet. "I bet I can fix that." She dropped the condom box on her nightstand and reached behind her to unzip the dress, letting it flutter to her feet. She'd worn her laciest, sexiest underwear.

He inhaled sharply, his eyes roaming her body like a starved man at a buffet. "Crisis averted," he murmured. "Christ," he said on an exhale, grinning at her as he moved forward. "Aren't you the prettiest thing?"

No one had ever said something like that to her before. Sure, a guy might say she was hot or sexy, maybe on occasion, and usually *before* they got her naked in an attempt to get her naked, but Shane . . .

Prettiest thing.

She blinked against the odd sting of tears. She didn't want to cry, or feel touched—at least not emotionally. She wanted the tide of heat and excitement to carry them away, and she'd deal with all those messy emotions later. When she was alone.

So, she cocked her hip, swept her gaze up and down his tall, broad frame. "Now who's overdressed?"

His hat had fallen off somewhere along the way, which was a shame, all in all. Still, as he lifted his hands to the buttons of his shirt, nothing was truly a shame. He unbuttoned the row with quick, efficient movements, his dark gaze fastened on hers the entire time. The corner of his mouth turned upward ever so slowly, all *cocky* cowboy, as he shrugged out of the fabric.

Cora inhaled a little sharply herself. He was bronzed skin and dark hair and just the broadest shoulders. She wasn't supposed to believe in fantasies, but Shane was one come to life. In a million little ways, and a few very large ones.

Very large.

She crossed to him, because, emotions or not, the odd little flutter of nerves or not, time was ticking. And she wanted to spend every second of that time touching *him.*

She pressed her palms to his abdomen, splaying her fingers wide. He was all hard ridges and warm skin. There was a delicious edge to his expression, restrained control. A hot bolt of lust arrowed through her.

That she knew how to deal with. She dropped her fingers to the button of his pants and unfastened it even as she pressed her mouth to his shoulder. She unzipped his jeans, allowing herself to linger in the taste of his skin, to brush her fingers lightly against the thick, hard length of him.

She shuddered with need as his large hand came up to cup her face, crushing his mouth to hers, a fierce kind of want she more than matched in the move. But then everything in him softened, gentled. His grip on her face went light. His mouth turned sweet.

And *that* she didn't know what to do with. Sweetness. Affection. *Care.* The way his fingertips, so rough from all that hard work he did, smoothed the bra strap off her shoulders and tugged her bra down. Scarred, calloused hands with the softest, most reverent touch over the tightened nipples of her breasts, all while his mouth gentled over hers as though she were something precious. Delicate.

It made those tears sting her eyes again, so she pulled back, away, flashing her sassiest smirk. "Lose the pants," she said, her voice a little rougher, weaker than she'd imagined it'd be.

But he lifted her off the ground again, still surprising her with the ease in which he did it, and, when he laid her out on the bed, that cocky curve back to his mouth, something dark and dangerous was in that brown gaze of his.

It was some kind of amazing he could be both. Sweet and light. Dark and dangerous. Here and somehow hers, for at least a little bit.

He pushed his jeans and boxers down in one easy push, so Cora wiggled out of her underwear. His gaze roamed her body, hot and heavy as a touch.

She crooked a finger at him, the other hand reaching behind her to the nightstand. "Come here," she said, because, if he kept staring at her like she was some kind of precious jewel, she was pretty sure she was going to break down and cry.

She was damn well going to get some sex out of the deal before she let herself do any of that. So, she tore open the packet and pulled out the condom, focusing on the very important task of rolling it onto him as he knelt beside her.

She made an approving noise in the back of her throat as she positioned the condom on him, then grinned up at him as she rolled it on. His expression was one of grim, fierce *control.*

And then it broke.

"Hell," he muttered, leveraging himself above her, positioning himself at her entrance. She grabbed onto his shoulders, pulling him down for a kiss so she could squeeze her eyes shut. Focus on sensation instead of feeling.

He slid inside of her, a slow, delicious invasion that had her groaning into his mouth. He kissed the corner of her mouth, her cheek, her bottom lip, whispering things she barely understood. Tried not to. Because every time she caught a word it was something like "beautiful" or "sweet," and she didn't know how those things could possibly be applied to someone like her. Especially from someone like him.

So she focused on the feel of his hard body above hers. The hot, heavy brand of his hand on her hip, the soft unexpected sweetness of his mouth in contrast to the demanding, needy, almost desperate pace he set.

She held on, trying so desperately hard to keep her heart separate from her libido. All those swirling, conflicting emotions drowned in lust and release.

But Shane filled her completely, moved inside of her with an ease and a fit that spoke of years together instead of firsts. *Meant togethers* instead of *just for nows.*

There was no keeping it separate. Not when he kissed her gently, or when the kiss went rough. Not as he slowed the pace down, or when she begged him to hurry.

There was only her heart swelling foolishly, unreasonably as his breath grew ragged with hers, as his heart beat hard against hers. Even when that climb to pleasure broke, pulsing through her like sparklers of ecstasy and wonder, her heart pulsed with it. Too big, too desperate.

She pressed her cheek to his shoulder, trying to keep a hold on the tears, the bolt of panic, and that all-encompassing need for someone to feel the same things she felt. To reciprocate even a fraction of what she wanted.

"Hold on," he murmured into her ear, and then, in a swift movement, his strong arm slid behind her back, and he rolled them in a fluid movement so he was on his back, and she was splayed across his long, rangy body—him still buried deep within her.

She let out a breathless chuckle, trying to find purchase in this new position, with his body under hers. Something like at *her* mercy, as if she had any control.

He grinned up at her, his hands sliding up her legs and then clamping on her hips. "Your turn to do some of the work."

Her heart flipped over at the mischievous look in his eye, but, with his gaze on hers, that lopsided grin half lost in pleasure, she could push that horrible well of emotion down, and focus on him. On fun. On making him go crazy.

She slid her hands up to his chest, pushing herself into a sitting position as she grinned down at him. "Buckle up, cowboy."

Shane was about ninety-nine percent sure he'd died at some point, and gorgeous Cora collapsed on top of him, warm and soft and perfect was a reward for some good he'd done along the way. Had to be.

She sighed contentedly against his neck, her cheek

pressed to his shoulder, breathing matching his as it slowly came back to a normal rate. He moved his hand up and down her spine, wishing they could stay here forever.

But he heard her stomach rumble, and he was getting hungry himself. Besides, if they lay here much longer he'd be liable to doze off and ruin the whole night. Reluctantly, he withdrew from her and rolled her onto her side. He pressed a kiss to her cheek. "Better wash up," he murmured.

He padded to the bathroom and got rid of the condom. When he walked back into her room, she was still lying naked on the bed. The prettiest damn thing he'd ever seen.

She yawned and stretched, her fingers grasping a fluffy, bright pink lump of fabric resting haphazardly across the headboard. "I'm starved. I can't cook, but I can occasionally heat up a frozen pizza without burning it." She slid off the bed, and he realized the fuzzy lump was a robe.

"Well, it just so happens I'm an expert at frozen pizzas," he offered, picking his boxers up off the ground and pulling them on.

She grinned, tying the robe with an efficient knot. She pulled her hair from underneath the collar, letting it fall onto her back.

He couldn't quite get over how he'd suddenly gotten so lucky. Aside from the ranch, good fortune wasn't generally in his corner, but he had no doubt Cora Preston was his very much good fortune.

"I'm going to have to say thank you to Ben Donahue."

She burst out laughing. "Why on earth?"

"If that bastard hadn't conned my mother into

marrying him, I'd have never met you. And I think you are even worth my mom's marrying the wrong guy."

She grimaced more than smiled, and he cupped her face, trying to read that odd reaction she had every time he complimented her. "How come you look like I'm about to land a punch every time I say something nice."

She blanched. Near bone white.

"Hey, what's wr—"

She stepped away, far out of his reach, and that bothered him almost as much as the way she'd paled.

"Cora."

"It's nothing." She smiled at him, but it was fake. Her lips might curve, but her eyes were downright haunted. "Hungry?"

He could have let it go, and maybe he should, but what had transpired in this bedroom was important to him, and he'd learned a thing or two from being burned by love in the past. He'd learned a thing or two since Cora had driven into his life.

Sometimes, you had to face the things you didn't want to verbalize for them to ever make any sense.

"Tell me," he said gently, looking right at her, treating her a bit like a skittish horse—not that he'd ever tell her that's what he was doing. He approached slowly, cautiously, hand out so she saw his intent before he did it. He smoothed his palm down her shoulder. "Tell me."

She looked up at him, and there was something like *fear* in that helpless look. A loss in those dark blue eyes he couldn't even guess at. But she closed them and shook her head. "It's just . . . Well, I told you, not a great many good guys in my life. So, it's always kind of jarring. A guy saying something nice. I don't expect it. I don't know quite how to . . . accept it."

He pulled her closer, drawing her into his arms, so

her cheek rested against his chest. "Every man in your life has been an idiot."

"Haven't they just?" She tilted her head back, looking up at him quizzically. "How come you're single? Doesn't seem natural after all the losers I've dated that someone as sweet and good as you is on the market."

"I'm not exactly . . . I'm not an easy guy to get to know. I tend to keep my guard up, I guess."

"It was easy enough for me to slip through."

"It's been a long time since I let someone." He reached out and touched one of the waves of curl that stuck out haphazardly. "You made that letting in hard to resist."

"Why was it a long time?"

Shane blew out a breath. Well, he really didn't want to get into that, but he supposed if he was standing here asking her for more information, she had just as much of a right.

"Well, how about this, I'll tell you all about my past broken heart, long as you tell me about yours."

Her eyes lowered, a heaviness washing through her. "Oh, who wants to talk about all that old stuff?" She flashed him a grin he knew wasn't anything more than an attempt at distraction. "Let's talk about now." She patted his chest and batted her eyelashes up at him. "And frozen pizza."

But he couldn't seem to let it go, much as part of him wanted to. Life was complicated, much as he hated that. But he was a practical man, and complicated could get solved if you faced it head-on. "I think I should know, Cora. If I'm going to be part of your and Micah's lives, I think I should know what happened with his father. At least the basics. At least so I don't end up saying the wrong thing to either of you."

"You won't."

"I'd like to know, and in return, I'll tell you why I've kept myself guarded. It's something I haven't told . . . anyone. Not the whole story."

She blinked up at him over that. "No one?"

He shook his head. "Not a living soul. My mom knows a few pieces, and Gavin knows a few other pieces, but no one knows the whole of it. I don't like talking about it. It's embarrassing as hell. But maybe it'd be good for us, to start on an open and honest foundation."

Again she looked down at the ground. He almost told her to forget it, to shove all those words back in his mouth and go back to sex and pizza and *fun*.

"He just didn't love us," she said in a small voice before he could.

"And you loved him?"

She made a scoffing sound. "I . . . I thought I did. I was desperate for someone to love me." She swallowed and waved a hand. "That can't make any sense to you, what with the family you have, but growing up I only ever had Lilly. So I just wanted someone who loved me, except I was too young and too dumb to know what love really is."

"No, I think I do understand that."

She gave him the most doleful look, reminding him for a second of Micah and his near-teenage disdain for so many things. "You had your mother and a whole big family and a ranch, Shane. You don't have to pretend you understand. It was a long time ago. I'm over it now."

"I did have a loving family. You're right. Maybe if my father hadn't died, I'd be oblivious, but he did die, and when he did I felt a lot of . . ." Shane wouldn't let the emotion clog his throat. He simply wouldn't. He'd be straightforward and plain and then maybe . . .

He'd loved Mattie and had wanted a life with her, but he hadn't been honest with her. Not about himself and how he felt, certainly not about what had happened with Dad. So, he'd do it differently this time. He'd give himself to Cora, and then it'd have to work out. Because she'd give herself back. If he did it all right, she'd have to.

Chapter Eighteen

Cora couldn't believe she was standing in her room, naked under her robe, after some seriously awesome sex talking about . . . *this.*

Feelings and heartbreak and awful pasts. She didn't want this, and she was more than grateful for her promise to Micah or she might have given in, given it all over to Shane, and where would that have left her?

It *had* been a long time ago, and she wanted nothing from *then* touching her life now. The only reason she'd given him the vague answer she'd given him was because . . . Well, she wanted Shane. The whole of him. His past hurts and scars and the crazy idea he could understand her, even if he didn't know all the pieces.

Maybe it was selfish, and maybe it was wrong, but she wanted all of his pieces. All for herself.

"I felt a lot of responsibility when my dad died," Shane said carefully, as though each word were chosen individually, with great thought. "I took a lot on myself, and because of that my family became more of a . . . *Burden* isn't the right word, but I didn't see myself as equal or as part of it. I was the protector. Finding someone who didn't need me to be that, well, I let that skew my thinking."

"She didn't love you?"

He blew out a breath and raked a hand through his hair, this gorgeous, tall, broad-shouldered man who only wore faded navy boxers.

"We dated in high school. I think we loved each other, as much as you can when you're a teenager anyway. Graduation loomed. I wanted to get married, and she wanted to go to and finish vet school first. It seemed reasonable. I'd be the rancher. She'd be the vet."

"She sounds perfect," Cora muttered, trying not to sound as petulant as she felt. Failing at it.

Shane laughed, bitterly, and Cora knew that shouldn't have soothed her, but it did.

"Uh, no. End of her sophomore year of college, she lost her scholarship, failed a few classes. Her parents cut her off, but she came to me crying about how she needed to prove she could do this. One of the stipulations of my father's will was that we each be afforded a certain amount of money, a trust fund of sorts, that we'd get at twenty-one, with the idea we'd buy or build our own place, on the ranch or off."

"Shane," Cora said on an exhale, afraid she knew where this was going. Maybe it was silly to hurt for him when she'd been beaten by the man she'd wanted to love, but Shane was so good. A betrayal like being used? It didn't seem fair.

"I figured we were going to be partners," he continued, standing a few feet away from Cora. "And she wouldn't mind living with Mom for a few years while we made it back. Long story short, she didn't have much intention of coming back home, of marrying me. I'm not sure she ever graduated. I paid for that semester and then she . . . disappeared. Well, I mean, not disappeared. Her parents knew where she was and all. She just stopped talking to me."

"She's the worst," Cora said emphatically. "I'd spit in her eye if I ever saw her."

Shane's mouth curved, just a pinch, though that heavy, something like guilty look remained in his expression. "It's possible that's part of why I'm a little concerned about Ben."

"Possible, yeah. I think I get that." Not that she had any doubt his behavior toward Ben had been based on anything other than that protective instinct. How could she find that so appealing and so bone-deep frightening all at the same time?

"Mom knows I lost the money. Gav knows I was pretty messed up over it for a while. Somehow made it worse that Molly went off and married some dipshit who did much of the same thing. And I never told her, you know? I never told her that Mattie took off on me, and I should have. Maybe Molly would have listened and not gotten suckered into the whole thing."

"Well, if she was in love, or thought herself to be, and her big brother was lecturing her, probably not," Cora offered, hoping to ease some of that guilt somehow. Someway. "I didn't listen to Lilly, and . . ." *I got into a lot worse relationships than one where I was stolen from.*

It was the strangest thing inside of her, the want to tell him, the utter fear that kept those words locked down tight. The promise she'd made to Micah.

"Why don't you come here?" he murmured.

She was feeling all too teary, but none of her flippant changes of subject had worked before. So, she took the few steps to cross the room to him and let him pull her into the warmth of his body.

Her shoulders relaxed somehow, that odd band in her chest loosening. He kissed her temple. A *good* man.

One who somehow thought she was something special. Worthy of his secrets. *Her.*

"So, all there is to the Micah's dad story is that he didn't love you guys?" he asked gently.

Cora stiffened, but she considered it progress she didn't pull away. "He didn't love us or want us," she said, and that was good enough. More than enough of that story. That was the bottom line. All Stephen had ever wanted out of her was someone to control. "I spent too long trying to make him," she whispered, the words sliding past her clogged throat. She was giving him too much, and the only thing stopping her from going further was her promise to Micah. His bone-deep certainty it would change everything.

Because it would, if Shane saw them as victims. It would change everything. "Guess I have a few of my own daddy issues." Which was the wrong thing to say, not because it suggested the tragic loss of his father was an "issue," but because he pulled slightly away, looking at her with those too-soft brown eyes.

"You haven't mentioned your dad," he said, again so gentle. Careful. As if she would shatter. God help her if he ever found out what she really was. He probably wouldn't even touch her. He'd be too afraid to break her.

But she wasn't broken. She couldn't let him think she was. "Technically my mom, Lilly, and I were my father's secret family," Cora offered with the best nonchalant shrug she could muster. "He'd swoop in with candy and pretty dresses every so often, never with anything that would keep Mom from having to work three jobs to keep us afloat, then he'd swoop out again."

"I can't imagine how hard that would be on a little girl."

"I had Lilly to offset it," Cora said firmly. "And, yeah, I chased the wrong kind of guy and the wrong kind of attention there for a while, but Micah changed my life. I'm not that desperate, needy girl anymore." *At least on the outside.*

She shoved that nasty Mom-sounding voice away and met his gaze with a cool, detached one of her own. "Childhoods and heartbreaks shape us, yeah, but kids shape you too. If you love your kid, parenthood shapes you into something better and stronger than you ever thought you could be." And she was strong for Micah, finally, after all these years. Because she was going to keep her promise to him, and she was going to have Shane and a career, and it was going to all work out. She wouldn't allow herself to bail or fail or sabotage. Not this time.

Shane's mouth brushed hers, soft and sweet, hands cupping her face. Not as though she were weak or fragile or something to be treated carefully, but as though she were *important* and *central.*

"I'm glad we talked," he said, still holding her face. "I said this about Ben, but it's true here too. It's because of you. Talking and dealing is not a Tyler strong point, and I wouldn't have acted on it then or now without your giving me a little nudge."

She smiled up at him, but inwardly all she could think was *you only have yourself to blame.* "Well, I'm glad. Now, if you don't get some food in me soon, I'm going to faint."

"I'll catch you," he offered cheerfully, and she had no doubt he would. A wonderful promise.

And a tiny little wiggle of impending doom.

Shane spent the night against his better judgment. He needed to be back at the ranch and ready to work by six at the latest, but Cora had been snuggled up to him, half asleep, telling him not to go.

What was a man to do?

No matter how late they'd stayed up, or how many times they'd turned to each other in the middle of the night, his internal clock was a powerful thing. Cora's room was still dark, but he was wide-awake.

He wasn't sure which was worse, the litany of chores he was missing piling up in his brain, or the scent of flowers and warm, soft skin next to him, making every single ranch thought vanish.

He was a practical man with serious responsibilities, and he did not have the kind of life or brain where shirking those would be easy.

But he wasn't used to having to resist anything, and Cora was quite the impossible thing to resist.

He shifted in the bed, and she yawned, snuggling deeper into the pillow. "Have to go, don't you?" she murmured, half muffled by the pillow her head was buried into.

"Better," he replied, running his palm over her tangled hair. "Come by tonight for dinner with Micah."

She yawned, her eyes opening, then fluttering closed again as if she just didn't have the energy to keep them open. "Isn't that a lot? Don't you want some space?"

He slid out of bed, grabbing his jeans. "Why would I want space from you guys?" He pulled on the jeans, watching her as she struggled in that half-asleep, half-awake middle ground.

"But . . ."

"Come by for dinner. We can talk all you want about space then. And maybe sneak off and make out somewhere."

Her mouth curved. "'Kay, you convinced me."

He leaned down and gave her one quick peck on the

cheek, wanting to linger and not allowing himself the pleasure. There was work to be done at home, and she'd be by later tonight.

He found his shirt and pulled it on, slipping out of her room. He found his cowboy hat and slid it onto his head before working on buttoning up the shirt as he walked down the stairs.

He looked rumpled and rather walk-of-shamed, but hopefully he could get back to the ranch early enough to avoid any familial prying.

He stepped onto the porch, pulling the door closed and making sure it locked. The world was still dark except for the faintest hint of light far away in the distance. He just might make it.

He drove through empty morning Gracely, though the lights in Em's bakery were already on. He possibly slid a little lower in his seat, despite the fact that she'd likely recognize his truck if she looked out and happened to see him drive past.

He sank lower still in his seat when he crossed the threshold of the Tyler ranch. And yeah, maybe he took the side way instead of the main drive, and maybe he parked his truck next to the stables and then hurried in a jog to the house in the hopes someone might fall for him already having been up and around.

Boone probably would have had no problem walking through the front door, bold and defiant, but Shane didn't have it in him. Not even because he was embarrassed, but because he didn't want his mouthy family saying anything that might embarrass Cora. And, Lord, was his family mouthy.

Shane slipped in through the back door, being careful to shut it quietly and flip the locks back as noiselessly as possible. He took two steps toward the stairs.

"Where have you been?"

"Jesus." Shane jumped a foot at the unexpected voice of his mother, and, when he slowly turned, Mom, Grandma, and Molly were all sitting around the seldom-used kitchen table, calmly sipping coffee.

Mom raised an eyebrow as Shane accepted his fate and stepped into the doorway of the kitchen.

"Seems to me you're sneaking in rather than heading out." She watched him over the edge of her mug.

"Seems to me those were the clothes you were wearing last night when you hightailed it out of here," Grandma said, also holding her mug up to her mouth.

Shane scowled at Molly. "What's your observation?" he grumbled.

But she smiled sweetly. "You look happy."

He grunted, because he didn't know what to say to all *that.* "Gonna shower," he muttered, turning away and moving out of the kitchen opening.

"Heed my advice," Grandma called after him. "Lock that girl down quick."

"Grandma's right," Molly added, even as Shane trudged up the stairs. "Plenty of nice-looking cowboys out there could sweep her off her feet."

"Ha." The thing was, locking Cora down didn't seem like such a bad idea. But he didn't have much to offer, and hadn't he made a few mistakes when deciding he was all in long before the other person did?

Hell, Cora had been asking about space just this morning, while she'd still been half asleep. Maybe he needed to heed the warnings of his past and slow down a bit.

He just had the sneaking suspicion that once she was in his orbit again, he wouldn't be able to help himself.

Chapter Nineteen

Cora hummed to herself as she drove up to Mile High headquarters to pick up Micah. She'd had a perfect day. Awash in a post-sex, post-sleep-in morning, she'd ticked off just about every stray errand and chore on her to-do list.

Once she got Micah home and showered, she had a dinner with the Tylers to look forward to. Micah got to hang out with his beloved horses, and the world seemed aglow with goodness and possibility.

Which was far too good to be true.

She forced that Debbie Downer thought out of her head as she pulled her car into the lot of Mile High Adventures. Sam, Hayley, and Micah were unloading things out of the Jeep.

She got out of the car, gratified when Micah grinned at her and scrambled over. All limbs and enthusiasm. Thank *God*.

"Did you have fun?" she asked, pulling him into a hug.

He let her hug him for about a second, then bounced out of her reach. "We saw a bear! Seriously!"

"From hundreds of yards away with my very high-powered binoculars," Sam assured Cora, still unloading things from his Jeep.

"It was *so* cool." Micah happily took the backpack Hayley handed him. "Hey, before we head home do you think we could stop by the ranch and see the horses?"

"Well, matter of fact, Shane asked us if we wanted to come over for dinner tonight."

There was the slightest hesitation at the mention of Shane, but the horses must have won out because Micah nodded. "Cool."

"I'm going to go give the babies hugs first. Coming?"

"Eh, sure, I guess," Micah said with a negligent shrug, but Micah had shocked the heck out of her when the twins were born. Oh, he acted tough and uninterested, but, any time an adult wasn't paying too close attention, that boy gave them nothing but love. "I have to help set up the tents to air out first."

She gave him another squeeze before he wriggled out of it. "My little responsible camper."

Micah groaned on his way over to help Sam and Hayley heft stuff out of the Jeep and then to the backyard of Mile High Adventures, where they'd do whatever they did with tents and tools. Cora tried not to know.

She headed inside and offered a greeting to Skeet, who merely grunted at her from his near-permanent spot behind the reception desk. He was wearing a T-shirt that read *my dog ate your stick-figure family*.

"Skeet, how do you feel about swords?"

The old man's white eyebrows drew together as he stared at her. "Huh?"

"I think I have the perfect woman for you."

Skeet scowled and made a shooing motion. "Lilly's in her office."

Grinning to herself, Cora walked through the main room and to the little hallway that led to the individual offices. She didn't bother knocking on Lilly's door since Lilly sometimes had the babies sleeping in there.

But when she pushed the door open, Cora groaned and squeezed her eyes shut. "Oh, God. Stop that you two." When she dared open her eyes, Lilly and Brandon had only moderately stopped *that*. In that their mouths were no longer fused together, but they still had their arms around each other.

Lilly grinned at her. "Well, knock."

"I was trying to be considerate of the babies." She gestured at the playpen where Aiden and Grace happily gurgled at each other. "Aren't babies supposed to cure you of all that?" she asked, gesturing at Brandon and Lilly's linked forms.

"Not cured, just desperate for the occasional moment of peace. We'll take it where we can get it."

Brandon, who at least had the decency to look a *little* shamed, unwound himself from Lilly. "I've got to go make those calls. Do you want me to take one?"

Lilly waved it off. "Make your calls first. They're liable to start screaming the minute you get a hold of someone."

Brandon nodded, kissing Lilly quickly on the cheek, then dropping a sweet pat on each of the babies' heads before exiting the office.

"I know it's a lot to ask. . . ."

"But you need a babysitter for the babies so you and Brandon can get it on."

Lilly chuckled. "Please. *Please.* I'll owe you eight million favors. I swear the second that man's penis gets anywhere near naked they start screaming."

"Little baby cock blockers," Cora cooed at them, earning a groan from Lilly. "Sure. I'd do it tonight, but I already told Micah we could go over to the Tyler ranch. What about tomorrow?"

"That'll work." Lilly's gaze zeroed in on Cora, that

I can read your mind if I try hard enough look. "The Tylers again?"

"Micah's loving the riding lessons," Cora returned, irritated to feel her face warming.

"Can you afford that?"

The warmth died into a cold chill. "Yes, I can afford that," Cora snapped.

Lilly winced. "I'm sorry. Old habits."

"Right," Cora said, smiling thinly. She didn't want to blow up at Lilly, and she really should be used to it, but it still smarted. Those old wounds never did seem to fully heal. She opened her mouth to make her excuses to leave, but Lilly spoke first.

"Tori said there was a cowboy at your door last night."

Cora's mood went even further south. "Tori is a loud-mouth."

"When were you going to tell me about him?"

Cora heaved out a sigh. "I don't know, when I thought you wouldn't question my judgment." So, *never*.

"Cora . . ."

Cora didn't dare look at her sister. She knew she'd see hurt there. "I . . . I just need to do some things without your old habits right now," Cora managed, being as non-accusatory as she could. Because none of this was about Lilly. It was about Cora trying to get herself together without Lilly's interference.

"I know. I've been backing off though. I've been doing a good job, haven't I?" Lilly nodded toward the playpen. "They've helped me mellow. But that doesn't mean I don't want us to be sisters or friends."

"Well, of course we're sisters and friends." Cora blew out a breath, forcing herself to look at Lilly and all that hurt. "We work together. I . . . I love you. I'm just still building myself up. I need to be strong enough to tell you to back off."

Lilly's mouth curved just a hint. "I think you just did."

Cora let that realization sink in. She had, without even second-guessing herself, pushed Lilly back. For possibly the first time in her life without being immature, mean, or petulant.

Every once in a while a moment like that washed over her, when she could see and *feel* the changes she'd made—the maturing and the healing—and it was something like hitting a brick wall at full force.

Followed by a welcome rush of pride and joy. She was *doing* this thing. Changing and growing and getting better.

Lilly stepped forward, gently grabbing her by the elbows. "I hope you know how proud I am of you. All you've done in the past year to get your life together. I've tried really hard to butt out. I'm sorry when I fall back into that place of wanting to control things for you."

"I know you mean well." People always did when they wanted to protect and care for a person. Maybe that was the true thing broken inside of her: she couldn't accept care or protection or maybe even love without turning into the worst version of herself.

She pushed that thought away. She wasn't broken. She was healing. What she felt for Shane wasn't that grasping, desperate need to fill an empty spot within herself. She hadn't been down and alone when he'd sauntered into her life. She'd been in a good place, and Shane only added to it, didn't torpedo her down into that worst version. He did that all without asking for anything in return.

"Then can't you tell me about Mr. Cowboy?" Lilly asked hopefully. "As a sister and a friend. Not as someone who might pass judgment or force her advice on you."

Cora stared at her sister. The identical blue eyes, and all that hope in them. Lilly had always had to be more mother than sister, more authoritarian than friend, but that *was* the past, and part of maturing and healing for Cora was trusting herself enough to choose relationships that could be equal. Being the one in charge of making sure they stood on equal ground, not letting or wanting anyone else to take over.

"Well, he's a rancher. Handsome. Sweet. And way too good . . ." *for me.* But she didn't allow herself to verbalize the thought. She deserved some good too. "He's so good I'm almost afraid he's a figment of my imagination."

Lilly propelled Cora into her desk chair. "I like where that's going," she said, rubbing her hands together. "He's good with Micah?"

"So sweet and patient. He's the oldest of five kids, and he takes care of the ranch and his family with kindness and protectiveness, and they all just accepted Micah right into that without a second thought. I've never seen anything like it." She glanced down at Aiden's dark head and thought of her brother-in-law, who had been kind and protective when it came to Lilly and the babies. "Rarely seen anyway."

Lilly smiled softly. "It's hard to believe, I know, but there are some really good guys out there. I'm glad you found one."

Cora stared down at her hands. The truth was, she wanted to confide in Lilly about not telling Shane about her past. About Micah's fears. But didn't that put her on uneven ground again? Asking for help instead of figuring it out herself.

"You don't seem ecstatic."

"I'm scared," Cora replied, the honesty falling right out of her. Then she laughed. How stupid she sounded. "I know I'm forever falling in lust with a guy and calling it love, or just wanting it to be love and calling it that, but this is different and scary and awful and too damn soon, and I think it might be love."

Lilly laughed. "Oh, that sounds all too familiar and thus all too possible."

Cora glanced up at Lilly's bemused face. "You were kind of a mess when you were falling for Brandon."

"Kind of?" Lilly scoffed. "The biggest mess I'd ever been. Rather determined to screw it all up out of fear too, because I could not admit to myself or anyone else I was afraid. I think you're a step ahead of me, sis."

Cora breathed in a deep breath and let it out. "Step ahead. Well, there's a first time for everything."

Lilly reached down into the playpen and picked up a fussing Grace. "I hope you'll let us meet him."

"Oh. Right." Cora tried to imagine the Tylers and Evanses together and . . . Actually, it wasn't that hard to imagine. Brandon and Lilly might be all business and polish, and the Tylers might be all no-nonsense ranch people, but they were one devoted group.

"I'm going to go change Gracie's diaper. Can you keep an eye on Aiden?"

Cora nodded. Lilly disappeared, and, when Cora's cell rang, she answered it absently without even looking at who was calling. "Hello?"

"You sound distracted."

She smiled at the sound of Shane's voice. "Funny how that happens when I was up all night for nefariously dirty reasons."

He chuckled. "Nefarious, huh?"

"The nefarious-est."

She loved the baffled sound to his laugh, as if he couldn't help himself but to find her charming, no matter how ridiculous she was.

"How was Micah's camping trip?"

It warmed her that he would call, call to ask *that*.

"Good. He saw a bear, though Sam assured me it was from an appropriate distance."

"I'm sure that eased your mind completely."

"Oh, yes, bears and my son didn't give me a panic attack *at all.*"

"Of course. You still up for dinner? Mom's planning a big old barbecue. Any special requests from either of you two?"

"No, we'll eat anything I don't cook," Cora returned, earning another laugh. Oh, hell, she was scarily in head over her heels with him. "You know, I was just talking to my sister. She wants to meet you."

"Well, I want to meet her too. Why don't you invite her and her family tonight? Mom put us boys in charge of grilling. Mol's in town getting groceries. I'll text her to pick up a few more."

"I don't want to—"

"Bring them," he insisted. Then there was an odd pause, and if she had been reading into things she might've called it uncertainty. "If you want to, that is."

"I do. I do want to." It scared her to want things like this, this much.

"It's settled then. See you in a bit, okay?"

"Yeah, okay." More than okay, really. "Shane?"

"Yeah."

"I . . ." What idiot said that after one not-even-date and over the phone? Not this idiot. "I wanted to say thanks for last night. Best date I've ever not been on."

He laughed. "We'll try again."

"Can we fail again, too? I really liked the failing part."

"I'll make sure of it. See you soon, Cora."

"Bye," she managed, feeling so many things at once she could hardly grasp any of them as she hit End on her phone.

She looked up to find Micah in the doorway giving

her one of those unreadable stares. She smiled at him, feeling a little too off-kilter right now to face that look straight on. "You ready to go?"

Micah only nodded.

Shane was flipping burgers when he spotted Cora's car on the crest of the hill. It was followed by a truck, which had to be her family.

Shane wasn't sure why he felt queasy. He was good with people, and Cora's sister and brother-in-law weren't likely to hate him on sight.

Probably.

"Looking a little green there, pal," Gavin offered with a grin. "Worried about the family's approval? Well, this is serious."

"Bite me," Shane muttered without much heat. He wasn't afraid of serious. Didn't particularly like getting razzed on it, but he wasn't afraid.

"Mattie's parents loved you. Maybe it'll be good luck if Cora's family hates you."

Cora stepped out of her car, offering a smile and a wave. Micah jumped out of the car too, already racing toward Boone.

"Cora isn't anything like Mattie," Shane mumbled, watching Cora wait for her sister and brother-in-law to pull two small babies out of the truck's back seat. Back then he'd loved Mattie, yes, but he'd wanted to marry her because he'd wanted things to be settled. He'd wanted to start his future.

With Cora, he just wanted to *be* with her. Much as he could.

"Hey, guys," Micah said breathlessly, his gaze bouncing from face to face. "Is Molly here? Can I get a ride in?"

Shane couldn't hide a grin. A kid's enthusiasm when

he was head over heels for horses was hard to beat. "Dinner is just about ready, but I bet if you're real sweet to her, Molly'll give you a lesson after we eat."

"Awesome," Micah managed, looking back at the approaching Cora and company. "Babies are gross," he offered, nodding toward the two bundles being carried by a large, bearded man and a woman who looked an awful lot like Cora, down to eye color and sweet dimple. "But my cousins are okay."

"You want to head over to the stables real quick? I'll take you over," Boone offered. "Gotta hear about this bear."

"It was *gigantic*," Micah said gleefully, and Shane tried to ignore the slight pang of jealousy. Boone would always be infinitely cooler, and Shane just had to accept it.

Micah scurried off with Boone, and Cora approached, looking nervous. He didn't mind it. "Take over the grill," he said, handing off the spatula to Gavin.

"Cora got any more sisters?" Gavin asked after a low whistle. "Damn."

"Manners, idiot," Shane returned before heading to meet Cora. "Howdy," he offered, tipping his hat because he knew it would knock at least a little of the nervousness out of her.

She rolled her eyes. "He's just being a dork. He does not actually say howdy," she offered to her sister. "Lilly, Brandon, this is Shane. Shane, my sister and her husband, and my niece Grace and my nephew Aiden."

The bundle of girl yawned. The bundle of boy babbled.

"It's nice to meet you all. We're just having a laid-back, picnic-type meal tonight. Everything's about ready." He gestured toward the picnic tables where Mom and Molly were setting up.

Mom, as if she could just sense the appearance of new people, hustled over, Ben trudging behind her. "Lilly, Brandon." Of course Mom already knew them from dealing with Mile High Weddings. "I'm so happy you could come over. And with your little ones." She held out her arms. "Oh, please let me hold one."

Brandon transferred the boy lump to Mom, and she sighed happily. "Oh, it's like I can't even remember when they were this tiny." Mom cuddled the baby to her chest while Ben shifted uncomfortably next to her.

"Better, uh, help Gavin with the burgers." Ben high-tailed it to the grill.

"Never had kids of his own. Babies make him squeam-ish. Well, come on, you two, well four, come eat. Eat, eat, eat," Mom said, ushering Lilly and Brandon toward the tables while Gavin and Ben took plates of meat to the warmers Molly had set up.

"I should go get Micah," Cora said, taking a step toward the stables.

Shane stopped her. "I'll grab him," he offered, squeez-ing Cora's arm. "You load up your plate."

She smiled up at him, then got to her toes and brushed her mouth across his.

"What did I get that for?"

She grinned up at him. "Guess you're just pretty or something."

He grinned down at her. "I know your sister is here and all, but I plan on sneaking you away later."

She bit her lip, giving him a once-over. "I'll hold you to that, cowboy," she murmured before sauntering off after Lilly and Brandon.

Shane walked over to the stables, more than just *pleased* with himself and how things were going. But as he entered the building, Boone's voice interrupted all that peace and contentment.

"Long as your mom says it's okay, you can come with us. It's about three days, and we drive the cattle—"

"No." The command came out of his mouth before

Shane even thought of it, before Boone or Micah had even realized he was there.

Boone turned slowly, that icy cold look in his eye. "You're not in charge of me, Shane."

"No, but I am in charge of this ranch, and, unfortunately, Micah's age makes him a liability." He noted Micah's mutinous expression and did what he could to assuage it, though he knew, thanks to Boone, he was going to be the bad guy no matter what. "I'm sorry, Micah. Those are the rules. They always have been the rules. I can't change them when they're there for safety reasons."

"But Boone said—"

"Boone was wrong and spoke out of turn. We can't have anyone on the cattle drive under the age of fifteen. That's the beginning and end of it."

"It doesn't have to be," Boone said.

"Yes, it does. You've been home for a few weeks tops. You don't get to sweep in and change things. We're talking about a kid's safety here. Not your pride."

"Fuck you."

"Maybe you should stay away from the kid since you can't seem to control your mouth."

"Whatever," Micah mumbled. "I don't even care." Then he stormed out of the stables, very clearly *caring*.

"You're being a dick," Boone growled, pressing his luck.

"You're being completely irresponsible. You cannot take a twelve-year-old who is still just getting used to horses on that kind of drive."

"You and Gavin went all the time when you were kids. I'm not stupid. You ended that practice because you didn't want the rest of us underfoot, not because it was *dangerous*."

"I ended that practice because people got hurt,"

Shane bit out. He did everything in his power to keep his temper under control, but screw Boone for always swooping in, trying to be the fun-time guy.

"Who?"

Oh, he wanted to go down this road? Fine. "You really buy the story Dad died accidentally with no interference?"

"What the fuck does that mean?"

"Nothing." He was not losing it like this over something so small. Much as he hated to admit it, he was more angry with Boone for making him the bad guy with Micah than anything else. That didn't excuse this outburst though. "Like I said, I'm in charge. On this matter, what I say goes."

"Oh, hell no, you don't get to shut it down. What did you mean? Dad did die accidentally."

"Yeah, he did."

Boone took a step forward and fisted his hand in Shane's shirt. Shane resisted the urge to push him away. He would not get in a fistfight with his *injured* brother. Not with Cora out there, that was for damn sure.

"Then what did you mean?" Boone asked in a low, threatening tone.

"It means it was an accident, but it could have been avoided." Shane hadn't told anyone this. Not even Mom. Not Cora, not Gavin, no one. "I was underfoot, about got myself trampled. Dad saved me, and *that's* how he died. Keeping my ass alive. So. Yeah, an accident, but one that wouldn't have happened if he'd kept kids out of it. Next time you want to include Micah on something, you run it by me first."

"Because you're his daddy?" Boone asked, giving Shane a hard shove as he released him. A bubbling fury in his gaze that stoked Shane's own.

"Because I'm the only adult around here. I'm the

only one who takes responsibility for anyone else. You're going to listen to me because I'm the foreman. Because I'm the oldest. Because I damn well know what I'm talking about. You ran away, Boone. You played with your bulls and got your ass handed to you. Now, you're back. Well, you're going to have to prove you belong."

"Fuck you," Boone said, limping toward the stable doors.

"Yeah, right back at you," Shane muttered, scrubbing his hands over his face. That had all been so out of control, so out of hand, and what had he been thinking, letting all that old, buried shit slip to *Boone* of all people?

Shane gave himself a few minutes to get it back together. To calm himself. To focus on what needed to be done. A nice dinner. Getting to know Cora's family. Hopefully smoothing things over with Micah.

And Boone could go straight to hell.

Chapter Twenty

Cora knew something was seriously up. If she hadn't noticed Micah running out of the stables, then insisting nothing was wrong, or Boone's follow-up storm out of the stables after which he went into the house with a loud slam of the door . . . and never came back throughout the whole meal, she'd still have known something was wrong.

Shane was tense. Oh, he tried to hide it with smiles and idle conversation with Brandon and Lilly, but everything in his posture, in the way he held himself was iron-rod straight. Painfully controlled.

Throughout the whole meal Micah was silent and sullen, sending Shane nasty looks when he thought Cora wasn't watching him.

Cora didn't want to make a big deal about it in front of Lilly, so she had to squash her curiosity best she could and fake her smiles and ease just like Shane was doing.

She helped the Tyler girls clear up the dishes while Shane cleaned the grill and Micah and Brandon took care of the babies. Lilly and Brandon and crew said their good-byes, and Cora knew she should too, but she needed to hear about what had happened from Shane as much as she needed to hear about it from Micah.

Micah was playing with Ben's dog, and most of the cleanup was accomplished. She caught Shane's gaze across the yard, and one corner of his mouth ticked up.

He crossed to her, and, before she even had to say anything, he held out a hand. "Walk?"

She nodded, noting that Shane nodded over at Molly, a clear sign to keep her eye on Micah.

"So, what happened?" she asked as they slowly walked what was becoming their normal path. Away from the house, toward the mountains, in the pretty glow of a fading summer day.

Shane sighed, adjusting his hat. Funny, he always seemed to do that when he wanted a little more control of the situation. She squeezed his hand, because she wanted to be here for him, and she liked that she could read him.

"Maybe I should let Micah tell you, but I'm afraid he might color my role in it a bit."

"I want the Shane version and the Micah version. I'm also curious about the Boone version." She smiled at him, hoping for a softening.

She didn't get it. If anything, Shane only got tenser. His jaw hard, that determined, almost cold look in his eye she remembered from their first meeting, when he'd been dead certain his mother wouldn't be marrying Ben.

But then he brought their joined hands to his mouth and brushed his lips across the top of her hand. He smiled ruefully. "Unfortunately, Micah was the middle man in a pissing match I shouldn't have gotten into with my brother."

They walked toward the mountains, hand-in-hand, and there was something so picture-perfect about it.

Yeah, there was a problem, but she was talking it out with a good, honest man who held her hand. Someone who wanted to fix it, not cast blame or land punches.

"Boone suggested taking Micah on a cattle drive the ranch is doing next week. I refused. We don't let kids on this kind of thing. Unfortunately, even if we did, Micah isn't experienced enough with the horses yet. So, I had to put my foot down. It's too dangerous. We can't risk his safety like that."

Emotion clogged Cora's throat. Micah's own father had once pushed Micah into a wall, Cora's last straw in the Stephen department. But this man, who was nothing to Micah all in all, wanted her baby to be safe even if it made Micah *and* Boone mad. Not because he was trying to impress her, but because it was good and right.

She stopped walking, and he stopped too, looking at her with something like pain in his dark brown eyes. "I'm sorry. I am. But I feel strongly about this. It's too dangerous."

She moved her arms around his neck, giving him a tight squeeze, afraid words like *love* would tumble out of her mouth if she dared open it.

Shane hugged her back. "What's that for?"

She kept her arms around him, but pulled back enough that she could look at him. Oh, she wanted to tell him she was head over heels in love with him. She wanted to tell him everything that had ever happened to her and have him soothe it away with his sympathy, his care.

That would never do. "You're the best man I know, Shane," she said, irritated with herself when her voice broke a little.

"Cora." He reached up, cupping her face with his big, rough hands, those brown eyes serious and intent on hers. As if he was going to say something important. Meaningful.

Oh, God, say it, maybe I'll feel a little less out of my mind.

"Cora, I—"

"Mom, can we go?" Micah demanded in a shout from a few yards off.

Cora eyed her son. Angry. Vibrating with it. She sighed. A year ago she might've given in to it. But Lilly and Dr. Grove had both encouraged her to set limits, to *discuss* anger rather than give in to it.

So, she pressed her mouth to Shane's, in a much more chaste display of affection than she would have given if they were alone. "Thank you for dinner. We'll see you tomorrow."

Shane looked over at Micah, and there was such a gentleness and an understanding in this man. "I hope I see both of you." He gave her one last brief hug before releasing her. He tipped his hat at Micah before walking back toward where his family was gathered.

"He's a jerk," Micah spat.

Cora couldn't remember the last time she'd seen him this *angry*. Sad or detached. Hurt or grumpy, yeah, but not . . . this. But he also wasn't used to not getting everything he wanted when he wanted it. She'd set a bad precedent of giving him too much leeway to try to make up for all the mistakes she'd made.

But she was a different woman now, and she would be a better mom. Like Deb. "You don't mean that," Cora returned calmly. "You're only mad he said you couldn't do something."

"Boone knows more than he does."

"Maybe about riding bulls or whatever it was he did in the rodeo, but I trust Shane's judgment when it comes to ranch things. I really trust his judgment when it comes to keeping you safe."

"Boone said—"

"Micah, I know you like Boone. I like him too. But Shane has your safety at heart, and that's the most important thing to me."

Micah didn't say anything, and she wouldn't allow herself to go further and apologize for not keeping him safe when he was younger. She'd made those apologies. She might never forgive herself completely, but she had to move on from that guilt-driven space. In the here and now she had to be the mom she hadn't been then.

"I know you're upset you can't be involved, but that doesn't mean you can't ever be. If you take your lessons seriously for the next few years—"

Micah scoffed. "Like we'll be around in the next few years."

"You don't know—"

"I know," Micah muttered, stomping off. "I'll wait in the car."

Cora stood in the middle of the Tyler ranch, wholly at a loss, but she looked back at the pretty house where Boone, Molly, and Gavin were sitting around talking with their mother and Ben. Not perfect, by any means, but good. Kind.

That existed in the world, and she would do everything in her power to keep it a part of her life. She couldn't expect Micah to believe her. He'd been through too many years of her worst, but she could prove it to him. Day after day. Year after year.

They finally had something good, and Cora was going to keep it.

Shane didn't head back to his family, though he'd started to. But before he'd reached them, Boone had come outside. Shane didn't feel like smoothing that over right now. He was too raw.

He'd never been the kind of guy to get worked up if someone didn't like him. Being in charge of his siblings, of ranch hands, he was used to making some enemies along the way.

It ate him up that Micah didn't like him, and yeah, maybe that was wrapped up in not knowing how to reach Boone. How to bridge that gap of bitterness Shane didn't understand.

Shane sighed and kept walking aimlessly around the ranch. He hadn't meant to end up at the family cemetery, but somehow that's where he was.

He slipped off his hat and walked the well-worn path to Dad's grave. He'd spent something like twenty years coming here: apologizing, bargaining, promising, begging for guidance.

Tonight he didn't feel much like doing anything. Twenty years of never quite explaining the whole of what happened with Dad. Keeping it buried below protecting and responsibility and a million other things.

"I don't know why I said anything," Shane murmured, gaze trained on his father's name. *Owen Todd Tyler: Beloved Son, Husband, Father, and Rancher.* "Doesn't change anything, does it?" Except maybe talking did change things. Could it heal the rift between him and Boone, or was it always going to be anger, bitterness, and blame?

"Hell if I know," Shane muttered. "Hell if I know anything, but you always told me to keep going. So, that's what I'll do."

"You really think the dead can hear you?"

When Shane whirled on Ben, he held his hands up.

"Don't try to hit me, your ma sent me."

"I wasn't going to hit you," Shane grumbled. He rocked back on his heels and sighed. "Who knows? Maybe the dead can hear you. Maybe they can't. I figure the talking is more for the alive anyway."

"Huh. You might be right."

Shane eyed the man, not at all trusting his solicitous tone. "Why did my mother send you?"

Ben raked a hand through his hair. "She's got me doing all sorts of shit. Help Molly with a lesson. Go shooting with Gavin. Talk bulls with Boone. You know, I fell in love with your mother. Didn't mean I planned on being some kind of fucking stepdad. I hate kids."

"You're literally ten years older than me."

"Yeah, well, *she* doesn't see you all that way."

"Why are you here, Ben?" Shane asked, too tired to fight or beat around the bush or whatever this was.

"Deb wants me to be part of this Denver trip you're all planning for next week. I put up a good fight, but she's having none of it, and I'm already in the doghouse for . . . Well, none of your damn business."

Shane tensed. "You're not—"

"She wants me to go, and I'm going. But I'll mostly keep my mouth shut."

"Mostly," Shane returned wryly. Because he needed Boone *and* Ben up his ass, while he took Micah to a baseball game, while the kid probably still hated him.

Silence stretched around them, just the breeze through the trees and the heavy quiet of the dead.

"You know, I had a brother just like you," Ben offered conversationally after a while of not taking the hint to disappear.

"Let me guess, you were best buddies," Shane said dryly.

"Couldn't stand the prick. Told him and the rest of 'em where to stuff it. Haven't been back in something like twenty-five years." He glanced at the gravestones. "Didn't think I'd ever care if they were dead or alive," he murmured. "Your mom is one hell of a confusing woman. You think you're forty-some years old and you've got your ways stuck deep down in you, then a woman comes along and messes it all up."

"Are we having a heart-to-heart, Ben?"

"Fuck no." He shoved his hands into his pockets. "Hell, maybe. And it's all Deb's fault. Always on me about feelings. Opening up. Being a better man. Spent forty years not wanting to be a better man. Then she comes along and . . . fuck."

Shane didn't want to be amused, didn't want to have to see all this *human* in Ben at this particular moment in his life. But, he hadn't wanted to lose Dad. Hadn't wanted a lot of things in this life, and yet he had a pretty good one.

"I know you don't see what I give her," Ben said, his voice hushed in the quiet solitude of the tree-lined cemetery. "But that's because she's your ma. She's not Deb to you. Just like I'm not the bad seed to her. Labels, good or bad, they make you lose yourself sometimes, and the people who remind you of who you are beyond it tend to . . . Well, it feels good."

Shane stared at his father's grave, thought of Cora and Micah and thought maybe he understood that a little bit. Here at the ranch he was the annoying older brother, or the boss man, but he wasn't often just *Shane*.

When Cora looked at him, hell even when Micah was pissed at him, Shane felt like something other than an automaton or dictator. He just felt like a . . . guy.

Mom had run this family and this ranch on her own for so long, and she'd done it all without ever appearing as a real, individual woman to Shane, or probably any of the kids. She was Mom. She was the boss lady. Maybe Ben was right and she deserved to be *Deb* every now and again.

"You came to me the other day, and you were upfront and honest," Ben continued. "I haven't been around that much in my life, so it's hard to trust it. Rather have a pissing match, have people think the worst so you can't fuck it up, but I'm . . . Well, I'm . . . Hell, I'll never be a good man, but for Deb I'll at least try. That's all I'm saying about this shit. You don't like it, that's your own damn problem."

And it was that, the way Ben had let his guard down and flung it back up, just like Boone and even Gavin were forever doing, that really got to Shane. Because guards were for safety, to keep your heart from being bruised or from hurting other people. It was why he'd never told the whole story of Dad's dying to anyone. It was why he'd only ever told Cora everything about Mattie. A guard around himself.

Ben was certainly not a good man, no, and Shane figured his mother deserved the best. But maybe the best out there was a man who would try, just for her.

Shane cleared his throat. "I want to be the one to tell her, but just FYI, I'll walk her down the aisle."

There was a long silence in the fading twilight, and for the first time since the fight with Boone, Shane felt a little peace. Maybe it was for the living to read signs into things, but he'd allow himself to believe it was Dad letting him know everything would be okay.

"I told her I'd sign a prenup," Ben grumbled, barely audibly. "Oh, she got all up in arms about it, but I don't want this ranch. Who wants that kind of responsibility? I'd rather shovel shit till I bite the dust."

"You know, if we'd talked this all out a few months ago, we could have avoided a lot of frustration and arguments." Shane slid a look at Ben.

Who grinned that irritating, don't-give-a-shit grin. "Where'd be the fun in that?" he asked, clapping Shane on the back once, and hard, before he walked away, out of the trees that shaded the cemetery.

Shane reached out and touched his father's grave. He still didn't know what to do about Micah or Boone, but at least progress had been made on one problem. "Thanks," he murmured, before heading back to the house himself, at least a little more determined to fix the problems still in front of him.

Chapter Twenty-One

Cora was nervous. If it had just been Shane and her driving to Denver and taking Micah to a baseball game, she'd have been fine, but this was a whole Tyler family excursion. There'd been talk of Micah "riding with the boys" and her "riding with the girls" and everything felt . . . big.

Weighted.

Which was her own head stuff.

"Can't we drive ourselves?" Micah grumbled as Cora checked the contents of her bag. This was technically a work excursion as she'd be accompanying Deb and the girls to try on dresses. They were way behind on that front with the moved-up wedding date.

"Not if you want to go to the baseball game. We're meeting you boys there. Would you rather come with me while the girls try on dresses?" Cora asked sweetly.

He merely groaned, flopping dramatically onto the couch for about the fiftieth time. She peered over the back of the couch at him.

"Is there something you want to talk about?"

His irritated expression blanked. "No."

"Because you can talk to me."

"Why? So you can take his side?"

"No." Cora breathed through her frustration, reminding herself twelve-year-olds weren't known for common sense. "I know you think agreeing with Shane is taking his side, but I'm on your side. I want you to be safe. So, on this, I have to agree with Shane."

"Whatever."

"Oh, gee, I just *love* that word," Cora muttered. "Next time you ask for dinner I'll just say *whatever* and move on."

Micah's mouth twitched, so she kept going. "Mom," she said, mimicking him. "I ran out of TP. Bring me some?" She adopted her own voice. "Sounds like a *you* problem. *Whatever.*"

He made a sound, clearly trying very hard to make it not a laugh.

"Believe it or not, I have a mind of my own. It's not infallible, but it does have your best interest at heart. You won't always agree, and when you're an adult you're free to do any number of things I don't agree with and break my heart."

"Yeah, yeah." Micah's expression did that blank thing again, the one that made her heart twist so hard she wanted to cry. "If he knew, he probably wouldn't want us around, you know."

Cora swallowed at the lump in her throat, wishing she could pretend she didn't know what he meant. "I don't believe that. He'd treat us differently, but he wouldn't disappear."

Micah shrugged, and she couldn't have that conversation. Not when she was so hung up on Shane. She had to find a way to arrange these pieces in herself a little better. Then she could calmly and rationally discuss it with Micah.

Dr. Grove would be proud.

A knock sounded on the door, and Cora forced herself to breathe in and let it all go out. She had a job to do with the dresses, then she had some fun to have with her boyfriend and son.

End of story.

She opened the door to find Shane standing there, cowboy hat pulled low. Her heart just *flipped* at the sight of him, but she'd be careful with that feeling. She *would*. No old Cora allowed. Shane would make all the first moves.

The scariest part was she trusted that he would. She *trusted* this feeling between him and her, no matter how many times the nasty voices in her head told her she was crazy and foolish.

"Hi."

His mouth curved into that knowing, sexy smile. She wondered if he was thinking about the last time he'd been here. *She* certainly was. "I don't suppose we could ditch everybody and head upstairs?" she asked on a whisper so Micah wouldn't hear.

Shane chuckled. "No, I don't think that one would fly. You guys ready?" He glanced at his watch. "Mom's getting antsy about making her appointment."

"Yup. Come on, Micah," she called, rechecking her bag one last time.

Micah trudged to the door. His response to Shane's greeting was a grunt, but Cora had to admit she was surprised he'd given that much.

She stepped out onto the porch, shoving her key into the doorknob to lock it. When she glanced at the two cars parked in front of her house, she squinted. "Is that Ben?"

Shane glanced back at the truck parked behind the little sedan. Ben was indeed in the front seat, Gavin standing next to the back door, waiting for Micah to crawl into the middle seat next to Boone.

Micah bounded over, clearly happy with the seating arrangements.

"Uh, yeah, Ben and I had a bit of a talk the other day."

"And you're just telling me about it now?"

"We need some alone time. Which is why I have a surprise for you tonight."

"Go on."

"It's called a surprise, Cora. I don't explain it to you. You wait and see what it is." He grinned down at her as they walked down the stairs of the porch.

"Hmm. I'm not sure I like surprises."

"Well, you can tell me after this one shakes out if you want more. You girls have fun now."

"Good luck with the troublemaker," Cora offered, nodding toward the truck.

Shane raised an eyebrow. "Which damn one?" he asked on a laugh.

"Would you hurry up?" Boone yelled irritably.

"He has to kiss her good-bye first," Molly shouted from her rolled-down window.

"A good one too," Deb added from the driver's seat.

"Don't listen to the women," Gavin called. "Brainless creatures."

"Don't think I won't kick your ass when we get to Denver," Molly shouted back at him.

"Be glad we're separated," Shane said quietly, brushing his mouth across her cheek. "Enjoy your day. See you at the game."

She couldn't help but grin all the way to the car, where she slid into the back, trying not to blush and look like, well, what she was. A besotted moron.

Molly grinned back at her. "You two are the sweetest damn thing."

Cora blushed deeper, her cheeks practically on fire. "Well, anyway." Then she heard the unmistakable sound of Deb crying. Cora's eyes widened. "What? What's wrong?"

Deb sniffled, wiping at her cheeks. "Oh, you two just make each other happy. I was starting to worry Shane wouldn't find that for himself."

Then Molly sniffled.

"No, don't start," Cora begged. "My God, we're just dating. It's nothing to get all . . ." But her own tears were starting to well up. "Well, hell, I didn't think I was going to find much romantic happy for myself either."

They all laughed and cried at the same time as Deb pulled the car onto the street. "Second chances are a beautiful thing." With one hand she reached over and patted her daughter. "You'll find one too."

"Oh, I'm not ready to think about that," Molly said, passing a box of tissues back to Cora. "But it's nice to know it's possible, I guess."

"I was incredibly blessed to love my first husband, and we lost him too soon, but he and his parents made me realize love is the best gift we can give each other. And the hardest damn thing we give to ourselves, but worth it. When you're both in it, it's so darn worth it."

The hardest damn thing we give to ourselves. Oh, wasn't that the truth.

"Fuck, are we ever going to get there?"

Shane glared at Boone in the rearview mirror. He opened his mouth to scold him on his language, but what was the point? Boone probably only swore more to piss Shane off.

They'd made it to Denver, eaten lunch, and walked around town a bit. Micah had slowly eased his *Shane is the devil* attitude, and Shane hadn't been able to resist buying him a cowboy hat.

Micah wore it now in the back seat as Shane navigated traffic for the baseball game.

"What, you worried about missing batting practice? Didn't remember your having much patience for baseball," Gavin said.

Boone shifted in the seat. "Sitting and walking around is killing my leg. You try getting trampled by bulls and then being shoved into a tin can of a back seat."

"How many bones have you broken?" Micah asked, though Shane noticed there was an odd note to his voice. Not that same hero worship, but something more . . . calculated. Weird.

"Lost count somewhere along the way. Bet I've got a fan out there who could tell you though," Boone offered.

Shane tried not to roll his eyes.

"Mom's had a ton of broken bones too," Micah said.

"Yeah, she a brawler on the side?" Boone asked, tousling Micah's hair.

There was a beat of silence, and, when Shane glanced in the mirror again, Micah's gaze was right on his. "My dad," he said precisely, carefully, as if he really wanted Shane to get those two words lodged into his brain.

Shane couldn't make sense of it at first, but a dread crept around the edges as it slowly clicked into place. The air in the car seemed to grow heavier as they all came to realize what Micah meant.

The truck hit the rumble strip, and Shane had to rip his gaze back to the road. He had to think, and breathe. Funny, he couldn't manage it until he cleared his throat. "Your dad . . ." He couldn't say it. Couldn't physically push the words out of his mouth.

"Used to beat her up all the time," Micah said, as

though talking about a slight inconvenience. "Only did it to me once."

Christ. He wasn't sure if he thought the curse or said it out loud. Shane stared hard at the road. He could feel Ben's gaze on him, but Shane had to focus on navigating the baseball game traffic.

No one said anything else, not as he drove, not as he parked. They filed out of the truck in a grim silence. Micah was the only one who seemed okay.

Shane didn't know what to do with that any more than he knew what to do with the information.

They started walking for the stadium entrance, Ben and Boone flanking Micah and Gavin and Shane walking behind them. While jovial attendees filed in around them, their little group was completely silent as they handed over their tickets at the gate, then found their seats.

"Hey, you want to come with me to get some snacks, kid?" Ben asked, standing and looking around.

"Sure," Micah offered, following Ben back up the stairs.

Shane let out a breath he hadn't realized had been caught in his chest. He couldn't . . . It didn't . . .

"You didn't know?" Gavin asked in a low tone.

Shane shook his head once. He couldn't manage anything else. Couldn't *fathom* this. What it meant. Why she wouldn't . . . Why hadn't she *told* him?

"Guess she'd have her reasons," Boone offered.

Reasons? For keeping something like *that* from him? He couldn't fathom what reasons she'd have.

How could she have . . . How could that vibrant, happy, sexy as hell woman have . . . How could she have survived it? Come out of it and still been . . .

He didn't even know, because he didn't know what she'd been through. He had a twelve-year-old's perspective.

God, he wanted to believe that perspective was wrong, but too many things made sense.

The way she'd reacted to his lecture to Micah on violence. The way she went pale when he gave her a compliment. *He didn't want us.*

Why wouldn't she have told him? It burned through his gut like acid.

Ben and Micah returned to the seats, and if Shane had been more with it, he might have been surprised and impressed by the amount of crap Ben had bought for the kid.

"There are the girls," Gavin said in a low voice.

Shane glanced up to see Mom leading Molly, Lindsay, and Cora toward them. They all looked happy, talking and laughing to each other as they filed in, filling up the rest of the row.

Cora slid into the seat next to him, smiling up at him. "I hope you know you're on the hook to buy me a hot dog and some cotton candy."

He tried to smile, didn't allow himself to speak, afraid all that would come out was a demand to know what the hell Micah was talking about.

"You'll be *thrilled* to know, your mom found the most gorgeous dress. Now I just have to find someone who can alter the hem in Benson, and things will be set on that front," she chattered, digging through her purse for something.

She pulled out a little piece of metal and handed it to him.

He took it and inspected what looked to be the remains of a horseshoe fashioned into a *T*. Small enough to fit in the palm of his hand.

"You're supposed to carry it around for good luck. I got one that looks like a horse for Micah." She grinned up at him, happy and sweet, and a lot of that anger leaked out of him. He loved this woman, and if she hadn't told him about things, maybe there was a reason for that. She didn't trust him yet.

It hurt, but it was okay. He'd make it okay.

Chapter Twenty-Two

Cora couldn't say she was a baseball convert, but she had a sneaking suspicion Micah was. At least a convert to the array of food offered to him over the course of nine rather long innings.

But the Rockies had won, and there was an air of joviality to the crowd funneling out of the stadium that she found a bit contagious. Maybe it was because Micah had been his normal self, well, mostly. A few times he'd glanced over at Shane and her with that *look* she hadn't figured out yet.

But she felt like she would. She just needed time, and they *had* time. Time to figure it all out and make it work.

Shane linked his fingers with hers as they walked to the car, and she managed to snag Micah's hand despite his trying to jerk it away. She pulled him to her side, until he gave in a little and leaned against her, though he did finally free his hand. They reached the truck the boys had driven in, and Deb tugged Micah out of Cora's grasp.

"All right, we're kidnapping this one for the ranch tonight and tomorrow. I don't know what you two are going to do, but you better make the most of it."

Cora laughed, thinking it was some kind of joke she didn't get, but Shane's grip on her hand tightened. "This way."

"But . . . What?"

"You two enjoy yourselves," Deb said, waving her away. "I don't want to see you before five o'clock tomorrow."

"But, Mi—" Micah was already walking to the car, happily chattering with Molly and no doubt making plans for horses, horses, and *more* horses. He glanced at her quickly enough to wave and offer a lame good-bye.

"Where are we going? How will we get home? How . . ." Cora asked, trying to make sense of it.

Shane kept tugging her in the opposite direction of his family. "The hotel is less than a mile away, so we can walk if it's okay with you. There's a rental at the hotel for us to drive home, or wherever we want to go tonight. I figured we could maybe make it to a restaurant this time since we have some time tomorrow too."

"This is . . ." She looked up at him in the middle of the baseball stadium parking lot. "Shane, this is too much. Cost and time and—"

"You try arguing with my mother." He stopped pulling and grinned at her. "This was not my idea, FYI. I mean, I agreed with it a lot more easily than you are, but Mom set everything up. Well, not everything. I had a say in a few things."

Cora opened her mouth, then shut it. Yes, there was no arguing with Deb, and Micah did seem more than happy to head off with the Tylers.

She shook her head, awed and a little dizzy with it. "It's so . . . We only had Lilly to rely on for so long, and then in this past year we've had this whole Mile High family, and now yours." She looked up at him, and some of her joy faded at the odd, serious look on his face. She traced a groove next to his all-too-serious mouth. "What's wrong?"

"I love you, Cora."

Someone bumped into her, and far off in the distance a drunk man yelled something really vulgar, and all Cora could manage to do was gape at him.

"This wasn't the venue I meant to confess that at," he added, but those dark, serious eyes never left hers.

"You . . . you *love* me." Love. That word she'd . . . Well, for so long she'd been desperate to hear it, or at least hear it on a day she hadn't also been smacked across the face. And he'd just said it. And gave her surprises like nights in Denver because his mother was wonderful.

"It's okay if you think it's too soon."

She laughed then, because too soon? "I've been trying not to say it for weeks, I think. Forever maybe."

His mouth finally curved at that, and he pulled her closer. "Say it then."

She kept her fingers on his face, brushing them across his jaw, keeping her gaze on his. "I love you," she said, and wasn't sure he could hear over the song more drunk people were singing next to them.

"Come on, let's get to the hotel."

They walked hand in hand, and Cora trusted Shane to lead them where they needed to go in the quickly fading twilight. It was weird not to see much of the sky, the mountains, weirder still to *miss* it. But Gracely and the Tyler ranch had changed her entire view of the world, and she couldn't help but be glad.

Shane stopped in front of an elegant building. It was the kind of place she'd spent so much time dreaming about. Fancy and sparkling. The kind Dad had always promised a trip to, and always failed to deliver. The kind Stephen would hold out like a pretty carrot, then always find fault with her and yank it away.

And Shane was the one who'd brought her here—
without a promise or a threat or a manipulation. He'd
just *done* it.

"*This* hotel?"

"I don't get off the ranch very often," he was saying
as he walked inside and toward the elevators. "I'm not
going to stay in a cheap roadside motel."

Cora could only stare at the lobby as they walked.
Chandeliers and gleaming floors and people in pretty
dresses.

"You don't have to check in?"

He pulled a key out of his pocket. "Lindsay took care
of everything before she met you guys at the dress
place."

"You Tylers are quite the handy, organized bunch."

"Most of us anyway."

They stepped into the elevator with a small group of
people. Shane's arm stayed around her waist, a nice,
tight grip. When they reached their floor, he confidently
headed down the hall.

He stopped at a door and smoothed the key in front
of the pad. They stepped into the room. A king-size bed
dominated the space. The only impression she had of
the bathroom was gleam and white as she stepped
toward the window.

Denver sparkled to life outside, and Cora had the
profound realization that her life had well and truly
changed. *She* had changed, and the world had opened
up to her, and suddenly she felt like she really could
accomplish anything.

"Mom said she'd call when they got to the ranch, so
you'll get a chance to talk to Micah tonight. I know she
kind of whisked him away before you could get a nice
good-bye in."

"He seemed okay with it," Cora replied wryly.

"Yeah, but I was worried about *you* in this case."

Because he would. Worry about her and take care of her and protect her. *Love* her, without her even having to try or manipulate or beg.

He came up behind her, wrapping his arms around her, pressing a kiss to her neck. It was like some impossible dream, and for a brief, panicked moment she wanted to tell him everything, what a mess she was, what mistakes she'd made. How she'd hurt Micah and herself for so long and was only just now coming out of it, and God, why would he love her?

Because you are *coming out of it. Because you got strong, and you moved on, and you're a damn good person now. That's why he loves you.*

So, he didn't need to know, because none of that old stuff mattered. She was a new woman, and this was her new life. He loved *her*, and she loved him, and things could work out. They would.

She turned in the circle of his arms and pressed her mouth to his, maybe a little on the side of rough and desperate, but she needed to convince herself that was true.

"I love you, Shane," she murmured against his mouth.

His arms slid down over her ass, then he hefted her up and against him, exactly the same as the last time they'd had a night alone together.

He lay her out on the bed, his long, gorgeous body sliding over hers. He smiled down at her, sweet and soft. "I love you, Cora."

They ordered room service. He'd really meant to take her out, but naked she made a million cases he could never win against. Besides, they could go out for breakfast. Probably.

He could mostly forget about everything from earlier today. What did the past matter when she was saying she loved him? When she was naked and pliant in his arms, wanting to stay exactly right here?

She was nestled up to him, and he'd lost track of time, practically dozing. Her fingers brushed back and forth against his chest, as if she were assuring herself he was there. Real.

He understood the feeling.

"You know, you never did tell me why Ben came," she murmured sleepily.

"I don't plan on telling you while I'm naked."

"You might as well get dressed then." She yawned, pulling away from him and stretching out in the giant bed. "Your endurance is impressive, but I think we're going to need a slight window of rest."

He grinned down at her. "Slight."

She laughed, but reached over the edge of the bed and threw his boxers at him. When she grabbed his T-shirt, she didn't hand it to him. She pulled it over herself.

It was this kind of thing. Not just great sex, but an easy camaraderie. A partner in things: to talk to, tease, enjoy. This was what he'd wanted with Mattie, all those years ago, and, with the mature twenty-twenty of hindsight, he could see he'd wanted that more than Mattie herself. The idea of what a partnership would look like.

With Cora, he didn't care what it looked like. As long as it was with her. So, it didn't matter if she told him about her past, because they had this. It was good enough. Had to be.

"That night Boone and I had a disagreement, after you and Micah left, I went for a little bit of a walk to clear my head. I'd forgotten how often I'd done that before Boone went off to the rodeo. Boone and I have never gotten along well. The age difference, his natural distaste for authority. It's always been oil and water."

"How come you and Gavin make it work then? He's prickly too."

"Gavin's natural state is angry, but it's not usually geared toward people. He's just . . . a grumpy asshole. Boone, he zeroes in on people, and he knows just how to get under their skin. I said some things I shouldn't have."

"Like what?"

He didn't want to tell her. In fact, he opened his mouth to change the subject to what they were supposed to be talking about—his and Ben's heart-to-heart, so to speak. His crap with Boone, the things about Dad, it wasn't important. It didn't *matter* anymore, but that was likely what she was telling herself about her own secrets.

She had secrets she didn't want to tell him, didn't *trust* to tell him, so maybe he needed to take the first step. Give her all his.

"He wanted to take Micah on that drive, and he just kept needling. Couldn't see that it was irresponsible and dangerous, so I said . . ." He blew out a breath, and Cora nestled into him again, placing her hand on his chest just above his heart.

"The thing is, *I* don't go on those drives. They're Gavin's, because the last one I went on was when my father died."

Cora's head whipped up as she leveraged her body up on her elbow. "Your father died on the drive?"

Shane nodded. "And that's about as much as was ever talked about. Horse kicked him in the worst possible spot, and he died. But . . . Well, there was more to it. I never did much talk about it. With anyone. Ever."

"Like with the money-stealing girlfriend?"

"Yeah. Only it wasn't out of embarrassment this time. It was . . . You see I was twelve, and, even as much as I loved ranching then, I was still a kid. Gavin had gotten to stay home because he was sick, which meant—to me—he got to sleep in and watch TV and play Nintendo and I had to work. So, I was pissy, lazy, and your average twelve-year-old asshole."

"I am familiar with those."

"I wasn't paying attention, and I led my horse right into a drainage ditch. The horse went down, and Dad tried to catch me. He managed to get me out of the way without any damage, but his horse startled and—"

Cora gasped before he could say the rest. "You were *there*?"

"Yeah. There. And, responsible, so to speak."

"Oh, no. No, you don't really think that." She cupped his face with her hands, staring at him sternly. "Baby, that's all accidents. Not your fault."

"I know, mostly. Intellectually, I know it, and I've accepted that in a lot of ways. I don't think I could ever truly shed the guilt, because if I'd done things differently . . . Well, but I didn't. It was a rough thing, and I . . . Well, the way the men told the story, Dad just fell. I guess maybe that's what it looked like to them. I went with it."

"You never told . . . You never told anyone?"

"No. Though I gave Boone the short version the other night, and I shouldn't have done it like that. But I was angry he didn't . . . He wouldn't listen. He never listens. I've been trying to protect that asshole for so long, and just having failure after failure. I just wanted him to *get it* for once, that it was for his own good. That *I* knew best."

"You just *lived* with that for what? Twenty years? You just . . ." She stopped, and a clear look of understanding passed over her features. "You decided you were responsible for everyone, because that would make up for it."

"That feels a little pat, but maybe not altogether wrong."

"Shane." She rubbed her palm against his cheek, and then she did the damnedest thing. She buried her face in his neck, and she started to cry.

"Hey, hey." He squeezed her tight. "What is it? What's wrong?"

"I just can't imagine. I just . . . *can't.*" She kissed his cheek. "And I think you're amazing." She kissed the corner of his mouth. "Just . . . amazing."

"I was supposed to be talking about Ben," was all he could think to say.

She wiped her cheeks and nodded, clearly working to pull herself together. "Well, you should tell me about that too."

"It's not quite as dramatic."

"Thank God," she said, the tears mostly gone.

"He told me, among other things, that my mother made him want to be a better man, and that he'd sign a prenup because he didn't want the ranch. So, I told him I'd walk Mom down the aisle, though I haven't had a chance to tell Mom yet."

Cora sniffled, and her eyes filled again.

"Why are you crying *now*?"

"Because you're the sweetest." She managed a wobbly smile. "And I know how happy your mom will be, and I . . . I'm just so glad you're mine."

They lay there for a while, and Shane waited, fruitlessly, for her to give that piece of herself. To offer it up, without any extra coercing. But it didn't happen.

He kissed her temple. "I hope you know you can tell

me anything too. Nothing would . . . You can trust me with anything, is all."

He felt her stiffen, and he waited for it. Any inclination she might fill him in, even a little.

"Okay," she said finally.

But she didn't go further. Didn't tell him. He wanted it not to matter. He'd try really hard to make it not matter.

Time, with time, they'd get there.

Chapter Twenty-Three

Cora couldn't remember the last time she'd been this relaxed or happy. And there was none of that horrible sense of impending doom that usually followed happiness.

No, this was hers, and it was going to stay hers.

She'd decided that she was being paranoid any time she caught Shane staring a little extra hard. It wasn't as if he could see through her to all her remaining secrets. He was just *looking*. Not examining her under a microscope, trying to find some hidden piece of her.

But there were none. Because that woman she'd been once upon a time didn't exist anymore. No hidden pieces. They'd all been obliterated.

So, the paranoia would have to go. She'd find a way.

The next morning, they finally made it out to a restaurant for breakfast, and enjoyed a little bit of a walk around Denver, though when Cora had admitted to missing the ranch, Shane had swooped down and kissed her hard on the mouth.

"Thank God," he'd said with a grin.

They'd enjoyed their hotel room for the remainder

of their time, then packed up the rental car to drive home.

Home.

She felt somehow exhausted and exhilarated all at the same time as the beautiful Colorado landscape passed by her window. She felt like a woman reborn, with a million determinations in her mind.

She was going to make Deb's wedding the best event Gracely had ever seen.

She was going to make sure Micah had as much Tyler ranch as he could handle, and, when school started, she was going to make sure he handled both. Because she was a good mom who loved her son, and he wasn't going to fall through any cracks with her at his side.

Shane was going to be the best role model for her kid without ever even trying. Micah could hero-worship Boone all he wanted, but Cora knew the older Micah got, the more he would understand the true mark of a good man because of Shane Tyler.

Her man. *Her* future.

Yes, indeed. Life was good.

So, somehow it didn't surprise her that, as Shane drove the rental car across the Tyler ranch property line, she could see an ambulance with lights flashing in the distance. Not at the house, but farther back.

She must have made a noise, some kind of gasp, because the car lurched to a faster pace. "Whatever it is, I'm sure it's . . ." But he didn't finish his sentence. He drove, too fast, but not up the drive. He cut through the fields, straight toward the ambulance.

Cora held her breath. It would just be a ranch hand. . . . A ranch hand with a minor injury. That's all. Maybe even a butt dial or a prank call or something . . . anything. Please God, anything other than what her heavy beating heart feared.

Don't overreact. Don't think catastrophe. She repeated those admonitions even as she held her breath.

As they got closer, Cora saw all the Tylers. Deb and Ben, Molly and Gavin. Boone, pacing back and forth next to—

"Oh, God." She had her car door open before Shane had even stopped the car, and only the seatbelt and his grabbing her arm as he slammed to a stop kept her from tumbling out while the car was still moving. But the minute it was stopped, he let her go, and was unbuckled and out of the car almost as fast as she was.

"Baby." She scrambled to a skidding halt, falling to her knees next to Micah, who the paramedics had fastened to one of those awful beds they put in ambulances.

"Sorry," he mumbled, face dirty and tear streaked. His eyes weren't focused, but he seemed to know she was there. There wasn't any blood. Then she glanced down, trying to take stock of his body, but his arm was twisted all wrong and her stomach revolted, so she had to look away from it and back to his face.

"Baby, sweetheart, Micah. What happened? What—" She reached out to touch him, just to brush that too-long hair off his forehead, but the paramedic gently restrained her arm.

"You're the mother?" the person asked, while a uniformed man did some awful thing with awful tools and oh, God, her baby. Her *baby.*

"Yes, she's his mother," Shane supplied, and it was only then Cora realized he was holding her. Kneeling behind her, arms wrapped around her.

"Can you give us some room? We're going to get him in the vehicle, all right?"

She didn't get to her feet, but somehow suddenly she was on them. Because Shane had picked her up, basically. Up, because her legs had ceased to work, and against him because, well, comfort she supposed.

But how could anything be a comfort when her baby was all strapped to something so awful she didn't even know its name?

"He's sedated," the female paramedic said gently. "He has a bad break in his arm. We have to transport him to the hospital where they'll have to do surgery."

"What? What?" Cora couldn't make sense of it. Any of it. "How? What . . . I don't . . ."

They were moving Micah into the ambulance, and the only thing keeping Cora upright was Shane. "Shane?" She looked up at him helplessly.

"Can we ride with?" Shane asked, his voice rough but even.

"The mother can ride with us. The rest of you can't. Ma'am? Are you up to it?"

Up to it? Her baby was in an ambulance, headed to the hospital. For surgery. She *had* to be up to it. Had to be.

She nodded once, firmly, and the female paramedic nodded at her partner, who walked swiftly to the driver's seat. The female paramedic smiled kindly. "I'll help you in," she said, holding out a hand.

Cora swallowed, found her feet, her strength, and stepped away from Shane.

"He's going to be okay," the woman was saying as she helped Cora into the back. She motioned her to something like a bench where she could sit almost next to Micah on the bed.

"It's a bad break, but it's a fairly common one. I know your kid's being hurt is scary, and you're still going to worry, but I just want you to know, everything is going to be okay." The paramedic reached out to pull the back doors closed, and Cora could only watch silently as Shane disappeared.

Gavin, Boone, and Ben were still holding him back from getting into the ambulance. Shane didn't think Cora had noticed. He hoped to *God* Cora hadn't noticed because he hadn't been thinking.

The minute she'd stepped into that ambulance, he'd lost it. He'd only wanted to be in that ambulance with them. He'd only wanted to be the one helping her while she looked so damn lost. All he'd known how to do was fight.

Thank God for everyone's stopping him from taking that fight to Cora. He had to get himself under control. Slowly, he stopped struggling, stopped *fighting* the arms holding him back. Tried to focus on the voices telling him to calm down, that everything was going to be okay.

The kid's arm was broken. *Broken.* Micah needed surgery, and Cora . . .

Focus.

Broken arm. Gavin had broken an arm in middle school, but he hadn't needed surgery. Mom had driven him to the hospital, and Shane had stayed home to watch the other kids.

But this was different. Micah hadn't been an idiot middle schooler showing off for Lou by jumping out of trees. Micah had been in the care of Shane's *family*, and they had failed.

He had failed.

Slowly Ben and Boone and Gavin let him go, and Shane focused on the cold ball deep inside his gut. A kind of numbness. A focus. He needed to solve this problem.

"What happened?" he demanded, low, cold, furious.

He couldn't even begin to try and get anger out of him. The boy was hurt. So, he focused on controlling it. On using it to be his center. Cold fury would get him to the next step.

"Shane."

He whirled on Boone, and it all came together in a painful blow. Boone looked pale, shaken. His voice had broken as he'd said *Shane.* "I'm so—"

"You fucking took him."

"I—"

Shane didn't think. He *couldn't* think. His body reacted of its own volition as his arm swung out, his fist connecting with Boone's jaw. He barely felt the blow. The crack of bone slapping against bone was nothing but a faint sound far in the distance. Dimly he heard the gasps of his family as Boone stumbled back, his leg buckling so he fell onto his ass.

"I told you no," Shane roared down at him, the rage and pain and betrayal and failure engulfing him. "I told you it was dangerous and he wasn't ready, and you took him?"

Boone didn't try to get up. He sat on the ground looking up at Shane, looking downright sick. "Look, I made a mistake."

"*A* mistake? You made *a* mistake? That boy's arm is broken so badly he needs surgery, and you made *a* mistake."

"There was a snake. The horse spooked. He fell and—" Boone snapped his jaw shut, clearly grappling with some emotion, but it didn't dim any of Shane's fury. "I'm sorry. You don't know how sorry. You were right, and I am sorry."

Shane wanted to hit him again. Kick him. Pummel him again and again. But Shane was afraid if he started, he wouldn't be able to stop, and clearly the fall was as much because of Boone's old injuries as because of Shane's punch. That flicker of weakness, of vulnerability, was the only thing that kept Shane from losing it completely.

"You're a worthless son of a bitch," he said, low and serious, because if he couldn't land a physical punch, maybe he could land one that would do some damage. Reach some part of him.

"Shane. I said I was sor—"

"Dad would be ashamed down to his soul, more so than even me," Shane continued. "That boy could be dead, and then what would your 'sorry' mean? You should leave this ranch and never show your face again."

"Shane Michael Tyler."

"Don't," he said, holding his hand up as his mother advanced on him. "That boy . . ." Shane couldn't swallow past the lump in his throat. "I was very clear in my instructions. No drive, and you keep him safe. *Safe*. Do you have any idea . . ." He'd been about to say *what they've been through*, but, hell, even he didn't know what they'd been through. Not really.

He turned and started walking for the rental car with its doors still open, engine still running. "I'm going to the hospital."

Molly hurried after him. "I'll drive you."

He shook his head, about to slide into the driver's seat. "No."

Molly grabbed his arm, stopping his progress into the seat. "You're shaking, Shane." She squeezed his arm, eyes soft and sympathetic. "I'll drive you."

"I'm going."

For the second time, Shane whirled on Boone, who'd gotten to his feet and was limping toward the car. "Like hell you—"

"You blame me, right? This is all my fucking fault?

Well, I know it, and I'm damn well going to apologize to that kid, and his mother, to their faces. No matter how much you hate me and wish I was gone, you don't get to decide how that shakes out."

"Shane, please," Molly whispered.

It was only because Molly was crying now, and he had the sneaking suspicion the noise he heard behind him was Mom crying, that he relented.

He might want Boone gone, but Boone did owe that apology to Cora and Micah both.

Shane didn't say anything as they climbed in the car. He sat in the passenger seat, jaw clenched so tight it started to throb, and all he could think about was how long the drive was taking for *them*. For Cora it had to feel twice as long, and she was alone.

Completely alone. Because of his fucking brother.

"I can't believe you did this," he couldn't help but say. "I can't believe after everything I told you, you went ahead and did it anyway."

"We were in the back. If we hadn't run into a snake, we would have been fine. I was watching him. I was—"

"He's getting surgery. God help whoever you decide to take care of next."

"We can't all be perfect, Shane."

"Get it all out right now," Molly said bitterly. "Get this dick measuring match out of your systems before you dare take one *step* toward that hospital. You want to be angry at each other, you have right at it, but I'll be damned if I let either of you walk in there and upset Cora further."

"I won't upset her," Shane retorted. "And if you do—"

"I'm coming to apologize," Boone exploded. "This isn't about *you*. I made a mistake, not to hurt *you*, but because I wanted to give that poor kid something. You heard what he said."

"Yeah, I heard what he said. That he'd been hurt e-damn-nough. So you thought you'd risk his safety?"

Boone didn't say anything to that, and they glared at each other in silence until Molly cleared her throat.

"We're here," she said before fixing them each with a hard stare. "You got your bullshit out of your systems?"

Shane didn't bother to respond. All of his feelings regarding Boone's disregard for a child's safety, Boone's disregard for him and every damn thing on this planet, they didn't matter.

All that mattered was that Micah was okay, and that Cora was holding up, and Shane would swallow down all the simmering rage he felt toward his brother.

At least until they were back home. Then, then maybe he and Boone would have it out once and for all.

Chapter Twenty-Four

Cora was in some awful waiting room after having filled out a bunch of paperwork that hadn't made any sense. Sitting, all alone, trying not to imagine worse-case scenarios where everything went all wrong and she'd lost her baby.

Because she didn't deserve happiness. Hadn't life taught her that?

She jolted when an arm came around her shoulders, then immediately began to sob into Shane's shoulder.

"He's just in there. Just in there."

"I'm so sorry, honey," he whispered, rubbing her back. It didn't take away the horrible dread, the awful thoughts, but at least she got to lean on someone.

"I need to call Lilly," she realized with a start. "I need—"

"Mom was calling Mile High when we left," Molly said softly. Oh, Molly was here. She blinked up at Molly's sympathetic face. That was nice.

Cora couldn't figure out why Boone hovered behind Molly, or why the air between the three was all tense, but she didn't want to. She leaned into Shane, and he rubbed a hand up and down her spine.

She breathed, trying to get control of her tears, of this weird, numb, nonsense feeling. She'd have to get clearer and more in control once Micah was . . .

God. Surgery.

"Cora."

It was Boone's voice, and it didn't escape Cora's notice that Shane tensed from head to toe. She looked curiously at Shane, but his face was blank and hard.

She turned in the waiting room seat to face Boone, who was holding his hat so tight in his hands he'd fairly crushed it. He stepped forward so that he was standing right in front of her. His gaze flicked to Shane, and his jaw hardened before he turned his attention back to her.

"I wanted to apologize, because as much as Micah's fall was an accident, I do feel responsible. Shane warned me not to take him on the drive. I thought it'd be fun for him. A snake spooked his horse, and, maybe if I'd been a hundred percent I could have fixed it before he fell off, but . . . Well, anyway, it was irresponsible of me, and I'm sorry Micah had to pay the price. I'm sorry you have to."

Cora managed a weak smile. "You don't have to feel responsible, Boone. I know you didn't—"

"Don't tell him that," Shane said, the sentence cold and flat.

Cora blinked over at Shane, utterly confused at that fury in his voice. "Shane, it was an accident. Accidents happen."

"An accident that would not have happened if he had listened to me for once in his life."

"Shane . . ." She didn't know what to say. Her head hurt too much. This was too much complication and emotion and upheaval.

But she had to be the strong one here. God, somebody did, and, maybe for once in her life, it should be her.

Her son was in surgery, yes, but he was in good hands. A broken arm wasn't a head injury or something truly serious. She sucked in a breath and slowly let it out.

The reason these two men were so angry, well, aside from deep-seated family issues, was because they cared about her son. Cared if he was all right, cared if he was happy. Somehow, the Tylers had opened their arms and accepted Micah and her as part of their circle of concern.

They were a messed up circle of concern, but it was nice to know even the best, most loving families made up of amazing people were a little screwy on the inside.

She met Boone's gaze, so like Shane's, and she smiled. "Thank you for apologizing. I appreciate it."

He nodded and stepped away, taking a seat a few chairs down from her. Molly gave her shoulder a pat, then went to sit next to him. Cora didn't understand why they'd put so much space between them, until she looked at Shane.

He looked so furious. Which, she supposed, made sense. He was angry at Boone for disobeying him, so to speak, but Shane . . . He took so much responsibility on his own shoulders, he probably felt guilty.

It was something like a relief to have something to focus on other than Micah. She'd comfort Shane, get him to understand this wasn't the end of the world, and it'd make her feel a little better herself.

She slid her arm around his shoulders. "Shane, I know you blame yourself for what happened to your father, but you shouldn't, any more than Boone should feel responsible for what happened to Micah. Even if he hadn't taken Micah on that drive, accidents happen. Boys break bones and hurt themselves. I don't love it, but it's . . . Well, there's a lot worse ways a person can be hurt."

"You know that pretty well, don't you?" Shane asked, and there was such *accusation* in his voice.

Something icy and cold rippled down her spine as she slowly met his gaze. "What does that mean?"

His mouth was a grim line, and she'd never seen him like this. At a sort of breaking point. So desperate to keep his control on all those emotions whirling in his dark eyes, but it was all close to the surface. Almost as though there was a visible crack in all his strength.

He looked down at his hands, which were clenched into fists, so tight his knuckles were white. "It doesn't matter."

She felt panic flutter in her stomach, just the leading edge of it. "It matters to me. What did you mean by that?"

Slowly, so slowly it felt like slow motion, his gaze moved from his fists to her face. "Micah told me."

"Told you what?" she whispered, even though she knew. Every hard beat of her heart against her chest knew exactly what he was talking about.

"We shouldn't . . ." He shook his head, looking away again. "Micah is what's important right now. We can discuss this later."

"No, that is not an option." Later? As if it could just be pushed off. That he . . . "What did my son tell you that made you say that?"

Shane shook his head, still staring at those fists, and how was this the way things were happening? They were supposed to be happy. They were supposed to *lean* on each other through hard things, not splinter apart.

"Micah told me his father used to hurt both of you, you most of all, repeatedly." Again, Shane's gaze slowly locked to hers. "I wanted to believe it wasn't true or was some kind of exaggeration, but it isn't, is it?"

It was her turn to look away. "Why do you want to believe all that? Is it really so awful that it changes how you feel about me?"

"Nothing changes the way I feel about you, Cora," he said, his voice low and fierce. "I told you that. This isn't about what happened. It isn't about what you've survived. It's about the fact you didn't tell me."

Survived. She hated that word. She hadn't *survived.* She'd been weak and stupid and had put her family through hell.

"Why would Micah . . ." She couldn't wrap her mind around all of this. That it was happening, that *Micah* had told Shane. When he'd . . . he'd been so adamant they not tell, but he'd told Shane anyway?

"Why would Micah tell me? Because it was the truth. And maybe someone thought I deserved it."

But it didn't make sense. It didn't . . . "When?"

"On the way to the game."

Cora tried to work through it all. So, not that long ago, but . . . Oh God, everything that had happened after the game. *I love you,* and him saying those things about . . .

Fury shot through her, and she grabbed onto it. Anger and blame was so much better than fear and shame.

"Oh, I see, so that's why you told me about your father? A little manipulative tit for tat. Is that why you said you loved me too?"

"No, it is not."

"Sure." Why should she believe that? He felt sorry for her. Wanted to protect her from things. Why wouldn't he just decide he loved her so he could bundle her up like he tried to do with everyone else? She crossed her arms over her chest, breathing not even, everything inside of her *hurting.*

"Don't you dare turn this on me," Shane returned, and everything about his voice was a vibrating fury she'd never seen from him, even when dealing with Boone. "I told you everything. Everything I'd never told anyone. Do you know what it's like to have a twelve-year-old upend everything?"

She looked at him dolefully. "Kinda regularly, Shane."

He sat there, breathing hard, but he was so strong. So much better than her. He fused that crack in his control back together right before her eyes. "Now is not the time to fight," he said, calm and sure and so in charge.

She hated it. "Oh, isn't it? When would be the time? Would you like to schedule it?" She pretended to check her phone. "I have time on the fifteenth."

"Guys—"

"Why are you mad at *me*?" Shane demanded. "I have done everything right."

"Yes, you're always right, and everyone else is to blame when something goes wrong, and, well, it must be nice, Shane. To never make a mistake. To be able to blame accidents on your brother and—"

"Guys," Molly repeated more firmly. "People are looking."

"I don't give a shit," Cora snapped. "Why don't you all take a good, long look?" she asked of the curious faces in the waiting room staring in their direction.

Shane abruptly got to his feet. "I love you, and I love your kid, so I'm going to step outside and not spew my anger all over you, because I'm not a worthless piece of shit like the man who did all of that to you."

That shut her up, because . . . He just . . . Why were they fighting? How had this gotten so damn twisted?

Because he knows, and now you're different to him. That's how.

"Cora, oh, sweetheart." Lilly slid into the chair next to her and grabbed her in a hug. "How's Micah?"

Cora leaned into her sister, empty and spent, and how many times had that been the case? "He's in surgery," she managed to mumble. "Did they—"

"Deb said it was a broken arm."

"Yeah, yeah. Where are the babies?"

"Brandon stayed home with them for now, though he can pawn them off on everyone else if we need him. Or anyone else can help. Whatever you need. What . . . Why was Shane storming out of here?"

Cora shook her head. "Everything's all messed up." Because she'd had the insane thought she could handle this, do this, be this. But a failure was all she was. Useless and stupid like Stephen had always said. A burden to him and Lilly and Micah.

"Cora, don't go there," Lilly whispered into her ear, hugging her fiercely. "I know it's hard when things are bad, but don't let those old lies back in."

Cora could see Shane pacing the sidewalk outside the windowed doors. Angry, so damn angry, and yet he was out there stomping out his anger on the sidewalk. He'd said he loved her.

"I wish I was strong enough to do it on my own." Wasn't it just weakness to need to know he loved her? To need Micah to need her and Lilly to remind her?

Lilly pulled back, searching Cora's face. "We can't do everything alone. What would be the point if we could get through without people who love us?"

"Ms. Preston?"

Cora blinked up at the nurse, who smiled kindly. "He's out of surgery and doing well, though he's still under anesthesia and will be for a while. You'll be able to go back soon, and a doctor will explain everything to you. Just give us a few more minutes to get him settled into a room."

Cora nodded silently. She inhaled and exhaled. "He's doing well."

"He's doing well," Lilly repeated, squeezing her close again.

That was all that could matter right now, but no matter how Cora told herself that, her eyes drifted out the window to Shane's solitary, pacing figure. All she could think was he *knew.*

The worst parts of herself. There was no taking that back.

Ever.

Shane didn't know how long he paced outside after watching Cora be taken back into the hallways of the hospital.

He'd wanted to rush in, to be with her. She didn't want that. So he walked and tried to find some solution for this. Some fix. Everything was broken, but he could fix it. He'd find a way to fix it.

The sad fact of the matter was, no one wanted that. His help, his guidance, his protection. No one wanted *him.*

That was a hell of a self-centered thought to have when a kid was in the hospital. So, he walked the sidewalk, thinking if he could just get his brain to *focus,* he could fix this. He could. . . .

"Man, I thought I had the market cornered on self-absorbed moping."

Shane didn't turn toward Boone's voice. He couldn't even work up a good mad. It had all leaked out of him. He'd done everything right. He'd been honest with her. He'd *loved* her, and here he was again having it not be enough.

Not remotely enough.

She didn't believe him. Didn't trust him. Was somehow furious that he knew. He didn't know what else he could do, what else he had to give. Certainly nothing to Boone.

"I'm done, Boone. I'm just done. Go home."

"Situations reversed, you wouldn't."

Shane stared into the dark evening around him. He wished for the quiet of the ranch, the dark shadows of the mountains, anything to ease these ragged edges inside of him. "Since when do you care what I'd do?"

"A little longer than you'd think. A lot longer than I'd ever admit."

Shane didn't have it in him for riddles. Especially Boone's riddles.

"Never seen you like this," Boone continued in that maddeningly conversational tone. As if this were any other day. As if everyone wasn't hurting.

"I'm begging you, Boone. Don't push me right now."

"I'm just interested to see how far you'll go." He rubbed his jaw with his palm. "Don't know how many years I spent *trying* to get you to hit me, then you finally did and I wasn't even trying."

"You want me to hit you again?" Shane asked, though he didn't think he had the energy. All this anger only made him exhausted.

"Maybe," Boone replied as if considering. "You could just go with the truth."

"Who cares about the truth?"

"Good point. Guess you could just fester and explode later. Sounds more like the Tyler way."

The Tyler way. Shane had always thought it was

superior. The best way. Look at him now. He thought he'd finally put all the pieces together, and they'd just . . . Well, they'd more than fallen apart. Everything was wrong and jumbled, and he didn't even know how.

"I just don't know why . . ." Was he really going to empty this all on Boone of all people? He shook his head. But no one else was here, and Cora had made it perfectly clear she didn't understand him. Whatever *love* meant to her, it was something different from how he meant it.

Felt a little too familiar.

"You don't know why what?"

"Why she wouldn't tell me. Why won't anyone *tell* me? I know I haven't always been the most open guy, but I've been trying. And all I get is secrets from her and shit from you and . . . and . . . Ben fucking Donahue is the most upfront person with me in this whole world right now, and I don't get it."

"Okay," Boone replied, so unceasingly *calm.* "You want to know why I took the kid on the drive?"

"Because I told you not to? Because you didn't care if he got hurt? Or if anyone got hurt because all that matters is that you have a good time?"

"No. Much as I'd like to blame you for all those answers, I figure I've cultivated that idea hard enough I can't blame you for believing it."

The worst part was Shane didn't believe it. Not really. For all Boone's faults, there *was* a good man under there. Shane had just never known how to reach that man.

"Sometimes . . ." Boone said, leaning against the hospital building, talking in a low, soothing voice. A voice that reminded Shane strangely of himself. "Sometimes you see yourself in someone so damn clearly it hurts. And it scares the shit out of you, so you do something dumb."

"That doesn't make any sense."

"To you," Boone said. "When that kid told you what his dad did to them, he looked right at you. He watched you, and he waited for your response. He planned that all out. It wasn't some accidental confession."

"Yeah. But why?"

"He had it good, and he sabotaged it—well, tried to—because he didn't know what to do with *good*. Or maybe he didn't think he deserved it. I'm not a shrink. I can't work all that out. I only know I've seen that look before—that look on his face when he told you about his dad. I've seen it in the mirror. In video. Felt it wash through me hard as a pelvis fracture. That was fear, plain and simple, and not of anything bad, but that good and right might be in front of you. Maybe even *for* you. Not everyone is comfortable with that, Shane."

Shane couldn't help but wince at the idea of a *pelvis* fracture, but then it only made him angry again. Boone had never told them. He'd hightailed it away and thumbed his nose at them, and what had Shane done so damn wrong?

Fear. But what had Micah hoped to gain out of . . . Clearly Cora didn't want Shane to know. Clearly it was going to require some . . .

Hell if he knew. He only wanted to fix it, but he'd never been so at a loss as to *how*.

Molly's head poked out of the door. "Um, Lilly convinced Cora to go get some coffee, and she said you two can come back and see Micah for a few minutes." She glanced from Boone to Shane, offered him a little smile. "He asked for you in particular."

Something in Shane's gut twisted so hard and painfully he couldn't even respond. Wasn't sure he was breathing as he strode inside to follow Molly, Boone at his heels.

Molly led them through a maze of halls, to an open

door. Inside, Cora's sister was sitting in a chair next to a hospital bed. Micah was lying still on it, though the bed was elevated so it almost looked like he was sitting.

His blue gaze drifted to the door, and Shane didn't know what to say, or do. He only knew that his legs were propelling him next to Micah's bed.

"Hey, kid," he managed to breathe.

Micah stared, wide-eyed, before his gaze shifted away. Down. "I'm sorry," he mumbled.

Shane breathed through all that horrible tightening in his chest. "It was an accident, bud. I think you learned your lesson, huh?"

Micah shifted in the bed, looking small and helpless and just breaking the hell out of Shane's heart. "Mom cried."

"Yeah, well, moms do that when they're worried."

"I'm sorry I messed it all up."

Shane stepped forward, bending over the bed. He placed his hand over Micah's forehead since it seemed the best place to touch him without hurting him. "You didn't mess anything up. Not a thing."

"You're not mad?"

"I was a little mad at Boone for taking you when I said no."

"I begged him."

Shane nodded. "The fact of the matter is, sometimes we make bad choices." He thought about what Boone had said about being afraid of good. Maybe he could understand that. Afraid you'd get used to it, lose it, break it, and it'd never last. Maybe Shane was starting to begin to understand the fear that you couldn't fix anything.

He brushed his palm across Micah's forehead. "You can't make a bad choice that would change how I feel about you. No matter what. We may not be related, but that doesn't mean we're not connected. Nothing you could do to change that now. Hell, break a bone on Tyler property, you're practically a Tyler."

Micah's eyes filled with tears, but the kid clearly fought them tooth and nail. "So, I can still ride horses and everything?"

"You'll have to get healed up, and probably do some major sucking up to your mom, but accidents happen." Which he said more for Micah's sake than because he believed it.

"You're not . . . with her," Micah said, sneaking a glance at his aunt who'd moved to a seat in the corner when he'd walked in. She quickly averted her eyes.

"You worry about getting yourself home and healed up," Shane offered, taking a step away from the bed. "You let me handle the rest, okay?"

Micah frowned, but he nodded.

But Shane could tell by his expression that Micah didn't trust him to handle anything, just like everyone else.

Chapter Twenty-Five

Cora knew she had to go back to Micah's room. She stared at her splotchy face in the bathroom mirror and knew even makeup couldn't fix this.

How on earth were parents brave for their kids? How did other people deal with this fear and guilt and worry all wrapped up in tears and failure? How did they look at their only child's face and see *pain* and not just break apart?

"Well, you're going to have to figure it out," she whispered to herself, fighting a fresh wave of tears by gripping the sink as hard as she could.

She had gotten this far because she'd *had* to, and that didn't stop here or now. It didn't stop, ever.

She felt strengthened by that. Determined.

Then she stepped out of the bathroom and saw Shane, Boone, and Molly walking away from Micah's room toward the waiting room. They all stared at her, then shared glances with each other. Nonverbally they seemed to agree Molly and Boone would keep walking.

But Shane stopped.

"Can we walk for a few minutes?"

She wanted to say no, but that was the coward's way out.

In the past few hours she'd come to grips with the very real fact that Shane and happiness and all those things she'd thought she had this morning weren't for her.

Besides, what would she even do with them? With him? Get married? Have a family? Live on the ranch?

Her knees nearly buckled at the horrible wave of *want* that swept through her. God, she wanted that life. That future.

But Micah's accident was her sign. Just like all those years ago when Stephen's turning his anger onto Micah had been her sign to leave. She believed in signs. She believed in Gracely's legend. She believed in herself.

If that one rang a little false, well, that was something to dissect at her next appointment with Dr. Grove. Not here with Shane.

She nodded and turned down a hallway that led outside. She wouldn't do this with the hospital staff or waiting room as an audience, but she needed to do it.

"I imagine they'll be keeping him overnight?" Shane asked, pushing the door open and waiting for her to step outside before he did.

Cora nodded stiffly. Some part of her wanted to reach out. Touch his face. Lean into what she knew would be willingly comforting arms.

Pity comfort. Charity sweetness. Because now he knew, and the illusion was shattered. She was tainted, and she couldn't stand the thought of still being with him with all that past ugliness weighing everything they were.

"Did they give you an idea of when you'll be able to go home?"

"Tomorrow, probably."

"I can stay put. Give you a ride whenever he's released. Whatever you guys need. Gavin and Boone have the ranch covered."

She didn't understand how that offer could somehow

make her heart soft and mushy, and yet somehow make her so damn angry too. It was a nice, sweet gesture, and if he hadn't known about her, she could have accepted it.

But he knew, so all gestures were now *I know better than you. I have to fix you.* "No, thank you. Lilly can do it."

Shane sighed. "Cora, I know we . . . I know you're upset, and you have to focus on Micah right now. We'll work out our stuff later, but for now I'm just offering help." He smiled kindly, reassuringly. The kind of smile a teacher gave a child he was trying to teach something hard.

Because that's what she was to him now. The same thing she was to Lilly. And Micah. And everyone who knew.

"I don't want to work it out," she said, looking straight at him, the words so honest-to-God truthful she nearly swayed on her feet.

Shane straightened, stiffened. "What?"

"I don't want a fixer, Shane."

He stared at her as if she'd lost her mind, and maybe she had.

He took a deep breath in and slowly let it out. "You're tired."

She laughed bitterly. "Tired? Don't know what I'm saying? Silly, stupid Cora is just so tired she's talking out of turn."

A flash of temper, one she hadn't truly seen until today, sparked in his eyes. "Don't put words in my mouth."

"I don't have to. I know what this does."

"What *what* does?"

"Knowing! Knowing everything about . . . about my past. I know what it does. I know how it changes how people see me, and I can't . . . I can't be what I've become when something I left behind is all anyone can see."

"So you don't want to be with me because I know this thing about you?"

"Yes! It changes everything. Everything. Because now every time you look at me and there's even a hint of pity I have to think about all the ways I was small and weak and—"

"You were none of those things. Someone's hurting you does not define *you*."

Which was nice in theory, but he didn't know what it was like to live with it. Maybe he had some warped father guilt, but it had all been a childhood accident. The things she'd allowed to happen . . . Maybe she'd been a teenager at first, but she'd let it happen into adulthood. "How would you know?"

"Because I know you. Because I *love* you. If the mistakes we make define us, then Boone's the cause of Micah's accident, and I'm my father's murderer."

"You believe those things, Shane. You blame Boone, and you blame yourself. You believe those things in your *soul*. So, why would it be different for me?"

"I . . ."

He looked as though she'd punched him. Right in the gut, with far more strength than she'd ever had.

But he didn't refute what she'd just said.

"It just can't work. It was a nice thought, but reality is a little tougher than nice thoughts."

"Cora, you can't honestly believe—"

"But I do. I honestly believe this changed everything, and for the worse. You know what? A few years ago, I might not have cared. A few years ago I would have been weak enough to let it all slide. To let you look down on me and live with it and think it was love, but I won't let Micah down like that again."

"There is a difference between love and pity. There is a difference between knowing something awful happened to you and thinking you're weak. You were a victim and—"

"I *am* a victim. Now that you know, that's what I *am* to you."

"No—"

"You used the word, Shane. Not me. You don't know a lot of *victims*, so you can't understand what it's like to be one. You don't know. Now, I have to get back to my son." She moved for the door.

"Cora."

But she couldn't stop. She couldn't go on this way any further without breaking down. Because it hurt to say all these awful things she didn't want to believe.

But they were all true. She saw the truth in him, in his inability to argue, in the way he felt about his own mistakes and failures.

"Good-bye, Shane," she managed, stepping back inside, doing everything she could to fight the swell of tears.

This was the *right* thing. She would always be the victim. He would always be the man trying too hard to make up for things that weren't his to make up for.

She had to want better for herself. For her son. No matter how badly, deeply, horrifically the wound cut.

When Shane finally got home after driving the rental car to Benson, and having Mom pick Boone, Molly, and him up, he felt as though he'd lived through a year rather than a day. A year that had done everything in the world to upend everything he felt and believed.

He trudged up to the house with his family, ready to just go to his room and sleep. Maybe with a bottle of Jack to aid the process. But as they got to the porch stairs, Mom hooked her arm with his.

"You and I are going for a little ride."

"Mom, thanks and all, but I don't feel like—"

"It wasn't a request or an invitation, Shane Tyler. It was a statement." And with that she gave him a hard jerk toward the stables.

"It's like four in the morning."

"Yes, just about the time you're usually getting up. The horses will think you're right on time."

"Mom."

"Not another word until you're in the saddle."

She pulled him the entire way, and he didn't know what else to do but be pulled. Two horses were already saddled and tethered outside the doors.

"Ben helped me out some. You know, he said you two talked the other day."

Shane grunted.

"It means a lot to me that you did that. That you were the one who reached out, and I know you don't want to hear that." Mom easily mounted her horse, gesturing for Shane to do the same.

Exhausted beyond measure, Shane got up on Mac-Gregor. It eased a little of that horrible tension inside of him, and he supposed that was why Mom had insisted upon this.

But it couldn't solve any of his problems. Of course, neither could sleep or even him, so what did it matter?

Mom nudged Templeton forward, and Shane followed, across the fields, around the familiar path toward the Tyler cemetery.

"This seems to be my go-to spot these days," he muttered. "Nothing like death to really solve a problem for you."

Mom didn't respond, but she brought Templeton to a stop and slid off. She hung the reins on a branch, and Shane followed suit.

Somehow, he knew where this was going, and if he had had any fight left in him, he would have fought. Refused to have this conversation. But he was plum out of fight, and Mom never fought fair anyway.

They stood in front of Dad's gravestone in the dark, yet Shane could see it all in his mind's eye.

"How is it possible," Mom said, in a low, hurt voice he hadn't heard too often from his mother, "that, for all these years, you never told us what really happened?"

In all his exhaustion, he didn't have it in him to wonder when Boone had told her or to find equivocations or anything other than the truth. "I felt responsible. I felt . . ." He wasn't sure he'd been this close to crying since his father's funeral. "You want me to explain something I did when I was twelve. I don't know. I did what I thought was right. I thought it would be better if no one knew. Better if I protected you."

"And yourself."

"Maybe. God, I don't know anymore. I just wanted to make it right."

"Yes, you've spent quite a lot of time and effort trying to make things right, haven't you?" Mom said, but it wasn't in the way Boone said things. Not scathing, but something more like proud.

Mom slid her arm around his waist. "Between that and Gavin letting me in on what Micah told you guys, and Molly texting me a little bit of you and Cora's fight, I've had quite a bit to think about all night. Trying to make sense of it all. You. Cora. I got to thinking, maybe you were afraid if people knew your father had died trying to help you, they might not just blame you, but they might stop loving you. Because all they'd be able to see was what had happened."

"Maybe, and I get that you're trying to make a correlation here, but I do love Cora, and I told her that. I told her what happened to her didn't matter. It doesn't. She might be afraid, but I didn't stop loving her."

"Yes, but . . . Do you remember your Aunt Sabrina?"

"No."

"My sister. She was around when you were a baby, but she married a man who carefully and slowly cut her off from her family. From herself. We tried everything we could to get her to leave him, and I felt such guilt that I never could. I don't know if he was physically abusive like Cora experienced, but it was abuse, nonetheless. Far too late, I realized I kept trying to change her circumstances, but I never tried to figure out why she felt that man's awfulness to her was love."

"That sounds . . . hard, Mom. And I'm sorry. But Cora told me a lot about how she grew up, and I can make a pretty easy jump to see how someone took advantage of her. It doesn't change how I feel about her. It doesn't change anything." Why did everyone have to assume it did? He didn't feel changed.

"But that's how *you* feel, Shane. What I'm saying is she has to feel it. She has to believe it, and you can't *make* her."

"So, I should just give up?" he demanded incredulously.

"No. No. But I think you have to give her time and support rather than solutions. Sometimes people don't want you to fix it for them. They want you to hold their hand while they fix it for themselves."

"I'm not very good at that, am I?"

Mom laughed, pulling him closer, giving him a squeeze. "It's not your strong suit, no, but I bet you could learn for that girl. I have faith that you will. You'll give her some time, then you'll let her know what you're willing to do, then you give her some more time."

"How much time we talking about here?" Shane asked wryly.

Mom chuckled. "Much as it takes, I'd say. You trust in that love and in that person, and it won't be so very bad. After all, I trusted in you to do the right thing when it came to me and Ben, and look where we are. You're practically best friends."

"Ha. Ha."

This time when she pulled, she pulled his face down and pressed her mouth to his cheek. "You are one of the five best things I've ever done, sweetheart. It has never been easy, but I would not change a second of it, because it has all brought you here, and I have never, ever seen you as happy as you are with Cora and Micah. Trust in that, Shane. Believe in it. Wait for it."

Shane rested his cheek against his mother's head. "If I manage to do all that, it's because of you. Well, and maybe a little bit the fear of Grandma's sword collection keeping me in line."

Mom laughed, and that soothed a little bit. There were still so many ragged edges, so many things he didn't understand, but Mom was right. It wasn't really about him.

So, he had to wait.

Chapter Twenty-Six

Cora felt like she hadn't been home in years instead of a few days. As she turned the key and pushed the door open, she tried not to think about everything that had changed.

Everything.

She let Micah walk inside on his own power, and tried very hard not to hover. She could tell Lilly was trying very hard not to do the same.

"Go home, Lil."

"Don't you need help?"

"Not right now. I'll get him settled. He'll probably take a nap. If he gets too antsy, I'll give him his video games. You have two babies who need their mama. This baby has flown the nest."

Lilly pulled her into a hard hug. "Expertly. Now listen, if you need anything we're all here to help. And before you say you don't *need* help, I just meant if you want it. You need an hour to yourself, or want us to run an errand or whatever. Help because we love both of you and want to be of some use to you."

Somehow those words struck Cora all wrong, reminding her of Shane when she shouldn't be thinking about him at all. She'd made her decision. For her and Micah. No more Shane thoughts.

"I'll be sure to let you know," she said to Lilly, fairly pushing her sister out the door, since it'd be the only way she left.

Once she got Lilly gone, Cora turned to the living room. Micah had sprawled out on the couch and was already turning on the TV. She'd give him another few days of laziness before she started poking him to do something requiring a little more brainpower.

The doctor had said Micah might still be sluggish for a day or two, but then he'd probably bounce back. Aside from his arm, which would take weeks to heal. Cora tried not to think too hard about the timeline.

"You want a blanket?" she asked, brushing her fingertips across the top of his head.

"Nah."

"You want *the* blanket?"

Micah eyed her, then slid his gaze to the TV and shrugged. Cora smiled in spite of her exhaustion. She went to the closet and dug out Micah's old safety blanket. It was ratty and so worn she couldn't even see the pattern anymore, which was probably for the best considering it had been a Noah's ark pattern, the baby animals something Micah would most definitely not appreciate now.

She placed it over Micah's shoulder of his bad arm. He didn't move except for the tips of his fingers wiggling till he touched the edge of the fabric.

"You hungry?"

"Yeah. Pizza rolls?" he asked hopefully.

"And broccoli?"

"I broke my *arm*."

"Doing something you weren't supposed to do. Broccoli for pizza rolls."

"Fine," he grumbled, trying to get comfortable on

the couch as he flipped channels. "Mom . . . How come Shane hasn't been around?"

"Oh, well." Cora blinked. She hadn't expected Micah to bring it up. She wasn't ready to get into it yet. Maybe when he was better. She went to the kitchen to make the pizza rolls. "I'm sure you'll see him next time you go to the ranch. Do you want some water?"

"But why isn't he here?" Micah persisted.

"I . . ." Okay, so maybe she had to discuss this right now.

"I ruined it, didn't I? I told, and I ruined it. He said I didn't, but he's not *here*."

"No. No. Nothing . . . Nothing is ruined," Cora said, and she knew she was completely unconvincing, standing in the kitchen giving him no actual details.

"He's not here, and he said . . ." Micah struggled into a sitting position on the couch so he could look over the back at her in the kitchen. "Mom, you have to tell me what's going on."

"Okay." Okay, she could do that. Somehow. "I just . . ." She couldn't think of what to say. Because, well, things had changed because Micah had told. Which wasn't his *fault*, but he'd think it was. How could he not?

She walked over to the couch, slowly. Really slowly, not because she was drawing out the inevitable, but because she was buying time to figure out what to say.

If she told him . . . If she told him the truth, she was afraid he'd apply it to himself. That he wouldn't want to tell anyone about his past.

But he hadn't been in charge. He hadn't been the adult. He hadn't *let* it happen. How on earth did she explain that to a twelve-year-old?

"Mom, come on."

She perched herself on the edge of the couch. "It's just adult stuff, honey." That was a good enough answer, surely. "Nothing to do with you."

"Except everything was fine until I told him."

"Micah, that isn't true exactly, but . . . Separately, aside from anything with Shane and me, why did you tell him? After I promised I wouldn't. I don't understand."

Micah's eyebrows drew together, his blue eyes a maze of emotions. The kind so complicated she wasn't sure she'd ever fully be able to untangle them.

"You know what, never mind. Maybe this is a conversation we have with Dr. Grove later, but—"

"Mom. I was scared."

"Scared of what?"

"When I was with Shane . . . he was always like . . . Dr. Grove keeps telling me I can have my feelings on the inside, but when they turn into outside actions, I need to say them to you."

He sounded so adult, talking about a therapist's coping mechanisms, and yet he was still such a *boy*. Her little boy working through this horrible thing.

"So, the thing was, being with Shane . . . He's like a real dad. Like my friends' dads. He says no and gives advice and stuff. And I wanted . . . I just wanted him to be my dad, but he's not. And I just felt sick all the time."

Micah clutched his blanket, looking down at it, and Cora understood, maybe a little too well, what he meant. That horrible feeling that all this good would come to an end. With Shane, she'd let some of that go—before the broken arm fiasco—but Micah wasn't at that point yet.

"Sick that I wanted him to be that, that he couldn't be. I wanted to stop feeling that way so I . . . I thought I'd ruin it. I'd tell him, and, well, I knew he wouldn't boot us out, but I figured you'd stop being with him, and it'd all go back to being the way it was before. But it's not. It's worse."

"Baby." She said it on a gasp, but she wasn't sure Micah paid her any mind. He was babbling ahead, and she was still reeling.

Like a dad.

"But we can make it better. Shane, he knew, and he never acted different. He even said I'd have to do some sucking up to you before I get back on a horse. And that I'd learned my lesson. He didn't . . . Nothing was different. So, it can be okay." Micah looked up at her hopefully.

Why did she have to keep disappointing her baby? "Micah, it isn't so simple. Because relationships, when you're an adult, it's all different. It's hard, and it's complicated. It's even hard and complicated to explain, let alone deal with."

"But you said you loved him, and he loved you, and he didn't treat us differently. He didn't. . . . Brandon and Will and Sam . . . I . . ." Micah ducked his head. "I love them and all, but they don't slap me on the back or push me as a joke. They don't grab me or anything. And even after I'd told Shane, right after I told him, and we were at the game and they hit that home run and he kind of picked me up and shook me around. It didn't change. You know?"

Cora nodded, because she didn't trust her voice enough to speak. Although nodding was making the tears in her eyes perilously close to falling. Yes, the boys at Mile High *were* careful with Micah. No roughhousing. She thought it was more for *her* sake than Micah's, but she understood what he meant about the difference.

He got to be *physical* at the Tyler ranch. A boy. And it hadn't changed even after Micah had told.

It hadn't changed.

"Mom, we can fix it."

We. She would fix anything for Micah, but this wasn't

about her son. It was about her. "I'm so glad things didn't change for you and Shane. I want you to be able to look up to him and spend time with him. What's happened with him and me is different, separate. It's about me."

"But he loves you. Like Uncle Brandon loves Aunt Lilly, and Sam loves Hayley, and Will and Tori. They're all getting married. Sometimes they fight, but you're always saying people in love fight because that means it matters."

"Micah—"

"Mom . . ." He reached across the couch with his good arm, grabbing onto her hand. "Mom, are you scared? Like me. Because it was good, and I was . . . Sometimes when everything's going well, I think Dad'll show up. Like basketball camp. Then I just want to ruin everything, and Dr. Grove said to talk before I act. If you're scared, you're supposed to talk before you act. I messed it up, I did it backwards, but you're an adult and stuff. You can do it the right way."

She wanted to refute it. The kid was *twelve*. How would he know what it felt like to be seen this way? She wasn't afraid of good. She'd been all settled into it. Happy and ready for a future until those flashing red and white lights.

And, oh, hadn't she jumped onto that as a *sign* awfully quick? Hadn't she *jumped* at the chance to make Shane the bad guy. To cut him off before he could prove to her things could still be good.

But he'd known. All that night before he'd known, and he'd loved her, and Micah was right. Shane hadn't treated her any differently. Not like she'd break or like he needed to second-guess how she felt or what she wanted.

But that had been short. So quick. How could she trust it?

"Dr. Grove says it's okay to be scared."

"I thought you didn't listen to her at all, and now you're spouting everything she's ever said?"

Micah smiled sheepishly. "She's okay."

Cora laughed a little, even as tears fell over. "I didn't think I was scared, but what you're saying makes a lot of sense."

"Really?"

She sniffled, reaching out to touch his sweet face. "Maybe you'll be a psychologist when you grow up and help people."

He jerked away from her hand and shrugged. "I don't know. Whatever. Maybe. Maybe I want to be in the rodeo like Boone."

And maybe I'll kick Boone's ass. But she kept that thought to herself.

"Mom, let's go to the ranch. If you're afraid to talk to Shane, I'll go first, and then you won't have to be."

"Baby, I don't know what I'd do without you."

"So, we can go? We can talk to Shane?"

She didn't want to. She practically recoiled from the idea, and that was when it truly hit her just how right Micah had been. How she'd let those old fears swallow up everything she'd been building.

Not because Shane would treat her differently, but because he might not. Because it might actually be good, and things like Micah's breaking his arm might not be signs, but accidents no one could control. That she'd never be able to predict. There were bound to be heartache and misunderstandings and loss.

It was easier to run away from all that than to stand up for it. Easier to hide in her insecurities than to lay them truthfully down. Easier to proactively dismantle a hurt than try to heal a misstep.

She blew out a breath, her body shaky with too

much uncertainty. Too much fear and that horrible, gut-twisting desire to do the *right* thing, and having no idea what the right thing was.

But Micah was looking at her expectantly, using all the things he'd learned in therapy. Wanting to talk it out, *work* it out. How could she say no to him and that?

"Okay. Okay, let's go."

Micah jumped up, winced a little bit, but it didn't stop his forward progression to the door. "Just, if you're going to kiss, can you like let me close my eyes or something?"

Cora laughed, though it was more nervous laughter. She had a bad feeling none of this was going to end in kissing.

Shane woke with a start to Gavin's staring down at him. Shane looked around, trying to figure out where the hell he was. A very uncomfortable chair in the barn, in the siblings' meeting room.

He didn't fully remember coming in here, or sitting down, and he really didn't remember falling asleep.

"Afternoon, sleeping beauty."

"Fuck off," Shane muttered.

"Fine, I won't warn you."

"Warn me about what?" Shane muttered, trying to work the kinks out of his neck. Everything hurt, and he didn't feel any more rested. God knows he hadn't gotten his work for the morning done. What time was it? Gavin had said afternoon.

"Saw Cora's car coming up the drive."

Shane was on his feet before the sentence was fully out of Gavin's mouth. "What?"

"Probably here by now."

Shane took a step toward the door, then stopped himself. Everything about the past few days tumbled into place. "She probably has a meeting with Mom."

"Doubt it."

"Why do you say that?"

Gavin gestured out the small window. "Coming this way with Micah. Doesn't have her fancy wedding planner clothes on."

Shane stood there, staring at their impending arrival, trying to work out what he was supposed to do. Mom had said trust and wait and all those other horrible things. Hell.

"Well, you just going to stand there like an idiot?"

Shane glared back at Gavin. "Maybe I am."

"Come on now. Man up. Get out there."

"Hey, how's Lou doing? You man up there yet?" Shane retorted.

Gavin flipped him off, but he didn't storm off or say anything. He nudged Shane out the stables door, so they were face to face with Micah and Cora.

"Hi," Cora offered, hands in her pockets, eyes darting from Gavin to Shane.

"Hi. Hey, how you doing, Micah?" Shane asked, shoving his own hands in his pockets because they wanted to do anything but stay at his sides.

Micah held up his cast awkwardly. "Kind of lame. Be cooler if it was like an Iron Man arm."

Shane chuckled. "Yes, that would probably be cooler."

"Hey, kid," Gavin offered. "I've got a chore you can do one-armed, if you're interested?"

"Really?" Micah looked up at Cora hopefully.

She smiled thinly and nodded. "Please be careful."

"Awesome." But Micah's gaze turned to Shane. "Um, before I go I just wanted to say . . . thanks for the baseball game and everything. It was really fun and I . . . I don't know. Um." He scratched his good hand through his shaggy hair.

Shane knelt down and held out his arms. When Micah hurriedly stepped into them, he knew he'd made the right move. Micah squeezed him with his good arm, and Shane expected that to be it.

"I'm sorry," Micah whispered.

"I already told you there was nothing you had to be sorry for. Accidents happen."

"Not about that," Micah said, still whispering. "I haven't always been nice to you, and all those things I said in the car, I said because I thought it would make you not want to be with us anymore. Not because I didn't want you, but because I was afraid to. Because you were like a real dad, not my crappy one, and it was scary to want that. So I did something dumb instead of talk, but that only made things worse. So, I'm sorry."

Shane couldn't speak. He glanced up at Cora helplessly, but she had tears in her eyes, and that was worse.

So, Shane just hugged Micah fiercely to his chest. "Apology accepted," he managed to rasp. "I love you, Micah. I want you to know that."

"I love you too, Shane." He wiggled out of Shane's grasp. "Can I, uh, go see the horses now?" he asked.

Shane and Cora nodded, and Gavin nodded toward the stables. "Come on, kid," he said, and even *his* voice was suspiciously raspy.

Shane managed to push to his feet, feeling a little more broken and a little more healed all at the same time.

"Yeah, so, we had to come over after he told me all *that*," Cora offered squeakily. She took a deep breath. "And maybe I realized a few things about myself and the past few days when he told me all that too."

"Yeah, what kind of things?" Shane asked cautiously. What he *wanted* was apologies and love and *we can work this outs*, but Mom had told him to wait. To be patient.

"Well, I've had some very real fear in my life, and I'd finally learned to fight it. To not let it win and make me just give up. But I guess . . . Well, there are different kinds of fears. Ones that are good and natural, like the fear of someone who hurts you, repeatedly."

"Cora—"

"And then there are the fears that something good isn't for you, and you don't deserve it. And maybe because part of me knew that was a little warped, or at least I'd been told that's not right by my therapist, because yes, I have one of those, I told myself I was afraid of you, and how you'd treat me. When in reality, what I was really afraid of was myself. What I thought I didn't deserve. You never gave me a real reason to fear you, Shane, and it wasn't fair to put it on you. It's my own baggage."

"You know, maybe I wouldn't have understood all this if I hadn't . . . I talked to Mom about what happened with my dad, and she pointed out it wasn't all that different. Hiding parts of ourselves we don't like or know what to do with. Fear that's hidden under the excuses we give ourselves. But whether I understand it or not, I only want to help you carry that baggage. I've got enough of my own. I know I can't take yours away, the same as you can't take away mine. I wasn't ever looking to be your savior, Cora. I just want to be your partner."

"Like want not . . . wanted?" She looked helplessly at him. "I wasn't nice."

"You don't always have to be nice. Or good. Or right or wrong. I don't want to fix you or change you. Sometimes I will want to fix *things* for you, but you are all I want. Just the way you are. I love you. And I am . . . I will be here whenever you're ready for that."

She chewed on her lip, studying him carefully. "Sometimes I'll need you to let me take care of things on my own."

"And sometimes I'll need you to let me protect you."

She waved a hand. "If snakes are involved, feel free."

He wanted to laugh, but there was still so much fear inside him. So much worry this wasn't what he wanted it to be. Mom said it would take time. Patience. He'd been so ready for that, but here Cora was . . . "So, you're really . . . You want to work things out? Now."

She nodded. "I love you. I *love* you. I want to be your partner too. I don't want fear to be the decision-maker in my life forever. I don't want to be the kind of person who lets love go because something bad happens, or because we don't agree, or because I'm feeling mixed up and don't know how to say it."

"I think you said it okay."

"So why are you still standing all the way over there?" she asked, throwing her hands in the air.

He grinned and crossed to her in a flash, all those heavy bricks on his shoulders dissolving to dust and blowing away, because he didn't have to *wait*, and they would make it all work.

Together.

"Thank God," he said into her neck, wrapping his arms around her and lifting her up off the ground. "I thought I was going to have to be patient and hands off for months."

"Months? You were going to wait months?"

He met her gaze, those dark blue eyes so confused as if she'd never imagined this, as if she couldn't fathom it.

He was going to damn well make sure she fathomed it.

"I'd wait years, Cora. However long it took." He set her down, gratified when she slid her arms around his neck.

She studied his face, tears in her eyes. "You are the very best man I know, Shane Tyler."

"Well, as long as I'm your man, that's all that matters to me."

She trailed her fingertips across his jaw, her mouth *finally* curving into a real smile. "Yeah, you're mine," she murmured.

He dropped his mouth to hers, but before he kissed her, he figured he might as well go for broke. "Hell, let's get married."

"What?" she asked on a breathless laugh. "Shane." As though she was fully realizing he was serious, she shoved ineffectively at his chest.

He held onto her. "If you're coming back to me this quickly, I'm going to push my advantage. I love you. I don't want to be apart or to pretend like I need more time to know I want you by my side for the rest of my life. You take all the time you need to answer. I don't plan on rushing you on anything. I just want you to know I want to. Whenever you're ready."

"I . . . I have to talk to Micah," she said, pushing less and less hard against him.

"Just say yes!" Micah called.

Shane and Cora both whipped around to see Micah's face pressed to the cracked glass of the window on the stables.

"Listen to the kid," Gavin called.

"I don't know. Marriage is kinda risky."

"No one asked you, Boone," Shane growled. Though he couldn't see his brothers, they must have been standing behind Micah at the window. "Would you all go away?"

"Say yes, Mom!"

"He can stay," Shane said to Cora, deadpan.

She grinned. "Oh, I'll marry you. Though in fairness we have to get through your mom's wedding first. I feel like I should get through planning someone else's before I start planning my own."

"Deal."

"But . . . what are we going to do? Live here? In the main house? And like, what about kids? We've never talked about having kids and . . ."

"Yes, to all of it, yes. Whatever you want. Because you and Micah are what I want, and the rest is negotiable."

A laugh tumbled out of her, a little lost but *happy*. "Living here, kids with you, it all sounds like a dream I had and tried to sabotage," she murmured, cupping his face with her hands.

"Well, lucky I was around to fix it."

She glared at him, though her mouth kept twitching up, ruining the attempt at severity. "I think we fixed it together."

Shane gathered her close, pressed a kiss to her forehead. "And we always will."

And then, paying no attention to the groans coming from the stable, Shane kissed his wife-to-be with everything he had. He knew without a shadow of a doubt he would love her and protect her, fight with her and make up with her, raise Micah and any other kids together, and it wouldn't ever be perfect or easy.

But it would be right. And it would be good.

Epilogue

Cora looked around the sparkling, gorgeous reception and breathed for the first time all day.

Deb and Ben's wedding, a wedding she had planned and worked her ass off on, had gone off without a hitch. Her very first wedding for Mile High Weddings, and it was beyond a success. It had been a gorgeous, fantastic spectacle of *joy*. And the great thing about it was, she wasn't just proud of herself and what she'd accomplished. She was happy. For Ben and Deb and their second chance.

"Does the prettiest wedding planner finally get to dance?" Shane asked against her ear, his arms coming around her from behind.

She turned in the circle of his arms, grinning up at him. The cake had been cut, the bouquet thrown— Lindsay hilariously fighting to the death for it. All that was left was dancing to the strains of old country music under a beautiful, starry sky.

"I think she can find a few minutes for the handsomest cowboy of the lot." And he was. Dressed in a suit, with a black cowboy hat to match. He'd walked Deb down the aisle, and just about everyone had cried as he'd given her away.

Cora got a little teary just remembering it. But Shane spun her onto the makeshift dance floor and she laughed instead.

"Don't try to butter me up just to get into my bed," he said, failing at hiding a grin. "I'm feeling a bit put out I haven't seen you in days."

Which was true. Despite the fact that she and Micah had moved into the Tyler ranch—totally for practical reasons with the school year starting and not at all for selfish, share-a-bed-with-Shane-at-night reasons—she'd only been home late in the evening, most of the time after Shane had gone to sleep.

"You'll have to get used to it during wedding season. I've found I'm determined to be the best damn wedding planner in all of Colorado."

They swayed to the music, and he kissed her temple. "I have no doubt you will be."

There were so many ways Shane surprised her, challenged what she'd thought a relationship would be. The fact he wanted her to succeed, even if it meant time away from him, was something that still amazed her.

"So, do we get to talk about our wedding yet?" he asked, drawing her closer than was appropriate for the beat of the song.

She didn't care. Not by a long shot. Though she was impatient too. Impatient to share this kind of night with him and the people she loved and pledge herself to him. It changed nothing, because she was already his, heart and soul, but there was something about the ritual that she knew would mean a little extra. "You are too impatient by half," she teased, because she was more than pleased he was as eager as she was.

"Yes, indeed."

"Well, Lilly did find this place that got me thinking . . ." Cora had to rest her cheek against his shoulder because she didn't want him to see her expression. They'd been talking about a summer wedding, when she let him mention a wedding that wasn't his mother's. "Do you know the Bartons?"

"Sure. Lindsay and Cal Barton were high school sweethearts. I always liked Cal. And that Christmas Tree farm of theirs is a Gracely tradition."

"It's a darling little place," Cora said. "Small, but so picturesque, and especially would be in the snow. Perfect for a wedding. A Christmas wedding."

He pulled her away from his shoulder so she was forced to look up at him. He glared down at her. "You better mean this Christmas."

She laughed, so happy it hurt. She knew it wouldn't always be this good or this easy, but she also knew he'd be there holding her either way. "Yeah, this Christmas. I don't want another year to go by where I don't get to call you my husband."

"I like the way you think. A Christmas tree farm, huh?"

"Snow and Christmas lights and most important, us. All three of us."

He still held her close, and they'd both sort of stopped swaying, though people danced around them, happy and oblivious.

"About that," Shane murmured. "I want to be the one to run it by Micah, or at least have us do it together, but I also don't want to get his hopes up because the legality of it might be tricky."

"Is this something underhanded, Shane Tyler?" she teased, having no idea where he was going with this sudden change of mood.

"No, afraid not."

He was so sober, so serious, something in her heart

shifted. Worry wiggled through her, but not heavy enough to be *fear*. Whatever Shane was talking about, they'd get through it.

"I want to adopt Micah. I want us all to be Tylers. I mean, we all will be no matter what. Don't get me wrong on that. But it'd be a nice symbol. The name."

She wasn't sure she breathed for a minute. Maybe more. She knew Shane would be an amazing stepfather, the kind who said no and gave advice, just as Micah had said. But she hadn't even thought about . . . hadn't considered . . .

"If it's okay?" he continued, clearly reading her shock as worry. "I thought—"

"It's okay. I mean, it might be tricky," she squeaked. "Hell, it might be impossible, but it's more than okay that we give it a shot."

He grinned. "Either way, I'll be a great dad to that kid."

"I know." She reached up and cupped his face. "I know." She brushed her mouth across his. "Oh, I don't know how I got so lucky."

"How *we* got so lucky," Shane corrected, holding her close.

And he was absolutely right.

And now . . .
Read on for a preview of

A COWBOY WEDDING FOR CHRISTMAS

by
Nicole Helm

Available in the anthology
Santa's On His Way
in October 2018
wherever books and
eBooks are sold.

Lindsay Tyler remembered exactly what she'd said to her oldest brother when he'd asked if she'd feel weird about his getting married at her ex-boyfriend's family's Christmas tree farm.

Why would I care about that?

No matter that Cal still lived in her head as the paragon of boyfriend-ness that no other man she'd dated had come close to. It had been *years* since she'd decided she wanted more than Gracely, Colorado and Cal Barton.

Why would I care about that?

As she turned onto the lane that would lead to the Barton Ranch and Christmas Tree Farm, she realized why she would care. Too many memories, sweet and increasingly nostalgic with time. There had been years of her life when she'd been so sure she'd marry Cal, move into the house at the end of this lane, and that would be it.

But he hadn't wanted her *more*, and she hadn't been willing to sacrifice seeing a different world for him.

A different world that hadn't fit her like the glove she'd expected it to. A different world that never quite lived up to *home*. Oh, she was glad she'd done it. Six years of independence and learning to be Lindsay Tyler outside of her wonderful but overbearing family. She'd *needed* that.

But coming home . . . Well, it was the right step now. Adult, twenty-four-year-old Lindsay needed home. And for good.

She still couldn't believe herself. Instead of traveling the world or becoming a famous artist, she was going to student teach, and then ideally get a job in the fall, where she'd once been an elementary school student.

It was such a joke after all her grand proclamations when she'd left the Tyler ranch. An embarrassing one. So embarrassing she still hadn't told her family she wasn't just coming home for Christmas vacation. She was home for good.

The thought of telling them made her a little sick, so she was more than happy to dive into wedding plans for her oldest brother and his soon-to-be-wife. Even if it meant driving up to the Barton house.

The arching sign over the entryway to the Barton Ranch and Christmas Tree Farm read just that in block red and green letters, and had for something like a century. She'd always liked that, that Cal had roots just like hers. Old and settled into the land. But unlike her family's straightforward cattle ranch, Cal's ranch had this amazing, festive, and unique history.

Cal was none of those things, which had always pleased her. Her gruff, taciturn cowboy whose smile was mostly just for her because he didn't smile for much else.

She needed to get over the nostalgia train and focus on what was ahead of her. Her brother's wedding. Christmas with her family. And at some point, swallowing her pride and telling them she was back for good.

Merry Crappy Christmas.

She pulled up behind a line of her family's trucks. The Barton house was decked out with an impressive light display. Before Cal's mother had abandoned the family, Cal's dad had always spent days and days getting it just right. After that, the task had fallen to Cal and his sister, much to Cal's consternation. He'd bitterly resented the Christmas tree portion of his family's legacy, especially after his mother had left a second time, but Gracely depended on Barton's for a festive Christmas tree-getting experience, and Cal couldn't say no to the influx of cash in the cold winter months.

Lindsay really had to stop thinking about Cal. Tonight was about Shane and Cora's wedding. The coming days were about celebrating that and Christmas with her family. Being on Barton property didn't really matter.

She stepped out of her car, finding her footing on the slick, snowy ground. The quiet of rural Colorado wrapped around her like a warm blanket. No matter that coming home involved swallowing her pride, she was happy to be here. Happy to be back where she could see the stars spread out like a canvas of joy above her, where she could go outside to feel perfectly alone and perfectly safe.

"I've missed you," she whispered fancifully into the dark. She carefully walked up to the porch stairs, then crested the gorgeous wraparound porch that was lit up to blazing with glowing white lights. Wreaths hung in every window, and two small Christmas trees sat in pots at the corners of the porch. It was the picture-perfect place to have a Christmas wedding. That was for sure.

Footsteps and grumbling interrupted the picturesque quiet. Lindsay lifted her arm to knock on the front door, but then the source of the noise came around the corner, and Lindsay forgot to hit her fist against the door.

Because bathed in the warm glow of the Christmas lights, the cowboy hat low on his head, was a man who could have been any ranch hand or friend of Sarah's.

But he lifted his gaze.

"Cal." Lindsay said his name on a whoosh of breath, because he'd always taken away her breath a little bit. Something about the midnight-black hair and the shock of summer sky-blue eyes.

And now he wasn't just tall and lean. He was broad. Sturdy. She'd always thought he was the most handsome man in Gracely County, but now that she'd spent some time outside of Gracely, she understood the truth.

He was one of the most handsome men *ever*, anywhere.

Crap.

"You seem surprised to see me on my own porch," he said, and she didn't remember his voice being that low and deliciously raspy. She didn't remember that hard, mean line to his mouth geared at anyone except his stepmother.

To be on the receiving end was more of a blow than she expected it to be. Still, she cleared her throat and forced her mouth to curve. "No, no. I just . . . You look so much different than the last time I saw you."

"Funny," he returned, giving her a quick once-over. "You look exactly the same."

Which shouldn't have sounded like an insult since he'd once considered her *the prettiest girl in Colorado*— his words. But the way he said it now . . .

Well, humph.

"Well, I, uh, my family is here. I'm meeting them. Shane's . . . wedding."

Cal grunted in assent, moving for the door. Except

she was standing in front of it, her hand still raised and ready to knock.

Cal. Cal was standing there in front of her, and she didn't know what to say, or even feel. She'd avoided him at all costs on visits home for six years. At most, she'd seen him across the street in Gracely proper once or twice, but Cal was happiest on his ranch, and she'd avoided anything and everything to do with the Barton ranch.

And now he was right there. Right. There. He clearly wasn't the boy she'd loved six years ago, but somehow standing on the same porch with him made her feel like that girl again. Naïve and so desperately in love.

"Darlin', either knock on the door or get out of my way."

Darlin'. He only ever pulled out that drawl with people he hated, but that didn't make sense. It had been six years. Surely he didn't still *hate* her. "I . . ."

"Did I sprout devil horns?"

"No. No. I just . . . No." Heat infused her cheeks, and she finally got herself together enough to step out of the way, drop her hand, not be a complete and utter dope.

Cal moved into the space she'd evacuated and pushed the door open. She could have done that. She *should* have done that. Instead, she followed timidly after him into the warmth of the Barton house.

Not that her face needed to be any warmer.

"Straggler," Cal announced simply, gesturing vaguely at Lindsay. Her family were sitting in various seats around the Barton living room, Cal's sister Sarah standing in front of all of them.

"Lindsay!" Sarah squealed, and rushed over to envelop her in a tight hug. "Oh my gosh, you look *amazing*."

Lindsay laughed uncomfortably, though she hugged Sarah back. "Me? You're all grown-up."

Sarah beamed and released her. "Come on in. You didn't miss much. We were just chitchatting, waiting for you to get here." Sarah ushered Lindsay to a couch where Molly and Gavin were sitting.

Lindsay took the seat in between her siblings. "So, let me guess, you're the driving force behind Barton Christmas Tree Farm as a wedding venue?"

"Er, well, sort of." Sarah looked back at Cal, who was standing there stoically in the corner. At his sister's glance he shook his head and disappeared down a hall Lindsay knew would take him to the Barton kitchen. "It was Cal's idea," Sarah said, over brightly. "But, I do most of the work on that front. But Shane and Cora's wedding is going to be our first."

"It's perfect," Lindsay said, grinning at her future sister-in-law, Cora. And she didn't let that grin or cheerfulness die, even though her head was anywhere but weddings or Christmas.

No, her thoughts were full of Cal.

Cal tossed a frozen meal into the microwave and took out at least some of his irritation on the microwave buttons.

Tylers in his house. Since he was alone, he could scowl. He had nothing against the Tylers in theory. Deb Tyler had been like a mother to him growing up, and Shane and Gavin were good ranch neighbors and decent men.

But no matter that he might like each person individually, they were all blood ties to the one person in the world he expressly did not like.

Lindsay Tyler.

Pretty as ever, too. He hadn't been lying when he'd told her she hadn't changed. She looked exactly the same as she had the day she'd effectively shoved a dagger into his heart.

Since he was not a man prone to hyperbole, the fact that he'd even think of that comparison proved what a betrayal it had been. Cal Barton was well acquainted with desertion and betrayal.

The microwave dinged, and Cal scowled at it. A burst of laughter from the living room invaded the quiet of the kitchen.

He wasn't a particularly *fun-loving* guy, but the laughter normally wouldn't have bothered him in the least. Especially if it meant Sarah was building a little side business for herself. Except *this* laughter was *Tyler* laughter, and he was almost certain he could pick out Lindsay's tinkling laugh in the midst of all the other people's.

He plopped himself onto a kitchen chair and attacked the microwave meal. It was only half hot, half still cold. He choked it all down anyway. The sooner he was done with dinner, the sooner he could head back outside. He didn't have any necessary chores left, but there were always extra chores to be scrounged up when he didn't want to be around people.

Especially Tyler people.

He would have avoided dinner altogether, but when he did that Sarah scolded him and pecked at him like she'd decided to be his mother, and he'd rather avoid watching her childhood issues bleed out all over him.

After all, he had plenty of his own.

He got up from the table and tossed the remnants of the meal. More laughter from the living room, and with all the damn Christmas lights twinkling around him, he really just wanted to punch something.

He hated Christmas.

He hated Lindsay Tyler.

He hated this ugly, black feeling inside of him. He

always wondered if it was the same one that had caused his mother to leave them. Twice.

Always on Christmas.

Cal needed to get out of here, but instead he stood and stared at the cabinet of liquor. It was tempting. A Barton Christmas tradition, after all, to get drunk and wax poetic about the woman who'd left you.

But Cal had decided a long, long time ago to be nothing like his father. That liquor cabinet was a reminder.

"You could have said hello."

Cal glanced back at his sister. She was only nineteen, and Dad had let wife number three (marriage number four, since he'd married Mom twice before moving on) talk him into traveling the world, leaving Sarah without the means or opportunity to go off to college.

She was stuck here, and Cal was damn determined she have something. Something that would fulfill her. Something that would make her happy.

Something that will keep her here.

"I did say hello."

"No, you didn't. You said exactly one word, which was 'straggler,' and then you stomped back here."

"I did not stomp. That's called a manly cowboy swagger."

She snorted in disgust, but grinned nonetheless, then her smile died. "You know I'm going to ask her."

"I know." He didn't have to like it to know.

"She's going to say yes."

"Of course she is. I don't know how long she's in town, but Lindsay would never refuse you. No matter what . . ." Which was why he hated Lindsay Tyler after six years, because he knew with everything he was that she was a good person. Pretty and good and helpful, and she and he belonged together.

But she'd needed more than him and this, and how could he ever forgive her for that?

The fact that Sarah needed some help with graphics and whatnot for advertising the Christmas tree farm as a wedding venue had nothing to do with him. Asking for Lindsay's art help had nothing to do with him. So, he wouldn't stand in Sarah's way. No matter how much he didn't want Lindsay hovering around, even for a short period of time.

"Okay . . . Well . . ." She trailed off, then shook her head and went for the pantry. "The chocolate ones went fast." She grabbed a cookie tin and opened it. She took two out and placed them on the table. "That's for being a good little rancher boy."

"Ha. Ha." But he took his sister's cookies, because she was a hell of a baker. Whether it was Christmas or old, bad memories swirling, he found himself swayed by an unusual wave of sentimentality. "You're really good at this. The whole entertaining thing. I'm not. I never will be. Lindsay or no. So, just ignore my manly cowboy swagger and focus on this thing you're really good at."

For a second she looked like she was about to cry, which horrified him enough to make him start edging toward the back door. But she straightened her shoulders and blinked a few times.

"You're not that manly," she offered gravely, before bursting into laughter as she headed back out to her waiting guests.

On a sigh, he ate the Christmas cookies and listened to the faint laughter of another family in his living room. Tylers. The whole lot of them. Up in his house and ranch for the next few days.

Christmases were never very merry around the Barton spread, but it couldn't be worse than waking up to finding Mom or Dad gone, so he supposed he'd survive.

He'd just do everything in his power to avoid Lindsay. It shouldn't be a problem. She couldn't possibly want to see him any more than he wanted to see her.

So, that was settled, and he'd eaten his dinner and talked to his sister, and now he could go back to the solitude of the barn and do something that didn't feel like a knife being shoved in his heart.